THE LAST MAN IN EUROPE

THE LAST MAN IN EUROPE

A NOVEL

DENNIS GLOVER

Polygon

This edition published in Great Britain in 2021 by
Polygon, an imprint of Birlinn Ltd.

West Newington House
10 Newington Road
Edinburgh EH9 1QS

www.polygonbooks.co.uk

9 8 7 6 5 4 3 2 1

ISBN 978 1 84697 534 9
eBook ISBN 978 1 78885 317 0

British Library Cataloguing-in-Publication Data
A catalogue record for this book is
available on request from the British Library.

Typeset in Bembo by Polygon, Edinburgh
Printed and bound in Great Britain by Clays Ltd, Elcograf S.p.A.

PROLOGUE

Jura, April 1947. It was his third day back on the island but the first he had managed to get out of bed. He knew what he had to do: transfer to paper the ceaseless, grinding monologue that had been working through his mind since . . . when? His days at the BBC? The betrayal in Barcelona? The discovery of the proles in Wigan? Those glorious summers of his youth? Prep school and H.G. Wells? He couldn't remember; perhaps the obsession had always been with him.

The view from his desk was desolate: the ground sodden and grassless, and the early spring flowers already spent. The late frosts and rains had played havoc with the place. He could see a dead calf in the next field, which meant rats. He roused himself and sat up straighter. Almost absentmindedly, he typed 'i.' at the top of the page.

He glanced at his watch. It was midday of the first day of Double Summer Time, meaning it was actually twelve plus one – or eleven plus two, depending on how you looked at it. What with the bolshiness of the islanders towards such matters, no one here could ever agree what time it really was. He took off his watch, wound it forward one hour and strapped it back on his wrist.

To mark the paper was the decisive act. He'd got somewhere the previous summer, but only with incidental parts, like Goldstein's secret book, and they'd all have to be redone. Now he faced the hard part: the story. *A Clergyman's Daughter* and *Keep the Aspidistra Flying* he had opened with the ringing of clocks, and *Coming Up for Air* with George Bowling nipping out of bed. It was an easy way in – perhaps too easy, but he could get it right in the next draft. He felt a jolt in his chest and his mind drifted to his illness, but he regained control before the thoughts could lead anywhere.

Then the right words came, the way good writing always does, in a rush. He put his hands to the keys and the letters began to indent the paper:

> It was a cold, blowy day in early April, and a million radios were striking thirteen.

He lit a cigarette and read the line over. Something wasn't right. There was a looseness about it. Connolly would have attacked the scansion, just as he had all those years ago at prep. And the radios – they smacked of Wells and Huxley and science fiction, which was the last thing he wanted. He picked up his pen and began amending. Satisfied, he read it back again:

> It was a bright cold day in April, and the clocks were striking thirteen.

There was no turning back now.

ONE

Booklover's Corner, Hampstead, March 1935. *He had reached that age when the future ceases to be a rosy blur and becomes actual and menacing.* It was a good sentence, and he set the pen down next to his notebook. Menacing. Yes, this was going to be his best novel so far, although sadly it was drawn directly from life – his own. It was about a failing poet, Gordon Comstock, in his early thirties, working in a dusty bookshop and living alone in an attic bedsit – halfway to the workhouse already. Good prose, he believed, should be like a windowpane, but in this case it would have to be a mirror.

He had expected becoming a published author to improve his life in noticeable ways, but little had really changed, except his name – from Eric Blair to George Orwell, after the river in Suffolk where he'd fished as a boy. As he had done from childhood, he still wrote all the time, even when at work in the bookshop, where he was allowed to scribble as long as there were no customers to serve or new stock to shelve. It seemed the only time he wasn't writing was when he was asleep – and even then he suspected his mind was secretly working on some book or essay or poem that only revealed itself later.

Despite all this hard work, despite years of tramping, policing the Empire and washing greasy plates to write about things that should have mattered, he had less money than ever. His appearance, even he could see, had the unmistakeable signs of failure: his hair too long, his fraying white shirts a dull grey, his unusually tall frame shrinking as his suits became baggier and more shapeless. There was a mouldering, moth-eaten-ness about him that without success and money he could never hope to shake. Even his voice – public school, but neither effeminate nor deep enough to convey the necessary impression of a successful writer – let him down. He certainly would never be mistaken for one of the sleek young literary lions whose frivolous must-read novels he was daily forced to sell. Bum-kissers!

He looked up from the page. It had darkened outside, and with the electric light on he could see his partial reflection in the shop window. Actually, he didn't look that bad after all. His collar was substantially intact, his jacket worn but decently tailored. Even his bedsit, he conceded, was clean and pleasantly furnished, quite a nice place to write, and just yards from Hampstead Heath. Maybe a quarter way to the workhouse, no more; he was not quite Gordon yet.

He doodled, thinking. By an act of willpower, he had turned himself into a writer, occasionally half starving himself in the process, but apart from the usual reasons of vanity and the search for fame, he didn't really know why. He knew instinctively what he was against, although even that required effort to pin down precisely. He was against the modern world, with its constant background noise of radios, its tinned food, thin bubbly beer, patent medicines, electric heating and contraception. He was against religion too – an obvious swindle, barely worth discussing. But what else?

He lit a cigarette. Looking across the street, he saw a poster for Bovril, its torn corner flapping in the wind. *Bovril, beef in brief.* Advertising – another evil! But what about politics? He realised he hadn't really given it much thought, except to hate imperialism for having sent him to Burma, wasting five good years of his life. In truth the things that really interested him were literature and being a writer. He sat back. A writer without any purpose or belief system, writing about writing – that's what he was.

He closed his eyes and, unbidden, a familiar vision came to him. He was outside, with springy turf under his feet and the warmth of the sun on his back. It was May, because the chestnut trees were in blossom and the smell of wild peppermint was in the air. He was at the edge of a clearing, completely alone, staring down at a sun-dappled pond, beneath which swam enormous fish, silent, contented, free. A breeze ruffled the elm behind him, and the only sound was the song of a bird – a thrush. It was the dream he'd had the night before, and now it wouldn't leave his mind. It had been a luminous dream, bathed in sunshine: a vision of straw-coloured grass and azure skies, with here and there a shell-burst of cloud lending contrast. It was a place where time moved slowly and death could never reach, giving him the feeling of not being hurried or frightened the way everyone around him seemed to be nowadays. He was certain he'd had the dream many times before, but had no evidence to confirm it. Perhaps the idea of having had the dream before was part of the dream itself – a false memory.

After all, you couldn't prove anything existed if the only proof of it lay inside your head.

The shop bell tinkled. A customer. Unlike Gordon, he actually looked forward to his battles with customers, and the chance to talk about the books he admired.

It was that girl. Her name was Eileen – Eileen O'Shaughnessy – although she forbade him from calling her that, being known exclusively as Emily, E or, to her closest chums, 'The Pig'. He had met her at the weekend, at a party his landlady held for students at University College. She was small, with thick, dark hair and a freckled face, and was, he reckoned, in her late twenties or thereabouts. She had fine features and swift movements and was distinctly attractive but rather intimidating – the sort who was probably head girl at a school where they played a lot of hockey. He pictured her as a schoolgirl, her sports outfit gathered tightly at the waist by a house sash, lending the plain costume an inviting dimension, the way a certain type of schoolgirl always managed.

'Hello!' She had caught him looking at her midriff. 'Frightfully busy, isn't it,' she said, in the ironic tone he recalled from a few days before, and which he put down to the fashion, rife right then, for imitating characters from the novels of Evelyn Waugh – another bum-kisser. 'I hope I'm interrupting some serious writing.'

He closed the notebook. 'You are indeed. An important scene.'

'An illicit one, I hope. You want it to be a bestseller.'

'Just slightly illicit.'

She pouted. 'Oh, how disappointing.'

'I could spice it up a bit, if you'd like.'

'Please do. Absolutely essential.'

'You know about such things? Lewd literature, I mean.'

'As you're aware, if you can remember, I studied at Oxford. English.' She lowered her voice conspiratorially. 'Read Lawrence when no one was watching.'

'One can't be too careful. I read Compton Mackenzie under the bedsheets at prep. They beat me for it.'

'I even have a degree. I warn you, though, it's only second-class.'

'Second-class is preferable; literature is always ruined when it's too good. Actually, you can help me complete an important scene. You see, my hero lives alone in a bedsit, with a snooping landlady, and hasn't anywhere to actually, you know . . .'

'How unfortunate.'

'Yes. It's rather causing him to go off his coconut. He's met a girl, you see. A peach.'

'A coconut with a peach. Sounds promising.' She sidled up to the counter and leaned her elbows on it.

He could smell her perfume. 'He hopes so.'

'I have to say, I can't believe an enterprising young writer couldn't invent some sort of bolthole in which to give this coconut and his peach a little privacy of an afternoon. Now, let me think . . .' She scanned the shop, fixing her eyes on the staircase at the rear. 'Maybe a room, upstairs from the shop where he works?'

He had thought her fairly drunk at the party, and that that was why she had seemed fast and flirtatious in a way other women never were with him. Without the attractions of money and fame, he'd always had to rather force things along. But now he saw she was the same when sober. Proper, yes, but corrupted in a way that excited him. It struck him that while he'd been in love before – in Shiplake, Burma, Paris and Southwold – he'd never really been loved in return. He'd only just met her, but already he could tell: this was the sort of girl he'd like to marry.

★

Burnham Beeches, May. They had arranged to have a picnic together. The choice of assignation had been dictated by the simple fact that even though they were both adults, they had nowhere private to make love. In a world full of eavesdroppers and nosey parkers, privacy was only a theoretical concept to the unmarried and unmoneyed. The bookshop and their bedsits were little use, with owners and landladies always threatening to burst in unannounced, constantly snooping, and seemingly bent on enforcing some standard of behaviour people their age couldn't possibly be expected to abide.

The weather had been beastly all the spring but today the sun had come out, making it a lucky day to have made a break for the countryside. They walked for near three hours, hardly seeing a living thing but for birds and rabbits; even the villages they walked through seemed to be asleep. It was hard to believe such solitude existed thirty minutes from the city.

Getting hungry, they topped a rise and halted, thinking not just of the picnic; a spot infallibly out of sight to passing strangers was needed. At that moment the sun, which had hidden itself behind clouds, reappeared, illuminating the valley below in a golden glow of sunshine, like one of those railway posters that enticed people like them to give up a few pounds for their annual trip to the Lake District.

'Oh, look, Eric,' she said. 'The sun is lighting everything up.' Down in the valley, cosy whitewashed cottages appeared against the green, blue and yellow background, so far away as to be little more than dots, their windows glinting in the sun and wisps of white smoke curling from their chimneys. A small river wound its way through the valley. England! It felt warm, like summer. He hugged her from behind and they looked out over the scene, he noticing the first signs of grey in the roots of her hair but not caring, knowing there was even more in his. In a life that had become harder and duller than he had expected, he felt a sort of unalloyed joy, a childish delight, and he knew right then that this was one of those moments, like the happiest days from childhood, that would never leave him, and which would return in memory to taunt him, always.

What he liked most about her was that she didn't have to be goaded into it. She actually wanted him to make love to her, although she could undoubtedly have done better and the act involved considerable risk. What the Sunday papers would make of it! 'Lewd Act in Forest', 'Couple Caught Coupling', 'Burnham Beeches Bliss' and so on. There they were in a world in which the moneyless middle-class like themselves had nothing but their respectability standing between them and ruin, and yet she was willing to pursue joy before all else.

And what did she have to gain? Without some sort of run-away literary success, he could never give her the material things most women of her class wanted. Despite being an Etonian, he wasn't going to inherit anything of much value – or become editor of *The Times* or make it to the senior ranks of the civil service. But she didn't seem to care. She really didn't. She wouldn't make him throw it all in for some bowler-hatted purgatory worth five hundred pounds a year and a green-doored villa owned by the building society.

'There's no one around. *Now*, while it's safe,' she said, taking him by the hand and leading him into the wooded field by the path. 'We can eat afterwards.'

A few rows of trees back and they entered a small clearing, almost completely encircled by a wall of saplings making a natural fortress of privacy. It seemed vaguely familiar, like a place he had been in his childhood. They stood opposite each other. Before she even kissed him, she began taking off her clothes, laying them on the ground as if to make a bed; he copied her, rolling up his jacket into a pillow. She'd done this before, possibly many times, he thought. Finally, she got down to her intimate items, which she removed without ceremony.

He watched her with awe, seeing her action for what it was: a defiant rejection not just of the moral system that bound their kind to lives of dreary conformity, but also of the poverty that held the happiness of their kind – the unmoneyed lower- upper-middle class – in check. Her disrobing was political, a strike at England, the sort of act that could only be performed in private, when the villa civilisation and its moral enforcers couldn't see you, and the salesmen with their advertising slogans and hire-purchase agreements and set-by schemes and never-ending bills were safely out of mind. It meant a sort of social annihilation if caught, which eventually they would be if they were foolish enough to do it over and again, but for now he pushed the possibility to the rear of his mind and got on with living.

★

London, January 1936. He had finished his novel the evening before, and the typescript and carbons felt heavy in the battered black briefcase he was carrying to the office of his publisher, Victor Gollancz. Although it meant a journey of at least two hours from Greenwich to Covent Garden, he had decided to walk – both to save the bus fare and to fill the day. Without a novel to write, what else was there to do? He might even think up a new story along the way.

He reached the river, feeling the wind whip up from its surface and cut through his thin coat. He halted and stared across the icy-looking water to the working-class quarter of the East End. Again his mind went anxiously to the manuscript by his side, but this time to Gordon Comstock's poem.

> *Sharply the menacing wind sweeps over*
> *The bending poplars, newly bare,*
> *And the dark ribbons of the chimneys*
> *Veer downward; flicked by whips of air,*
> *Torn posters flutter.*

It was bleak, admittedly, but not bad; he just hoped Gollancz would agree.

He started walking. Bleakness. Why did he have to be good at bleakness? Obviously, to represent failure, bleakness was inevitable. But how many writers had become successful by depressing everyone? Such writers were usually famous *after* they were dead – men like Gissing. You didn't buy books in order to feel gloomy, did you? For 10/6 you wanted a little happiness and pleasure. Waugh, for instance . . . but he cut off his own line of thought. Bleakness, it occurred to him, meant he would never be able to afford to marry. He picked up a piece of brick and threw it over the embankment at the water, but it landed in the mud. Eileen had put him off again – not wanting to be a burden on him, she said, which of course meant not wanting to sink lower than she already had. It was for that reason he had changed his novel's ending.

Rather than have Gordon, the starving poet, moulder and die of consumptive illness, as he'd originally plotted it, he decided to let him be happy, marry his girl Rosemary, take back his old job at the advertising agency and settle down to suburban contentment, complete with an aspidistra in the entrance hall. It was wrong, obviously, but making the novel a bestseller would solve his problems. He could quit the bookshop and buy a nice house, like Waugh had, although maybe one not so grand.

Any other publisher would be pleased at this approach, but Gollancz – a socialist, and likely also a communist – probably wouldn't. Bleakness – that's what people like Gollancz wanted: failure on a national scale. Only by making people miserable could they get their revolution. He thought of the letter he had written, setting out all his ideas for this new and more upbeat ending, making a case for a larger advance against a more popular novel, and realised what a fool he had been. Bleakness was his destiny.

Never again would he artificially sweeten any book he wrote. Down into the mud – that's where he'd go, and never come up.

The briefcase once again felt heavy. Why not just fling it over the embankment and watch the filthy current carry it off – the way he'd thrown the manuscript of his first novel down that drain outside the Gare du Nord? Gordon – the original, true Gordon of the first draft, not the gutless, saccharine Gordon of the second – would have done just that, and then leapt in after it.

He was distracted by a buzzing sound. Watching an aeroplane making for Croydon airport, he wondered what magic a few bombs would work among the shipping in front of him at the West India Docks. That's what he needed, he thought: a good war. Civilisation getting the unhappy ending it so thoroughly deserved! Everyone knew the war was coming, so why not have it now? The thought should have depressed him, but compared with the alternative of scurrying around like a penniless beetle, even the trenches seemed inviting. He could be a war correspondent. He forgot about the weight of his briefcase and walked on.

On reaching Henrietta Street, he found Gollancz – balding, with a mass of grizzled hair at each temple framing a sheep-like face – seated in a scuffed brown leather armchair, flicking through a wad of galleys.

'Ah, Orwell. Good. Sit.' The publisher pointed to the settee opposite.

He pulled the typescript from his briefcase and handed it over. 'You got my letter? About the new ending?'

'Yes, well, let's see how it reads.' Gollancz appeared to

weigh the typescript in his hands, before leafing through it rapidly and setting it on the floor next to the other piles of paper.

He seized the moment. 'I know you like your books to have . . .' He searched for the right word. 'Realism.'

'Don't be worried, Orwell.' Gollancz reached over to his desk and grabbed a book with a bright yellow dust jacket and held it up. *Jamaica Inn* by Daphne du Maurier. 'Just arrived back from the printer. Now, if you want bleak, this makes your stories read like comedy. But I'm expecting it to do well, regardless.'

He felt like a fool. 'I mentioned an advance on sales . . .' Gollancz smiled and waited for him to continue.

'It's just that . . . You know what it's like. I'm going to need some income to get on with another book. And get married.'

'Actually, I've thought of that,' Gollancz replied.

A wave of relief flowed over him. A decent advance, at last!

'A project. Call it a commission, to tide you over, until royalties come through for this one.' Gollancz picked up Orwell's new manuscript and read out the title. '*Keep the Aspidistra Flying.*'

'A commission?' His mood deflated.

'I'm starting a new imprint. We're calling it the Left Book Club. Strachey and Laski are going to help edit it.' Communists! Or as near as can be.

'We're after a book about unemployment, in the north.'

He groaned inwardly. He knew it! More slumming. More compulsory bleakness. Was that all they thought he could do? They didn't send the likes of Waugh 'up north'.

'And, of course, we immediately thought of the author of *Down and Out*.'

'Haven't Priestley and Morton already taken that trip?'

'Not with your eye, Orwell. Too sentimental. I don't want a travel brochure. As you said, we like realism.'

'I feel like I've done it before.'

'I can offer fifty pounds in expenses, and a hundred advance, with an agreed proportion on signature. That's for the trade edition.' Gollancz leaned forward. 'And if Strachey and Laski agree to accept it for the new club, quite a deal more.'

– II –

Barnsley, February 1936. Who could possibly take British Union of Fascists seriously? Just look at their flag, hanging behind the podium of the town hall next to the Union Jack: a bright red background, with a navy blue circle cut by a white lightning bolt, like some absurd parody of Nazism and communism. Really, he thought, even Hollywood couldn't make this up. Then there were the Blackshirts. He counted about a hundred of them, lined up either side of the aisle and at the front of the stage.

He knew what they were *supposed* to look like: stormtroopers – tall, broad-chested and hard-bodied, with prize-fighters' jowls, tight slits for mouths and frightening, pitiless faces like wax masks – but the reality was rather more comic. The one nearest to him had close-cropped greying hair, a crooked nose and so many missing teeth that the few discoloured ones left looked like fangs; the tight black fencing sweater of his uniform tucked into his black trousers revealed a soft belly and flabby arms. What came to mind was an ageing, overfed and unintelligent sewer rat.

He had been brought along by the local National Unemployed Workers' Movement organisers Tommy Degnan and Ellis Firth, and sat with the communist and

Independent Labour Party contingent, whose members were making something of a scene, catcalling the Blackshirts and ragging them. He could see the Blackshirts muttering among themselves as they looked over the crowd, probably sizing up his hosts and maybe even him for special attention afterwards. They were all clutching lengths of rubber hose; one was slipping on a knuckleduster.

The hall was called to order by the meeting's chairman, and an organ started on 'God Save the King', for which they all stood and sang. Strange, the English! As the song ended the yelling began, just like at a football game: 'Hitler and Mosley mean hunger and war!' versus 'Out with the Jews!' This was allowed to go on for some minutes, though whether deliberately or not he couldn't tell. Then the Blackshirts began a slow, rhythmical chant – 'Mosley . . . Mosley . . . Mosley . . .' – each repetition carrying an unmissable undertone of violence. They were trying to drown out the cries of the communists and socialists, but the real object, he suspected, was to drown out even the possibility of thought.

A searchlight suddenly illuminated an entrance door behind them and, announced by half a dozen off-key trumpeters, a lean and insincere-looking man with a full moustache and short black hair cropped at the temples entered the hall. He was wearing a black uniform like that of the Blackshirts except for the riding breeches and boots of the officer class. Amid the loud and growing boos there were shouts of worship. Flanked by a number of more impressive guards, the Chaplinesque figure made his way to the stage, stopping at one point to trade kisses with a gaggle of upper-class women no doubt placed there for just that purpose. After their leader had passed, he saw one of the women drop to her knees and bury her face in her hands in what he took to be the act of prayer.

With the chanting joined by the sound of people stamping their feet and pounding their hands on the backs of chairs, the leader reached the podium to applause and jeering in equal measure. It was Sir Oswald Mosley: inheritor of an estate worth ten million pounds, the reputed lover of beer-baron scioness Diana Guinness, former Tory MP, former Labour cabinet minister, former leader of the New Party, Britain's number one admirer of Hitler and Mussolini, and now the self-appointed Fuehrer of the British Union of Fascists.

What a contrast with the German dictator he had seen on the newsreels. Even at his smartest there was something obviously wrong about old Adolf 's appearance that added to his menace: the uniform slightly ill-fitting, the hair that fell over his pathetic dog-like face, the pale skin that spoke of failure and mustard gas, and explained the fixed, monomaniacal hatred of his speeches screeched out in common, guttural German. Yet here was Mosley, neat as a pin, speaking of the struggle for the new world order as if it were a pep talk before a house rugger match at Winchester.

'I have come here to this great meeting tonight to outline the policies and faith of British fascism,' Mosley began.

'You mean *German* fascism, you Kraut-loving bastard!' one of the miners near Orwell yelled out, audible amid the jeers. 'We fought your pal Hitler at Eep!' The rat-faced Blackshirt eyed up the offender and gripped his hose tighter.

Mosley ignored the hostility. 'If you think the present state of things can really see you through, then it's idle for this virile faith of fascism to come to you with a new and revolutionary conception of politics, of economics and of life itself.'

Really! Hitler never used terms like 'revolutionary conception'; he had hate, which he directed against his enemies like a machine gun.

'And now our men of 1914, our brave men of 1914 to 1918, the grim ranks of ex-servicemen who have again and again been betrayed by our politicians—'

'Yeah, bloody right, mate, after fighting your German pals,' yelled out someone close by, but he could see some of the older men nodding.

'. . . we need a Britain worthy of their sacrifices; not a Britain of idle mills and closed pits and dole queues.'

Mosley was sounding more like Adolf now. He noticed how Mosley had moved from fascism to socialism without so much as a change in syntax. Start mild and reasonable, build up the resentment and hate. A good old hate, that's what his people had come along for.

'Those brave, forgotten men of the last war should join their hands with the new youth, the new generation that has studied the past and says that England is not dead.'

A new chant now went up: 'England! England! England!' The words were repeated slowly, over and over again.

Up on the stage, under the spotlight and in front of the huge microphone suspended from the ceiling, Mosley barely raised a sweat as he went through his theatrics, flinging his right arm back and forth like a Roman senator. The chanting continued, interspersed with eruptions of outrage as more vocal members of the audience were dragged from their seats by groups of Blackshirts and thrown through the auditorium's swinging doors, where others were waiting to deal with them. Finally, Mosley quietened the crowd with a wave of his hand.

'Think of your lives, men and women of northern England. You are born, fed on broken biscuits, forced to toil long hours underground or in mills until the last ounce of your strength is gone, then you are thrown into the workhouse when you can't work a minute longer, or forced onto the dole with its iniquitous means test when the international financiers decide it's time to cut production. You, the steelworker; why should you be on short-time, your children shoeless and in rags, when Britain needs tanks and battleships and aeroplanes? Why should you, the unemployed miner, scrabble for coal and watch your children go malnourished to support the earnings of foreign bondholders?'

The booing continued, but only from the communists and ILPers, and soon was drowned out by the applause, which was growing louder.

'Why is this happening? Is it because Britain isn't capable of supporting the people who work for it? Or is it because your work and the fruits of your work are being stolen from you?'

'By rich buggers like you,' someone shouted. 'By capitalists!'

'By the Jews!' someone countered. The applause detonated.

'You said it, sir, not I,' Mosley went on. 'I say we need a new government of men who can make decisions.'

Degnan stood on his chair. 'We can't all live off the estate of our dead wives, Mosley!' he yelled.

'Or our mistresses,' another added.

'Aye,' Firth cried out, 'no more drinking Guinness for us!' This provoked laughter.

'You're a millionaire and a murderer, Mosley. When's the last time *you* worked? Where's your money invested? Traitor!'

Mosley nodded a signal to his Blackshirts. 'Send all the world a message: England lives on and marches on! We can make Britain stronger!' He was purple now. 'One nation united – miner and shopkeeper, mill-worker and farmer. Yes, indeed, even the Jews putting Britain before Jewry.'

At this, audience members from both camps rose to their feet, either applauding or shouting abuse. The air throbbed with concentrated hate. As the chant of 'Mosley!' went up again, hundreds of fascist salutes appeared across the room in unison, as in a theatrical production. The activists around Orwell raised their voices in response but had no effect. Degnan was still standing on his chair, shaking his fist, his red face a mask of rage, screaming out: 'Swine, swine, swine!' A group of Blackshirts was heading towards him.

Mosley's screeching continued. As he raved, the rat-faced Blackshirt and his comrades dragged Degnan to the aisle, shoving him towards the rear, where he stumbled and was set upon, large boots thudding into his groin and face. A broken set of dentures fell into the dark pool of blood from Degnan's mouth. Firth, sitting a few rows ahead, tried to get across to the aisle to help but was blocked by a wall of Blackshirts. Instead he ran forward and tried to mount the stage, thinking this the quickest way across to the other aisle, but as he reached it he too was punched to the ground and whipped with rubberhoses.

'A typical example of red tactics!' Mosley commented to the crowd, pointing to the scene, which was illuminated by one of the roving spotlights. 'We do not want to fight, ladies and gentlemen, but if violence is organised against us, then we shall organise violence in reply.'

'Mosley, Mosley, Mosley . . .' The rhythmical chanting reached a crescendo.

– III –

Wigan, March 1936. The scene that met his eyes only made sense as science fiction. It was shift changeover time, and thousands of shortstatured, black-faced men in filthy overalls were emerging from the ground like Morlocks. Soon, he and Albert Grey – a small, powerful and balding man of about forty-five, whom the wealthy socialist editor of *The Adelphi*, Sir Richard Rees, had suggested to Orwell as a guide – were like rocks in a tide as waves of miners surged past, swigging from their bottles and spitting black gargles of tea and coal dust onto the shale and mud at their feet. There was no pithead bath here; these men would go home to be washed by their wives.

After the morning shift had dispersed, he shuffled to the lift cage, surrounded by the experienced miners with their bluescarred noses and bad teeth. They were packed like pilchards in a tin; at six-foot-three he had to take off his wooden helmet and stoop, but still his head rested against the roof. Then the floor dropped away, queering his guts, and they plunged into the void. It was only as they decelerated that he noticed the sensation of movement, and that strangely counter-intuitive feeling that one was actually going upwards. As they slowed to a halt, he could make out through the wire cage door passing hints of whiteness, which he took to be the fossilised bones of long-extinct animals. This far down they must have been truly ancient – perhaps enormous reptiles that walked England before the first man was ever seen.

They stopped, the cage door slid open and they emerged into what looked like a pea-soup fog. A draught of circulating air carried particles of coal dust into his lungs, setting off a tickling cough. He looked around, expecting to find men hacking away at a ledge with picks, but saw only confusion and movement as another pod of men squeezed past him to take the lift for the upwards journey.

Grey, a miner himself, pointed to one of the smallish holes that opened off the concourse. 'Pit face is that way, Eric. Mind your head.'

He had decided to leave 'George' for the literary world. The going underfoot was bad – rocky and muddy with puddles, like a farmyard in autumn. After a few hundred yards the pain of stooping – far worse for him than the others, most of whom stood a foot shorter – became by turns tiresome and debilitating. The base of his spine, his neck and his calves ached simultaneously, and he felt an overwhelming urge either to stand up straight or lie down and stretch out. At some points the tremendous pressure of half a mile of mountainside had buckled the props holding up the roof, and he had to bend double to pass through, several times scraping the vertebrae of his back on the jagged rocks, an exquisite form of agony.

Just as he thought he could no longer go on, Grey yelled out cheerily, 'Four hundred yards to go.' He might as well have said four hundred miles. Then, as his hamstrings and thighs were ceasing to obey his mental commands, they reached the coal face. 'We're here!'

As the other men picked up bundles of tools to begin their day's paid work, he flung himself to the ground, in too much agony to care what the others thought. 'Sorry, chaps.'

'That's alright, Mr Blair,' one of the men, Ken Goodliffe, said.

'It's always hard first time. It's not so bad for us, coming down first time as lads. We normally run most of way.'

He sat up, his back against a pit prop, and watched the miners at work. The shot men on the departing shift had exploded a brace of charges into the seam, cracking the solid mass to make it more gettable. To loosen the coal further, a team with an electric drill the size of a Lewis gun was cutting a deep groove along the base of the black wall, undermining it. The drill was unbearably loud in the confined space and raised a fog of black dust so thick that Davy lamps and electric torches could barely penetrate the gloom. These added to the increasingly unbearable heat; it was like a sauna bath where you went to get dirty instead of clean.

The whole effect was to overwhelm the senses. Even the powers of smell and taste were assaulted by the steady progress of coal dust through the nose and mouth to the back of the throat. While he watched, the team disassembled the conveyor belt that carried the cut coal back to the waiting tubs, and then reassembled it closer to the end of the seam. It wasn't long ago, the miners told him later, that the coal was dragged by women and children to carts drawn by pit ponies. Now it had all been electrified. So this sight before him, he thought, was considered a wonder of modernity!

'Job was much harder in our fathers' time, Mr Blair, much harder.' He wished they would call him Eric.

Now the real work began. Naked from the waist up, sitting on their knees with their padded knee-caps jammed tight against the surface, the miners drove their short, sharp shovels into the loosened face, cutting the coal free in various sizes.

Grey beckoned him over and shouted above the din: 'Have a try.'

He got on his knees and did his best to drive the shovel into the shiny black wall in front of him, but barely made a mark. He kept going, the men around him smiling wryly, and managed to dislodge a lump the size of a cricket ball. It fell to the floor and was picked up by one of the younger men, who spat on it and made out to polish it on his grimy trousers. 'Here you go, Mr Blair,' the boy said. 'Keep it as a souvenir.'

He stumbled back, exhausted, and watched the men working at the face. He felt humbled, humiliated almost, but it was a feeling devoid of shame. With their bodies that looked like hammered iron statues coated in coal dust, exerting themselves with stupendous force and speed as they shared the frightening dangers of their jobs, they raised in him a pang of envy. *How can educated people continue to feel ourselves superior?* It was only because magnificent men like these smashed away at nature like moles, and lived lives of misery and slum-squalor, that the rest of England could enjoy comparative comfort and advantage. He could see the miners now, just as Wells foretold, coming up from the ground one day to wreak revenge on the rich, and he wondered if it wouldn't be an entirely bad thing.

On the way back to the surface he failed to duck at the right moment and knocked himself flat on his back, almost unconscious.

★

After cleaning themselves up, the miners insisted on taking him to the pub. He was adamant about buying the first round and got a packet of cigarettes to share. While ordering, he noticed the afternoon newspaper lying on the bar. The headline had one word: ABYSSINIA.

He returned and passed around cigarettes and pints of the local beer, which was thick and dark. 'Thanks for showing me how the mine works, chaps.' He wasn't sure how they might receive *comrades*.

'If you have any sense, Mr Blair,' said Goodliffe, 'it'll be the last mine you go down. Writing – now, that seems much cushier. And better paid too, I'll bet.'

'Please, call me Eric.' He thought about it for a moment. He'd collected some miners' pay dockets for his research and reckoned that, at about £2 10s per week, he'd not earned as much as a miner in any of the years since he left Burma. 'Well, it's certainly a lot more comfortable than mining. I've never seen a man killed by a typewriter, that's for sure.'

'Aye, true enough. But none of us could do what you can do, Mr Blair – I mean, Eric – writing books and all. I'll bet your family thinks you right clever.'

If only they knew. He was about to tell them his parents had hoped he'd stay a policeman, then thought better of it. 'Writing's not so difficult, once you know how. Anyway, have you seen the latest news?'

'Yeah,' said another man. 'The bloody FA stopping us betting.' It was the strangest thing. Here were men with political contacts – real rank-and-file members of the militant ILP – but the talk wasn't of the world situation or Mosley's sally into the north, but the decision of the Football Association not to publish the season fixture in advance, in an attempt to quell the football pools. The local newspapers wrote of little else.

'Lousy bastards,' the man continued, 'trying to rob us of the only chance to make some real money.'

'I don't quite understand . . .'

'Sorry, Eric. I was just saying, those of us who follow the football reckon we've got a good chance of winning the pools, and it's not right of those that control the Football Association to ban betting.'

'Have you ever won yourself?' asked Orwell.

'Wouldn't be mining coal if I had, now, would I? But I know football and reckon it's only time before I do win.'

'Always bets on Barnsley, that's his problem,' said another.

'Do you know anyone who has won the jackpot?'

'Well, no; but you read about it in the papers, don't you? Friend of mine says he has a mother-in-law whose dustman won. A dustman! Bet he won't be picking up no one's slops from now on.'

'Quite.'

He was eager to hear their political views. 'I say, what do you think about the international situation? The Italians are in Abyssinia. The German army has crossed the Rhine.'

'Parley-voo?' said Goodliffe, producing laughter.

'Don't mind the lads, Eric,' said Grey. 'They're not old enough to know what's coming. Weren't in Flanders, like me and their dads, but they might be a few years from now.'

'Don't you think it's serious? Fascism is on the march everywhere. Mosley's round these parts right now, breaking some of your friends' heads.'

'Friends? Communists, you mean,' said Goodliffe. 'Bloody troublemakers. Just looking for a fight.'

'Do you think you might have to? Fight the fascists, I mean. In a war.'

'Oh, aye. We'd fight alright. Germans and Italians. But for England and the King, not for Russia and *Comrade* Stalin.'

'And for better jobs,' another added. 'Look what our dads came back to.'

'Well, what would you change about the way you live?' From the expressions on the men's faces, he could see immediately that to them this question was absurdly abstract.

'The way we live? I'd say we were happy enough.'

Happy enough, he thought. He had seen their slum houses, with cancerous mould growing up the walls, no bathrooms and the only WC fifty yards away and shared by dozens of other families. 'I mean to say, what about the social question? The economy, social conditions generally?' Again a look of incomprehension.

He got up to buy another round, but was stopped.

'We can buy our own drink, Eric,' said Grey.

'Let me. My publisher gave me money for expenses. Beer's as good an expense as any.'

'That's not how we do things around here,' one said, slapping him on the shoulder and heading up to the bar. At least beer was cheap, he thought, but it struck him that few starving writers would have had such a sense of honour. The conversation turned back to the football pools.

★

Later that evening he was sitting at Albert Grey's dining table. It was a council house, but one of the largest and neatest he had seen on his trip north; he had even been luxuriating in flannelette sheets. He was typing a letter, part of his interminable correspondence with Gollancz about *Keep the Aspidistra Flying*, which the gutless lawyers were slowly bowdlerising as efficiently as any state propaganda service.

At his shoulder, Irene, Grey's ten-year-old daughter, was fascinated by the typewriter. He completed the letter and rolled another sheet onto the platen. He moved the machine in front of her to let her have a play. 'Now, Irene, write me something about your dog. Don't forget the space bar, here.'

She began tapping slowly: 'my dogs name is jimmy he barcks a lott and sleeps at my feet on my bed we all love him . . .'

Mrs Grey, who was sitting by the fire sewing, looked over and smiled. Her husband, in his rocking chair in shirtsleeves and no collar, and absorbed in a tawdry sensational murder tale that was then filling the local newspaper, looked up. 'Now, Irene, don't be annoying Mr Blair; he has important work to do. Go on, off with you.'

Orwell patted her head and she went to the rag mat in front of the fire and sat down next to her sister, who like her was sucking on the mint humbug that was their evening treat. The girls were giggling, giving their small dog his favourite thrill – the simultaneous scratching of his stomach and ears. At their age, he reflected, he barely knew his father. He tried to imagine Grey or his wife allowing deranged sadists like his masters at St Cyprians to beat their children into submission. How much better was this childhood? He rolled a fresh page into the typewriter and commenced typing.

Curiously enough it is not

He hit the backspace bar three times and underlined the last word.

Curiously enough it is <u>not</u> the triumphs of modern engineering, not the radio, nor the cinematograph, nor the five thousand novels which are published yearly, nor the crowds at Ascot and the Eton and Harrow match, but the memory of working-class interiors – especially as I sometimes saw them in my childhood before the war when England was still prosperous – that reminds me that our age has not been altogether a bad one to live in.

★

The next morning it was time to leave. Grey, who had bronchitis – although of course everyone suspected something worse – and was too ill for his shift, was at home to say his farewells.

'Every success with your book, Eric,' said Mrs Grey near the front gate. 'We're looking forward to reading it. And thank you for helping me with the washing-up.'

'The least I can do. Your house is the most welcoming in England.'

Grey, who was in the doorway, quietly coughing into his palm, stepped out and offered his hand, which he had wiped carefully on his handkerchief. 'We're relying on you to help set things right, comrade.'

Taking the proffered hand, Orwell said simply, 'Comrade.' It was the first time he had ever used the term without a sense of shame and embarrassment. For a man like himself – despite his poverty, he was still an Etonian – to call another man *comrade* seemed somehow hypocritical, absurd even. But only if you were not a socialist.

– IV –

Kingsway Hall, London, 26 October 1936. With his pixie-like frame, hatchet face and long mane of dark hair dragged unwillingly across his large skull, the radical MP James Maxton was tuning the crowd to the required angry pitch. His long and bony arms clawed aggressively at the smoke-filled air before the grand backdrop of giant organ pipes, from which hung the huge scarlet banner of the ILP.

Eileen, whose idea it had been to come, took the cigarette from her mouth, leaned over and put her lips almost to his ear.

'I've just figured out who this Maxton fellow reminds me of. You'll never guess.'

'A clue?'

'From a children's fable.'

'Rumpelstiltskin.'

'Uncanny, isn't it?'

Maxton was reading out a speech which was to have been delivered by a Spanish revolutionary leader, who had at the last minute been turned back at the airport. Amplified through loudspeakers, his metallic voice screeched with the usual slogans – 'fascist nightmare', 'imperialist dreams', 'crimes against working humanity', 'stand side by side' – riveted together with facts about the recent massacres in Badajoz, the reporting of which had incensed Orwell and Eileen as it had every socialist in Britain: the reason she had suggested they come. The impression was of a disturbing clanking noise, grinding away like some industrial machine badly in need of oil. With a slightly altered message, and some of the words rearranged, he figured, he could have been back in Barnsley, listening to Mosley; and yet he didn't care. The fascists, no matter what faux sympathies they professed for 'the people', had no interest in ending the miseries of the workers in Wigan; he now realised they simply had to be stopped.

As Maxton worked himself into a near delirium for the peroration, it occurred to him that although the man hadn't written the speech, and indeed its author wasn't even English, it would have been almost impossible to tell.

'Workers of Britain! Workers of all political sections in Britain! Comrades – brothers! Our party, the Worker's Party of Marxist Unity, has dedicated itself under this banner: "Unto the end – conquer or die!"'

This was met by wild cheers and the raising of fists, the most enthusiastic of which came from the ILP's youth section.

'Where did he say he was from, darling?' he asked Eileen.

'The POUM. Anarchists or some such, I think.'

'Already some of our heroic comrades have died. If it is necessary that we should all die to gain the victory, then die we will! Workers, comrades, brothers – help us! Help us against fascism, help us against war, help us for the complete emancipation of the workers!'

From up in the gods of the grand theatre, they looked down through the thick blue smoke to see the crowd heaving, yelling slogans that could be heard with difficulty against the stamping of feet: 'Fascist swine! . . . Revolution! . . . United front!' The speech was complete. Wild, angry applause went on.

Maxton, who was the chairman of the ILP, gave way to the general secretary, the taller and better dressed Fenner Brockway, whose round spectacles glinted like mirrors in the footlights, obscuring his eyes. 'Comrades, I have a resolution,' Brockway announced, waving a sheet of paper, and the crowd bayed at him to read it. Brockway set it down on the lectern and adjusted his glasses to the end of his nose in a characteristic gesture. The audience quietened.

'This meeting believes that the threefold duty of the British workers is: One – Action to support the Spanish workers in the struggle against fascism. Two – Action to prevent capitalist intervention to destroy the Spanish workers in favour of capitalist liberalism. And three – Action to resist any war of rival capitalist imperialisms.' He was stopped by applause.

Orwell groaned. Something about it sounded vaguely contradictory, but it was difficult to say just what. Why couldn't these people just speak normal English, the way the workers did?

'Comrades, if carried, this pledges us to intensify our efforts to send shipments of food, medical supplies and other necessities to Spain. We have already sent money and an ambulance. Give of yourselves, comrades! Give!'

Young men wearing Spanish-style berets (he had noted this fashion taking hold in the last month) began moving through the audience carrying buckets, which they shook up and down.

'What about fighting, Fenner?' someone yelled out. 'What about troops? Arms!'

'Tanks!' screeched another, to wilder acclamation.

Brockway hesitated, thinking no doubt of the police informers who were almost certainly in the hall, but, carried away, he soon continued. 'Comrades, the National Administrative Council has voted to raise an armed labour battalion of socialist volunteers to fight on the front lines. Comrade Bob Edwards is developing the plan. We will begin advertising for willing fighters shortly.'

The room erupted, and all around the younger party members – too young to have seen the trenches – raised their fists even higher, smiling in happy anticipation of being spattered with somebody else's blood.

He looked at them. A good old-fashioned fight, against someone truly worthy of hate, smashing their faces in with clubs, kicking them in the genitals, breaking teeth, blowing their children up with thermite – that's what socialists really wanted, when it came down to it. In that, they were just the same as the fascists. He had thought his book about the workers' lives in the north would attract the sort of literary attention he craved. But, overnight, Spain had changed everything, altering everyone's priorities. Unemployment, hunger marches, poverty, slums and bedbugs – the very things that had constituted the political struggle until then – had dissolved as issues, leaving him with a half-written book about yesterday's news. He had visions of it covered in dust, in piles out the front of bookshops, where no one really cared whether or not it was stolen. Other writers, firing off war dispatches from luxury hotels in Madrid, would get the front-page reviews and the runaway book sales, leaving him once again a failure.

He looked around at the audience members, seeing a young woman in blue overalls and a bright red headscarf yelling slogans in an educated voice. Who wanted to read about bedbugs anymore? No one.

'I shall take it as carried, comrades,' Brockway concluded. With the exception of a scattering of cardigan-wearers – pacifists, he suspected – who determinedly remained seated, the audience stood, fists raised and eyes closed, as if in prayer. The organ sounded and a Scottish voice at the microphone – Maxton – began singing: 'The workers' flag is deepest red . . .'

Although he was unsure of the words, he found himself singing along, humming through the bits he didn't know. Eileen joined in too – with an enthusiasm that suggested seriousness rather than the irony he had expected. The Spanish business, with its suspiciously neat choice between good and evil, its bayoneted children and raped nuns, had had that effect on seemingly everyone he knew. He doubted there was a thinking person in the whole of Britain who hadn't taken sides. It was even funny, in a way, listening to himself taking part so fully, when six months earlier he had barely given socialism or even politics a thought. It occurred to him that, along with Eileen, he was probably the only person among the two-thousand-strong crowd who didn't think about Marx more often than about beer or sex, and yet this act of joining in still seemed, somehow, the right thing to do. Fascism had to be stopped if socialism was to have a chance.

This, he now saw, was what he must write about. Any fool could see that there was only one issue that mattered, and only one place where a writer could really make his name: Spain.

– V –

The Republican trenches, Huesca, Spain, May 1937. It was the most curious sensation, being shot. Even though he was certain he was dying, he desperately tried to commit the effects to memory, just in case. Not many writers had been shot, or at least had survived to write about it.

It was only when he regained consciousness, face-down on the bottom of the trench, to the sounds of his comrades arguing about the source of the blood soaking his clothes, that his mind tried to make sense of what had happened. As he recalled to the best of his capacity, it went in roughly this order, the whole thing only taking a second or two. He heard a loud explosion and was surrounded by a terrific burst of light. As the bullet entered his body a violent tremor ran through him, like an express train through a tunnel. Then he dropped forward in two separate movements to hit the ground – knees first, then head, like a calf stunned by a hammer. He tried to hold on to these impressions, fearing his memory might muck them up before he got the chance to write them down.

While these thoughts were flashing through his mind, the others were fumbling beside him, clumsily cutting away at his shirt and applying a field dressing, waiting for the stretcher party to arrive down the support trench.

'His neck,' one said. 'Bullet's gone clean through.'

The neck! You didn't survive those; he'd seen goats, pigs and other creatures shot in the neck and they were always goners. He tried to open his mouth to talk but all that came from his lips was a spurt of blood; not a good omen.

★

Five months earlier he had arrived on the slow train via Toulouse, singing the 'Marseillaise' to the raised fists of the peasants they passed. Revolutionary Barcelona he remembered as a sort of carnival, complete with gay songs about love and brotherhood which played through the loudspeakers hanging on the lamp-posts. Almost every wall was painted red and black and daubed with the slogans of the various left-wing parties and unions: PSUC, UGT, CNT-FAI, JCI, JSU, AIT, POUM. The last was the only one he recognised, remembering it from Maxton's speech in London.

Shops and cafés carried signs proclaiming they had been collectivised. The various hotels carried their party flags, and at the Hotel Colon, headquarters of the communists, he saw enormous portraits of Lenin and Stalin, looking benevolently at the people below. At the barber's having his morning shave, he sat beneath a slogan which his poor grasp of Spanish took to be a solemn explanation that barbers were not slaves. (All barbers, he later learnt, were anarchists.) And while everything else bore the unmistakeable signs of a city at war – the litter-filled pavements, the bomb-chipped walls and broken windows, the shabby and half-empty shops with queues of people outside, tobacco at terrifically inflated prices – the dun colour of the streetscape was more than made up for by the garishly rendered posters of triumphant worker-soldiers pasted on every wall. *Obreros a la Victoria!* Workers to Victory!

He recalled, vividly, stopping at a bootblack, a small man of late middle age who was wearing the regulation grey overalls and tattered beret. Before placing his shoes on the man's polishing box, which like everything else was painted black and red, he used the greeting he had learnt in schoolboy Spanish classes: '*Buenos dias.*' But the man, on noticing him, looked him in the eye, gave him the raised-fist salute and replied, '*Salud, comrade!*' Instinctively almost, he returned the gesture. '*Salud!*' It was an unremarkable exchange, but one that was inconceivable back in England. A gentleman and a bootblack on equal terms! Brothers!

In that brief encounter, his understanding of his surroundings suddenly became complete. He realised, for instance, that the irregular, un-mortared cobblestones on which he constantly stumbled spoke of hastily torn-down barricades. Then there was the complete absence of the well-to-do upper classes. In Wigan this had felt like some sort of betrayal, but in Barcelona it seemed comely, a symbol of something positive: victory, perhaps. Yes, he remembered thinking, in a kind of rapture, *this* is what socialism looks like; a society with the working classes in the saddle. He had come to Spain in search of a story, hoping to gain fame as a correspondent, and maybe write a book, but he had known from that moment that he must also fight.

Within a week, Nye Bevan's glamorous wife, Jenny Lee,

had directed him to the militia of the POUM, where he was soon joined by other British volunteers. Eileen turned up some weeks later to make herself useful, helping with the unit's pay and administration. The POUM may have been the sister party of the ILP, but in Moscow its members and fighters were 'Trotskyists' or 'masked fascists', and therefore to be exterminated at the first opportunity. The man known as 'Stalin's Midget' – Nikolai Yezhov, chief of the party's secret police, the NKVD – had already drawn up the plans. But he and Eileen hadn't known that then.

★

The Republican front line, Monte Oscuro, February 1937. He was sitting on an empty ammunition box, smoking. At that time of day the sun slanted into the trench, warming his bones and reviving his spirits. When the early fighting of the war petered out the previous autumn, the Republicans and fascists found themselves perched on high razorback ridges of limestone on opposing sides of a rocky valley, and there they remained. It was less a trench line than a series of fortified positions within signalling distance, and the white cliff-face topped by stone parapets gave him the impression of being atop a medieval castle.

In the era of the machine gun (even including the rusty specimens they had been given), the almost vertical terrain made a successful infantry assault all but impossible; as a result, the only options for either force were stagnation or suicide. As the crow flew, the two ragged lines were only about seven hundred yards apart, but he reckoned it closer to a mile by foot. At that range bullets limped overhead meaninglessly, made even less lethal by the woeful standard of Spanish marksmanship. What fascist shellfire there was was desultory, rationed to a few rounds a week, the worn-out barrels of the antique artillery pieces causing most shots to fall well short or fly long. The real weapons and the real war – and the real opportunities to write and report, the way Hemingway and others were doing – were elsewhere, in Madrid, and he longed to be there.

His sentry duty was coming to an end, and he heard a scrabble in front of the trench as the patrol – the warlike name given to scrambling for food and firewood in an old potato field in noman's land – returned through a gap in the pitiful barbed-wire obstacle twenty yards to the front. He yelled out the challenge:

'*Seremos!*'

'*Invencibles!*' came the reply.

As the men were sliding down into the trench, they heard the noise of an aeroplane. In this part of the front that could mean only one thing: a *fascist* aeroplane. All the Russian-supplied aircraft were near Madrid, supporting the communist-led units, which also had Russian tanks, artillery and even serviceable rifles. Why would Stalin give arms to Trotskyites in Spain, the POUM members argued, at the very moment he was executing them in Moscow? If only he'd known before he'd signed on!

He motioned to the machine gunners, who picked up their ancient French weapon and carried it into the open, where they perched it on a rock so as to traverse the sky. After a dozen shots the clip jammed, as usual. As they set about extracting the bulbous bullet from the breech, they saw something white and glittering tumbling from the rear of the ancient-looking biplane. Newspapers.

'We can burn them,' he said, and the men scrambled about the ridge under harmless rifle fire, collecting the fallen bundles. It was the fascist newspaper *Heraldo de Aragon*. One of the better Spanish speakers translated it for them but he could make out the general picture himself: Malaga had fallen. They didn't believe a word of it. But by that evening word had filtered up from the rear that it was true – and, worse, the communists were alleging that the town had been betrayed by the Anarchists and the POUM.

After dark, he managed to bed down on the rocky floor of the dugout, which had been driven into the reverse slope of the limestone ridge they were defending. There he lay, with the Spanish machine-gunner Ramon snoring away behind him, when his commander, the ILP heavy Bob Edwards, stuck his head in the dugout. 'They're attacking.'

They scrambled up the steps through mist that swirled about their ankles like a cold stream, presenting their rifles at the firestep. The fascists had moved up some extra machine guns – he counted five lines of tracer – and their fire was closer than usual. They began firing their rifles at the sources of the flashes, hopelessly, and a few shells lobbed well wide of them, half of which failed to explode.

A series of ricochets sounded behind them – they were surrounded! His entrails turned to jelly – in this war there was no taking of prisoners. But the threat to their rear turned out to be one of their own guns firing in support, but at the wrong target. On cue, their Hotchkiss gun jammed, and in their exposed condition there was nothing they could do but stand and be shot at, and try to make a fight of it with the bayonet. When you're under fire, he realised, the thing that runs through your mind is not when you will be hit but *where*, causing one's whole body to tense up, giving it a most unpleasant sensitivity. After an hour or two of drama the attack faded away, and in the morning they could see that it had merely been some sort of patrol, and it had soon retired. They had suffered only one casualty, which turned out to be a minor wound. Though petty and unremarkable, it was his first real fight against fascists.

Two days later in their dugout, he and Bob Smillie listened incredulously as Edwards translated a news report about the fascist attack which appeared in the POUM newspaper *La Batalla*.

'"In a great battle that took place on the night of February 20,"' Edwards was saying, '"our lines opposite Zaragoza repulsed a major fascist offensive. The famous English contingent of the 29th Division, led by Comrade Robert Edwardo, defended their trenches like lions, using machine guns and bombs to beat off numerous waves of determined fascist stormtroopers backed by cavalry and tanks. If not for the bravery shown by the valiant Englishmen, our line may have broken leaving the road to Alcubierre and even Barcelona itself open to the enemy. This glorious victory once again shows the superior power of international working-class solidarity over the conscripted hirelings of Fascism . . ." It goes on, comrades. Mentions young Bob here – "son of the famous working-class leader", etc., etc. Even quotes Lenin!'

'Of course,' Orwell said. 'Wouldn't be publishable without a quote from the big cheese.'

Smillie was laughing. 'Obviously written by someone back in Barcelona or Madrid.'

'Or perhaps back in London,' said Orwell. 'Pure fantasy. I doubt there's a single tank between here and Gibraltar. And even if there were, how would the fascists get them up the cliff below our position?'

'It's preposterous, I'll admit,' said Smillie. 'But my grandfather will be pleased when he reads about it in the *New Leader*. "Comrade Smillie, the miners' leader's grandson, a hero repulsing fascist tanks on the Aragon front."'

'He'll be right to be proud,' said Orwell. 'It's all there in black and white, and who's to say otherwise? As far as future generations are concerned, Comrade Smillie here will be a hero of the revolution, and when we're all dead and unable to refute it, our pathetic little skirmish will exist as a great battle on more evidence than history has for Thermopylae and Senlac.'

'Well, at least it's good to know we're not getting cold and lousy out here for nothing,' Edwards said.

'Problem is, of course, that if we ever get beaten, like those chaps did at Malaga, history will record us as traitors. The English Trotsky-fascists who stabbed the revolution in the back. The truth will be whatever Comrade Stalin wants it to be.'

★

The weeks following being shot he barely remembered, apart from the discomfort and the pain: the jolting ambulance rides over potholed Spanish roads; the filthy Spanish hospitals with their greasy, tin-tasting food and slovenly nurses; the doctors who gave him up for dead before calling him their lucky charm (one millimetre to the left, they said, and the bullet would have severed his carotid artery); and the strange electro-shock therapy they gave him to stimulate his damaged throat and arm muscles into life again. At the end of it all, finding himself still breathing, he had had to retrace his route back to the front line to get his discharge papers signed, only to be lined up, handed a rifle and cartridges, and told he was in the reserve for the assault that would finally take Huesca. In typical Spanish confusion the attack was postponed, and he managed to get his papers signed and hitch a ride back to Barcelona.

He reached the city after days of hitchhiking and sleeping rough, and was surprised to find Eileen waiting for him in the lounge of the Hotel Continental, holding his travelling bag. She rose and intercepted him before he could be seen by the man at the reception desk, took his arm in hers and walked him towards the entrance again. 'Shh!' she said.

A hotel worker – an anarchist, most likely – opened the door and said, 'Quickly!'

As they entered the harsh sunshine of the Ramblas, he slowed, making to stop and turn around, but she dragged him on, with a firm tug of his painful arm, causing him to stumble slightly.

'Do you want to be shot?' she said in a firm but low voice.

He struggled against her again, but again she powered on. She whispered: 'They've outlawed the POUM.'

It couldn't be!

'They're executing everyone. They say Nin is already

dead.' Nin! The POUM's charismatic leader, whom he'd met during the street fighting of the weeks before.

She pulled him across to the far side of the wide boulevard, which was packed with Civil Guards, and soon they plunged into the warren of the old city – its prole quarter, the anarchist bastion – where they were more likely to be safe. In a side street they found a quieter place and ordered coffee, hoping the proprietor wasn't listening in.

'What shall we do?' he asked Eileen.

'Get our papers stamped and leave. But you can't go back to the Continental; it's swarming with spies. They mustn't know you're back in the city or they'll scoop you up too.'

'I'll have to find another hotel.'

'They will betray you; all hotels must report their guests. No, you'll have to go into hiding. I've worked it all out. To leave, we'll need our travel documents stamped by the British consulate.'

'But that will take days.' He was tired and unwell from his wound, and the prospect of sleeping rough filled him with dread.

'No, I'm going back to our room; this is paranoid nonsense. I've done nothing against them. If they're after everyone who took part in the street fighting, they will have to arrest forty or fifty thousand people. No!'

She grabbed his wrist tightly and roughly, pinning his hand to the table. 'Listen to me! Stafford Cottman and Williams – they were at the Sanatorium Maurin with you, remember? They said the police came looking for POUM members there and hauled them away, even the severely wounded ones, probably to execute them. They managed to hide, but they said the police took a particular interest in *your* whereabouts, and took away all your possessions, even your laundry.'

'The Spanish? Carry out a purge?' He laughed. 'After the *mañana*, perhaps.'

She forced his hand down onto the table again. 'This is *not* something you can dismiss, Eric. Everything is not going to be alright. They're arresting and shooting everyone they think is a Trotskyist.'

'But I'm not a Trotskyist.'

'And neither is Nin – *was* Nin. This isn't England!'

'This is nonsense . . .'

She forced his wrist down once again, this time more painfully. Her voice was as insistent as one could be without raising a scene. 'Can't you see, the truth doesn't matter here, Eric. Everyone we know has been arrested. And they will arrest you too, and maybe shoot you – and probably me as well. You're going into hiding, and as soon as we get our passports stamped we're taking the first train we can board.'

In his tiredness he hadn't wanted to believe it, but it finally hit him. This was a purge. They were in a police state during a reign of terror, and on the losing side. While getting shot by fascists might set him apart from other writers, getting shot by communists was an entirely different matter. They would be shooting from point-blank range and wouldn't miss.

'Empty your pockets,' Eileen ordered.

He did so, placing his wallet and papers on the greasy tablecloth. She took his militia card and discharge papers, which had 'POUM' stamped prominently on them, along with a photograph taken at the front with a POUM flag visible in the background, and tore them into tiny pieces.

'These are the things they'll shoot you for. Now, I've arranged for John McNair and Stafford Cottman to meet us at the British consulate tomorrow at ten; they're to leave with us. The whole British contingent has orders to disperse immediately. I'll see you there.'

His notebooks! He had gone to Spain to write, and to leave without his notebooks was unthinkable. 'I need my papers.'

'Seized from my hotel room.'

'When?'

'In the early hours of this morning – they came in and arrested Kopp.'

'Kopp!' he exclaimed, loudly enough that anyone snooping on them could hear. His militia commander. A momentary disbelief drove all discretion out of him. He regained control. 'I thought he was in Valencia?'

'He came back.'

'You and he . . . While I was . . .'

She started to cry. 'Are you angry with me?'

Strangely, he found he was not. He had told her once, before they were married, that he believed marriage should involve freedom as well as love. Matrimony must never be a prison. He leaned over the table, took her face in his hands and kissed her hard on the lips. 'What matters is that when it counts, we stay loyal to each other and the things we believe in. We must never betray each other. That is all that counts.'

'Yes, darling.' She was crying, but for a different reason now.

'If they take me at the hotel, you must get out of Spain.'

'The hotel! You mustn't go back. You know more about

the entire British detachment than anyone. You'll be more valuable to them than me.'

'It's you they're after,' she said. 'If I disappear now, it will look too suspicious. They'll leave me alone as long as they think you haven't yet returned from the front. By the time they realise, we'll be long gone, hopefully. Don't come for me.'

'If I'm not at the consulate tomorrow, get yourself across the border on the first train.'

'No, it's neither or both.' She stood and left.

He made an instinctive attempt to follow her, to keep her within sight for possibly the last time, but became tangled in a knot of people and gave up.

– VI –

He wandered alone through the streets, looking for somewhere to sleep. Barcelona felt eerily dissimilar. The streets seemed duller, less cheery, as if he had just disembarked from a tropical ocean journey into a city in the grip of winter. At first he couldn't quite figure out what it was that was different. Then he noticed. The loudspeakers had changed their tone. The uplifting revolutionary tunes had been replaced by more martial sounds, and even though he couldn't make out all they were saying, the voices of the speakers seemed somehow shriller and more threatening. The colourful posters and banners of the revolutionary parties were also gone. Here and there, blowing down the Ramblas, he could see a shred of brightly coloured paper or fabric flapping from a wall or lying in a gutter, blocking the drain. Given the sheer volume of propaganda the left-wing parties had pasted over the city in the previous year, removing the posters must have been a prodigious task.

When he had arrived in Spain, he had assumed naively that the POUM and the anarchists had been the natural allies of the communists and the socialists; now it was obvious they were deadly enemies, and that all traces of their former alliance were being systematically eliminated. New posters had appeared. He stopped at a particularly ugly one that seemed to be on every wall thereabouts, and scanned it closely. It was a hideous image that struck him immediately as a threat to his own life. The picture showed a powerful-looking man carrying a large, knotted club, stamping his boot down violently on a group of POUM and anarchist members caught helplessly at his feet, like animals in a net. *DESCUBR ID Y APLASTAD SIN PIEDAD A LA 5a COLUMNA*, it read. Uncover and crush the Fifth Column without mercy. *Without mercy.* In the corner of the poster was the hammer and sickle of the Spanish Communist Party. So this is what the Bolshevik revolution had come to: a boot stamping on all who resist, forever.

There were no POUM safe houses that he knew of; even the party's headquarters at the Hotel Falcon had been turned into a prison. Walking for hours, he ended up nosing around the city's outskirts, noticing new graffiti on the walls: *Gobierno Negrín: ¿dónde está Nin?* – Government of Negrín: where is Nin? He found out later that on that very night, Nin was liquidated although the communists were claiming he had made his way to Berlin, where he was working for his old paymaster, Hitler. Even in death, Nin had to be kept alive as a threat.

He first tried an empty air-raid shelter, but it had been newly dug and was dripping with damp. He then came across an abandoned church, gutted and burnt during the anti-clerical frenzy at the start of the revolution. In the dim light of the Barcelona blackout, he could just make out four walls and the remains of the belfry, and wondered to what century it belonged; probably the Middle Ages. The air inside was hot and stagnant and smelled overpoweringly of pigeon dung, but it was dry and unlikely to attract the prying eyes of the patrols. He rooted around in the rubble and found a hollow that provided a hard bed of broken masonry.

The next morning the streets thronged with the patrols: Civil Guards, Assault Guards, Carabineros and ordinary police, as well as who knew how many plainclothes spies. He wandered about, going from café to café, killing time. At one point he passed the Hotel Falcon and the POUM *comité general*, noticing that the semi-circular windows just above the front doors had been smashed and the revolutionary slogans on its walls imperfectly painted over.

Scattered about the city he saw groups of men he recognised as old comrades, some just back from the front. They winked to him as he passed, too afraid to talk. Midway down the Ramblas he spotted the two ILP comrades – McNair and Cottman – whom Eileen had arranged for him to meet, and by means of signals and whispers arranged to talk to them. They chose a market in a small *plaça* in the labyrinthine back streets of the medieval working-class district, where it seemed possible to talk in the middle of a thronging crowd without being detected, as long as you kept moving from stall to stall, like tourists out shopping. Along the way the pair gathered another fugitive, a 24-year-old German who went by the pseudonym Willy Brandt; Orwell knew him as the POUM's liaison man with the German Socialist Worker's Party, the SAP. They greeted each other warmly, lifted by the fact of being able to share their deadly predicament.

As they moved along, Cottman, who was a short man,

reached up and touched Orwell on the shoulder. 'Comrade, the news is the worst. Bob Smillie is dead.'

He said nothing.

'The communists are saying he got ill in prison – appendicitis – but it's rumoured they beat him to death.'

Young Bob, beaten to death? He felt an inward shudder, as if his body was anticipating the pain of his own beatings. Up to then, being gaoled by Spaniards had seemed a sort of chaotic administrative formality, where they first wasted your time in some disordered holding pen, then checked your papers and eventually pushed you back over the border to get you out of the way. Of all the people for so-called fellow socialists to kill – a Smillie, the son of trade union royalty.

'What are we doing?' said Brandt, ashen-faced. 'Workers killing workers? It was bad enough having to kill fascist workers, but socialist ones? What has gone wrong?' In a moment of despair he cupped his face in his hands. 'What have we done?'

A moment later Brandt gathered himself. 'Comrades,' he began more firmly – and, as in Wigan, the word seemed natural, emotionally powerful. 'Our cause is the right one, but the military struggle has soured it. We should never have put winning the war before securing the revolution. Can't you see? War degrades all of us. Without the revolution, what's all this fighting about but killing? Who will fight for that?' One by one, he looked each of them in the eyes, holding their stares until by some exchange of mental energy each responded with a nod.

'This war is lost, but there are other battles to come; we know that. And we have to win them. Stay true. Are you prepared to fight and die for the eventual victory against the fascists and the communists?'

This Brandt, he saw, had the capacity, common to natural leaders, of being able to cut through the side issues and state what was truly important. The communists posed the same threat to freedom as the fascists. Even though Brandt was the youngest of them, there was a moral force about the man: a sort of crystal spirit that nothing, not even the most powerful of bombs, could shatter. It was infinitely admirable. How strange, it struck him, the quick affection, bordering on love, you can feel for someone you hardly know.

He glanced at his companions. 'We've learnt our lesson,' he said, backing up Brandt. 'Never trust the communists.'

They couldn't linger; the patrols, though sparser in the working-class quarter, were still a menace. Before departing, he turned to Brandt. 'Come with us to France. We can try to smuggle you into England.'

But Brandt just clenched his fist low by his side, in a clandestine version of the Republican salute, and disappeared into the crowd.

★

It was incredibly stupid, like taking a step into their own graves. He and Eileen should have been on the last train, but they had decided to visit Kopp in gaol. He couldn't let his old commander be murdered without at least some show of solidarity, even if all he could do was take him food and cigarettes. On the face of it the idea seemed insane, but they had heard the prison was a shambles.

On entering the gaol, which was really just two rooms of a shuttered shop, he saw two POUM militiamen he knew from the front, including the American who had been with him when he was shot and had carried him down the line on a stretcher. They exchanged winks.

Kopp's huge bulk ploughed its way through the crowd – there were at least a hundred inmates in the two spaces, each about twenty feet by twenty feet of fetid gloom – and he greeted them both with hugs. 'Well, I suppose we shall all be shot,' he said cheerfully.

When arrested, Kopp told them, he had been carrying in his briefcase letters of recommendation from General Pozas, who was known to be on good terms with the communists; the letters, which stated that Kopp was needed for urgent matters at the front, were now somewhere in the office of the chief of police.

A crazy resolve possessed Orwell: he would find the officer to whom the letters were addressed and ask him to retrieve them from the police. It might get Kopp released. He left Eileen and Kopp talking, and minutes later was walking around the labyrinth of corridors of the war office, where the man to whom Kopp's letters of recommendation were addressed supposedly worked. So complex and rambling were the ministry's endless network of corridors that he almost gave up, but eventually found the right office.

Ushered in, he explained why he was there.

'This Major Kopp, what force was he in?'

'The 29th battalion.'

'The POUM!' The shock and alarm in his voice was unsettling. 'And he was your commander?'

'Yes.'

'Which means that you too were serving in the POUM?' He swallowed hard. Lying wouldn't help him now. 'Yes.'

'Wait here.'

The man left the room, and he could hear an animated discussion ensue outside. He was about to be arrested. His entrails turned to ice and his legs began to shake uncontrollably. He could feel it already, the truncheons, the fists, the humiliating grovelling on the floor, crying out for mercy . . . The man returned, put on his cap and asked Orwell to follow him to police headquarters. Momentarily he thought of running, but when they arrived the man entered the police chief's office and began a loud argument, emerging some minutes later with the envelopes containing Kopp's letters.

He thanked him, and, as they parted, the man awkwardly shook his hand. It seemed a small thing, but happening right there, in front of the police headquarters and all it signified, and within sight of posters screaming that he was a Fifth Column traitor who had to be exterminated, it was an affirmation of something much more significant. He struggled to define it; in the end he could only conclude that, somehow, amid all this, the spirit of man still existed.

*

He, McNair and Cottman spent three evenings sleeping rough, first in a forgotten cemetery and then in the long grass at the end of a derelict building lot. By means of a morning visit to the public baths, a shoeshine (the anti-fascist salutes were long gone) and a shave, they managed to look quite normal, although they heard the patrols were onto this ruse and had taken to raiding the public baths at random. They spent their days playing the role of well-heeled English tourists, seeing the sights and eating in the more expensive restaurants, where the waiters had taken once again to wearing their boiled shirts and behaving in the most obsequious manner.

Before leaving one fashionable restaurant, he went to the bathroom. With the door locked, it was one of the few places in the whole city where he could feel free from prying eyes and flapping ears. So this was what the revolution had come to.

He combed his hair and, looking into the mirror, noticed how he had changed since he had arrived in Barcelona seven months ago. There was the scar in his neck, of course, and a few more grey hairs. He was only thirty-four, but he now knew something he hadn't known back then. It wasn't the conclusion others had reached: that all revolutions were a fraud and politics should be shunned. It was that people like him were on the way out. He was already a relic – not because of any physical decline, but because there was no longer any place in the world for those like him, pathetic romantics who believed in the truth and that men should be free to think as they chose. The future, he now understood, belonged to a new generation: to streamlined men with streamlined minds packed with lies, hate and power-worship – the sort of men who had rounded up Nin and Kopp and killed Bob Smillie and were now hunting him and Eileen.

He reached into the breast pocket of his jacket and pulled out his pen, unscrewed the cap and wrote on the wall in as large a script as he could: *Visca POUM!* – Long live the

POUM! It was reckless, but he didn't care. The communists, he concluded, would shoot him anyway if he was caught, no matter what he did; even if he had committed no actual crime, the case against him would be faked. In truth, no real laws existed anymore, the only crime being to oppose those in power.

Just as he was about to leave there was a knock on the door. Already! They must have been followed; or perhaps the proprietor was an informer who had lured them into a trap, maybe with some sort of two-way mirror in the bathroom. The folly; the sheer, suicidal folly! He froze. The knock was repeated. He realised the worst thing would be to delay – which would be taken as a sure sign that he was hiding from someone. Carefully, he opened the door to find that it was only Cottman, who, like him, had drunk a lot of wine and needed to use the urinal.

The next morning he, Eileen, McNair and Cottman boarded the train for France. Upon crossing the border, they purchased a French newspaper which carried a report on its front page saying that Cottman had been arrested as a Trotskyist spy. What to do but laugh?

– VII –

The Stores, Wallington, March 1938. He ignored the approaching storm. In Wallington, ignoring the present came naturally. It was this quality – the feeling that this was somewhere they had forgotten to modernise, a vision of nostalgia turned into reality – that had attracted him to the tiny, two-street village in the first place. That wasn't the sort of thing you admitted freely, of course. Nostalgia, they would say, stupid and useless nostalgia; only a fool would waste his time with it; all that really mattered was the future. But he never saw it that way. The moment he entered the village one half of him was back in another time. It was hard to say exactly what set him off: the familiar smells of chaff and sainfoin, the sweet mustiness of the ancient church, the sight of the burly farmhands drinking thick, dark ale outside The Plough, the shady pond with its lurking dace, or maybe just the warm sunshine; in the past, of course, it is always summer. All he knew was that once his mind was back there, before August 1914, it seemed a good time to have been alive. Far better than now. The problem of the present, he reckoned, was that people couldn't remember just how good the past had been.

Wallington seemed just the place for them after Spain.

The fleets of bombing planes, which he knew were on their way, likely wouldn't waste their loads on so small a dot on the map. He and Eileen took up the lease of the village store, bought a bacon slicer and placed large bottles of boiled sweets behind the counter to sell to the local children. They spent their time writing and managing the shop, and their evenings in front of the fireplace reading and talking. On weekends they entertained friends up from London, she sitting on his lap, telling them of his many failures in animal husbandry. But no matter how much he and Eileen tried to run from it, the Spanish business wouldn't let them go. They had escaped, but Kopp was still in prison and the bodies of his POUM comrades lay decomposing in front of Huesca. And of course he had his Spanish book to finish. He returned to it, thumping away at the keys.

> When you have had a glimpse of such a disaster as this
> – and however it ends the Spanish war will turn out
> to have been an appalling disaster, quite apart from
> the slaughter and physical suffering – the result is not
> necessarily disillusionment and cynicism. Curiously
> enough the whole experience has left me with not less
> but more belief in the decency of human beings.

He had begun by placing great hopes on the book – it was the wake-up call the left needed – but already he was assailed by doubts. From the notices in *The Times* and the political newspapers, he guessed the market for books on Spain was already glutted, and it occurred to him that it was only intellectuals who bought books of this kind. He couldn't imagine his northern miners reading and discussing it at the pub, or even knowing of its existence, even though they, not the intellectuals, were the ones who could stop the nightmares being repeated here. If only they could be made conscious – but of course the moment they became conscious, they would cease to be themselves, and would instead surrender themselves to 'objective political realities'. His mind was full of such paradoxes. Revolutions, he now realised, were all about paradoxes.

The tiny cottage shivered, rattling its windows in their dried putty. The darkness was arriving, sped up by the arrival of a high, sprawling thundercloud of the deepest purple. From his window on the second floor he regarded the village. The pond where he and Eileen picnicked and fished the previous summer was black and icy, and the winter-stripped elms which bordered it were starting to bend under the approaching gale. Thirty or forty yards across from his rented field a light appeared. It was the farmer rounding his pigs, goats, milking cows and horses into the warmth and safety of a great and ancient-looking barn, on which he could just make out a rusting sign carrying the property's name: Manor Farm.

The first surge of the storm snapped a tree branch somewhere close by, making a loud crack. It was going to be violent; probably blow the roof off the henhouse again, and he'd just got the damned thing back on. Time to get his own motley collection of animals in. He headed out into the yard, pausing to tell Eileen he was 'battening down', and ushered the hens and ducks into the henhouse, and his goats, Muriel and Kate, into one of the two sheds. He let his black poodle, Marx, into the house, where he could sit on the rag mat by the fire.

In honour of his imminent completion of the book on Spain, Eileen, who had finally mastered the cottage's shambles of an oven, had roasted their troublesome rooster, named Henry Ford, and got the once squalid cottage in reasonable order. After the main meal she sat on his lap, spooning her speciality – apple meringue pie – into his mouth. She contemplated the scene: a fire in the grate, his slippered feet perched on the fender, a pile of unread newspapers and magazines on the floor, the typewriter in the corner.

'You think you're back in Wigan, don't you, in your council house with me and the dog.'

'This is far too bourgeois.'

'By gum, ye be right,' she said.

'Not such a bad idea, though, living like the proles. We could head up north, disguise our voices, get jobs in a mill and have ten children.'

'Nine kiddies only; I have my figure to think of. And I'm not wearing wooden clogs.' She paused, thinking about it. 'We'd probably have more money, though. I did some calculations today. It's only our chickens and goats that are keeping us alive.'

'Good old Ford. He was delicious.'

'Let's hope the hens don't go on strike, or we'll starve.' She gave him the last piece of pie.

'This won't go on forever, you know,' he said, 'living like this.' He turned to her, more eagerly. 'I've got a new idea for a book. It's about a man who sees there's a war coming and tries to escape, to the past.'

'You're far too young to be writing your memoirs, darling.'

'I'm serious. I think it will hit a chord.'

'Yes – how to be a socialist, but Tory at the same time. Not much of an audience for that nowadays.'

'It will be the first book about the next big war. This war's going to have its great novel before it even starts. Should keep us fed for a while.'

'Unlike our little farm.'

'Except tonight. Survived another day.'

'Well, it be a right good thing they don't give you money for to write books about farming,' she said, laughing.

He kissed her.

'That's the pudding done. Would you like some Pig now?'

★

The next morning, he stepped into the kitchen to boil water for his shave, only to get his slippers soaked. The house was like a sponge. The storm-blasted village looked like a battlefield, the belting rains petering out in the middle of the night, but succeeded by a heavy frost. The laneway to Manor Farm had turned into a drain full of freezing water.

Later, as he was feeding Muriel on the frozen, muddy patch opposite, he observed that old Field's van, which was doing its regular weekly rounds, picking up some of the town's livestock to take to market in Baldock, had become badly bogged. Field, who was renting him the patch of land, waved and walked off in the direction of the farm entrance for help. Ten minutes later, he heard a loud 'clop, clop, clopping' and saw Field returning with a little boy, perhaps ten years old, who was driving the great big brute of a carthorse, whipping as it shied away from its duty, which was to haul the stranded van clear. If only the poor creature knew its own strength, the tables would be easily turned.

'Imagine,' he said to Muriel, scratching her ear, 'Marxism from the animals' point of view.' She licked the bowl of mash he was holding. 'Actually, when you consider it, old girl, it makes a lot of sense, doesn't it?'

His fall made Muriel start.

It was half an hour later that Eileen spotted him.

'It is my lung,' he said, in a small voice. A stream of blood had trickled from his mouth. His long neck was stretched out, and he looked too weak to do so much as lift his head. Unable to move him, Eileen raced over to The Plough and raised the publican's daughter, who told her to wait while she searched for her father, who was soon found in the basement, moving great barrels of beer.

Eileen dropped to her knees by his side and raised his head onto her lap. In the two years since they had married, his appearance had gradually altered, and it was only now that she saw it clearly. When they had first met, there had remained a vestige of smartness about him, and while his tall, bony body had never been fat, there had been a solidity appropriate to his frame. Now his shoulders looked sharp and shrunken, and his hips had lost their fleshy padding; his patched and frayed suit, expensive and well-tailored when bought, hung about him like the rags on a scarecrow.

She started sobbing. 'Darling, now do you see you must slow down?'

He reached up and patted her head, which helped her regain her composure, but conceded nothing.

'No more work until the summer's over. That's an order from The Pig.'

'Darling, there's really nothing to worry about,' he managed to say. 'Probably just pleurisy. I've felt something coming on. Anyway, I've been looking forward to a rest.'

'Good. I shall put you out to pasture here with the goats. Muriel can keep you company. Don't give her fleas.' But her sobbing continued. She could only be so brave.

The publican appeared and carried him back to the cottage, where a bed was made up on the couch by the fireplace. His temperature climbed and the spitting of blood continued. On the third morning, after vile black liquid began oozing from his mouth onto his blankets, she went to the telephone at The Plough and called her brother, Laurence. For all the hopelessness of the situation, there was a kind of providence in it – Laurence O'Shaughnessy was one of the country's foremost specialists in the treatment of tuberculosis. He would see to everything.

The next day, as the rain pelted down, he was led into the back of a large ambulance. With the door closed and the vehicle starting to move, he watched Eileen waving to him through the window, disappearing as they accelerated away.

★

On his third day at the sanatorium, Laurence appeared in his doorway, tall and stern in a well-cut double-breasted suit, waving a file in his hand. 'No more bloody trooping off to fight for the brotherhood of man.' He knew Laurence had never really taken to him, and he could see his point: after all, what famous surgeon would be happy about his younger sister marrying an Etonian who spent his time writing about consumptive beggars, miners and anarchists, and who didn't have five pounds to his name?

'I don't want any charity, Laurence, and it's bad form that I've got my own room when the veterans are in common wards. They're talking, I hear. I shan't object to being moved.'

'Oh, don't worry, old boy. You're earning your keep as a case study for my forthcoming monograph.'

'On?'

'TB.'

He nodded.

'I want you isolated so I can keep a good eye on you. Don't want to corrupt my statistics.'

There seemed no point in resisting.

'It seems an old lesion, likely from some filthy old tramp or miner you met. But these things are uncertain. Complete bed rest, fresh food and vitamin injections. And no typewriter. I promised The Pig, and The Pig, as we both know, is always the boss.' With that he left, shoving the file under his armpit, not having conveyed to his patient the calculations it contained: if the case was serious, there was a seventy per cent likelihood he'd be dead within six years, and ninety per cent he wouldn't last a further five after that.

He thought of what to do, now that he couldn't write. Luckily, Laurence had left his copy of *The Times*; one could read it all day and still not finish. The news had been depressing for weeks. Blum's Popular Front government was in chaos. Hitler's troops had entered Austria, and again the Tories were counselling doing nothing. The debate on the war estimates was in full swing, and to ram it home there was a photograph of the RAF's newest monoplane fighter. And now, from the arrows on the maps, he could see that the Republican siege of Huesca had been lifted, meaning his old trenches at Monte Oscuro were in fascist hands. It was going to be one of those summers, he thought, like 1914, a sleepwalk into disaster and misery. He turned another page.

The instant he saw the photographs he grasped their significance. Perhaps to another they might have seemed ordinary enough: three portraits picked out from a larger tableau – probably a group photograph of Bolshevik congress delegates. Their faces looked calm, happy even, not hinting at anything sinister; and yet he knew that in some essential if not wholly obvious way, their images explained everything.

The first photograph was of a man in a uniform that he guessed to be that of the NKVD. He looked to be in his midforties and therefore must already have been a grown man when the revolution began, twenty years before. He looked surprisingly clean-cut, with a noble yet stern bearing which, combined with *that* uniform, suggested idealism gone wrong in some undefined way. The second man, far older, had a more conservative appearance – he was bearded and wearing the old-fashioned high collar of some European government minister before the war. If he had to guess, he would have placed him as a liberal-radical or socialdemocratic lawyer, of the sort you seldom met in England. The last was the giveaway: balding at the front, with a goatee beard and the mischievous eyes of a man who read too much Balzac – features that identified him with absolute precision as a Marxist intellectual from the same generation as Lenin. There was even a smile on his face. Their names were in the caption at the bottom: Yagoda, Rykoff and Bukharin. And above the story stood the headline:

EXECUTIONS IN MOSCOW
18 PRISONERS SHOT
THE CHIEF VICTIMS

He had mostly ignored Stalin's show trials until then, thinking them too absurd to be taken seriously. Yet he now grasped that it was their absurdity that explained their meaning. The accusations and evidence were obviously lies, but they were conducted in such a way that no one who mattered could gainsay them without forfeiting his life. In the absence of public contradiction this made them incontrovertibly true.

The first of the men, Genrikh Yagoda, had until the previous year been the head of the Soviet secret police, yet he looked more like a bureaucrat than a mass killer. The other two had also been among the original leaders of the revolution, the rest of whom, with the exceptions of Stalin and the exiled Trotsky, had been swallowed up in the great purges that had started the decade before. Now, it appeared, the last of them were being wiped out once and for all.

Horrified and yet drawn to know more, he asked the nurses to bring him back copies of *The Times* from the sanatorium's library. As soon as he read each edition, he dropped it to the floor and reached for another, having cut out the most interesting articles for future reference.

He could see that this particular trial – distinguished

from the rest by the name 'The Trial of the Twenty-One' – followed the same absurd trajectory to the graveyard. Like Kamenev and Zinoviev before them (whom Yagoda himself had disposed of), the three accused had previously been denounced and rehabilitated, but this time they had run out of luck, being forced into fulsome confessions to an absurd list of crimes: plotting with Trotsky to murder Lenin and Stalin, to undo collectivisation, to restore capitalism, to dismember the Soviet Union, and even to wreck the Soviet economy by blowing up trains and putting glass fragments in packets of workers' butter. Thousands of pornographic photographs had supposedly been found hidden in the walls of their dachas. At various times, he began to chuckle to himself at the comic nature of it all. At one point in the trial, two of the twenty-one defendants had confessed to having plotted a coup d'état with Trotsky, only for it to be revealed that, at the time of the correspondence, Trotsky was at sea, on his way to Mexico. It made the verdict a nonsense, and in any other country the trial would have been aborted, but the victims confessed their guilt regardless, logically impossible though it was. Now being on the official record, and repeated endlessly in the communist press, the lie had become the truth. It wouldn't be long, he thought, until all the original Bolsheviks – bar Stalin and Trotsky, whom Stalin needed, in the way God needed Satan – were written out of the Party's official histories and ceased to exist.

The whole confected story now lay across his bed, table and floor. He reached for another issue and kept reading. He circled a passage from one of *The Times*' special correspondents: 'According to Soviet law, crime and the intent to commit crime are virtually the same thing . . . In the coming trial the prosecution expects to show that the accused premeditated certain crimes although they never committed them – and therefore are little less guilty than if the crimes had actually been committed.' *Thought itself has become a crime.*

The stupidity of it! How could they expect the workers to take socialism seriously in the face of such nonsense? He felt restless, and, getting up, began pacing the room, the better to think. The Soviet debacle was now total. As a socialist, it should have made him angry, yet it left him inwardly exultant. Here was proof – physical proof, spread about his room, that he could feel under his feet – that the picture he had painted of communist madness in *Homage* was essentially correct; anyone could see that now. The revolution was finally dead, and some dreadful new form of society had taken its place.

His agitated mind filled with questions. Were all revolutions, all attempts to create a better world, doomed? Were all men ultimately irredeemable, incapable of living up to the hopes idealists had invested in them? Were they all now unworthy of the brave comrades he had left behind, who at that very moment were being squeezed into the shrinking Republican redoubt to face death, but determined to fight on to the end? Could a brotherhood of man really exist in this world?

He put on his slippers and dressing gown and wandered down the corridor, and in short order was struck by a memory. Perhaps it was the sanatorium's dormitory, built in the nature of a school, but his mind turned to the first time he had pondered these questions: Eton.

★

Eton College, June 1918. The almost blind Aldous Huxley was by all agreement a truly hopeless teacher. He was tall and gaunt, dressed after the fashion of Oscar Wilde, and was considered an eccentric fop. Blair was one of the few who admired him.

Emboldened by Huxley's myopia, the boys at the back of the class were playing cards. In an effort to quell their increasingly rowdy behaviour, made worse by the fact it was the last day of the school year, Huxley set the class regular tests, which, he assured them, though unconvincingly, would reflect on their standing in the grades. This test was simple: *Whom do you consider the ten greatest men now living?*

'Pens down, gentlemen,' Huxley said, feebly. 'Pass your papers to the front.' He stood before the blackboard, flicking rapidly through the papers, which he held close to his face. 'Who is going to volunteer to tell me their answer?'

'I can, sir. It's Blair.' He wasn't by nature a keen student, but thought the class's mocking of the afflicted Huxley scandalous.

'Yes, Blair, I *can* see you.' He handed Blair's paper back to him. 'Your top ten, please.'

Sitting at his desk, he read it out. 'Wells, obviously, sir. Shaw, equally obviously. Galsworthy. Jack London. Henri Barbusse.'

'Barbusse, Blair? Bravo,' Huxley said. 'But where on earth did you get a copy of *Le Feu*?' The anti-war novel was considered almost seditious.

'From the provost, sir.'

'That's five so far, Blair. Continue.'

'Bertrand Russell—'

'Oh, Blair!' one boy called out, 'this is just too funny. I knew you were a Shavian and a Red, but a conchie? This is hilarious.'

The card-playing boys threw screwed-up papers at him.

He dodged the missiles and kept going. 'Keir Hardie—'

'Dead!' someone yelled out. 'You of all people should know that, Blair.'

'Bukharin—'

'Never heard of him!'

'Editor of *Pravda*,' said Huxley. 'Reputedly the most brilliant of all the Bolsheviks.'

More laughter and missiles.

'Trotsky.'

'That's nine, Blair.'

'And Lenin.'

'Lenin indeed, Mr Blair. I've just had a glance at all sixteen papers, and fifteen name Lenin. Why do you think that is?'

'He represents the future happiness and freedom of man, sir.'

'Do you really think so? Blair, does the future happiness and freedom of man lie in Jacobinism? Did Cromwell and his Ironsides deliver happiness?'

'It lies in equality.'

'Imposed by force? As under Robespierre and the Terror? You've read Carlyle?'

'Yes, sir. Violence . . . well, it seems necessary, sometimes.'

'Ah, so you think the two things – happiness and

equality – are the same? What about freedom?'

'The poor are always unfree.'

'I take it you got that from Jack London? What if, instead of mandating communism, we gave the people what they wanted?'

'You mean equality, sir?'

'No. What they're actually asking for. I mean happiness – peace, nice clothes, an annual holiday at the seaside, an ice every day, free beer, oriental mistresses, everyone with their own motorcar and aeroplane. No work, no need to think or worry.'

'A society based on the principle of hedonism?'

'Yes, Blair. Shallow, gutless hedonism. Happiness! With little to complain about or agitate for, people will be easily governed, don't you think? Isn't that ultimately what Mr Lenin is promising the Russians – a complete absence of material hardship for everyone forever? Universal happiness? An end to politics?'

'He's promising it to *all* the working classes of the world, sir, not just the Russians,' added Cyril Connolly, his friend. 'Or was that Trotsky? I can't remember.'

'Which will make it all just that much more difficult to achieve, Connolly, when the dictatorship eventually ends,' Huxley continued. 'And if its goal of material progress and equality fails, what will be left? Mr Blair, what do you think will be left?'

'I don't know, sir.'

'Think about it, Blair. What will be left will be the very things you started with: force and terror. The dictatorship of the proletariat, forever.'

Huxley heard the bell ring for the end of class. 'A holiday

assignment, gentlemen – or should I say *comrades*. An essay, please: *Why dictatorship will be impossible in the future.*' With that, Huxley put on his wide-brimmed hat and his cape, turned and went through the door before any student could protest.

★

June 1938. The days and weeks in the sanatorium passed rapidly, spring giving way to summer. Watching from his hospital window, he began to feel like a character in Wells' *The Time Machine* as he saw the brown fields turn green, the flowers bud and burst into life, then wilt under the assault of the sun. They said the days dragged when you were ill and forced to do nothing, but they were wrong. Unable to work, he felt time burning up like the petrol wasted by the idling engine of a motorcar. He sat in bed, smoking absent-mindedly, filling an ashtray balanced precariously on a pile of books on the bedside table. He realised he was being watched.

Laurence, unexpectedly in the uniform of a Territorial Army captain, leant on the doorframe. He tossed over a packet of Player's Navy Cut, and then a heavy parcel which thudded onto the bed. Orwell picked up the parcel and peeled off the brown wrapping. It was a book: *Assignment in Utopia*, by someone called Eugene Lyons. He didn't recognise the name, but on the jacket it said he'd been the Moscow correspondent for the United Press Agency between 1928 and 1934. 'Another book for your collection,' Laurence said. 'Are you sure you have space for it?' There was a note inside, on the letterhead of the *New English Weekly*, which he pulled out and read. 'They want a review.' He set it aside and looked up. 'I guess I shall have to return it.'

'I think you're sufficiently recovered to resume supporting my little sister. We don't want her wasting away.' He had been putting on weight and getting stronger. 'But only an hour a day.'

'I'll need my typewriter.'

'I'll have a nurse bring it in.'

No intellectual in Britain, he thought, would have believed a tenth of what appeared in Lyons's six-hundred-and-fifty-page book, which he devoured in little more than a day – but none of them had been hunted by the NKVD. Here was the workers' state: a nightmare world in which the leader's portrait hung in every apartment, children routinely denounced their parents as counter-revolutionaries, and even an inappropriate facial expression at the wrong moment could lead to a late-night arrest, a show trial and a bullet in the back of the head. Small details he found particularly chilling – the way, for instance, people methodically removed from their address books the names of colleagues who had failed to turn up for work for more than a couple of days.

There was something in the book, though, that disturbed him even more than the secret police's terror. In the early 1930s huge billboards had appeared in Moscow and Leningrad bearing cryptic slogans such as '5-in-4' and '2+2=5'. They were part of a campaign to fulfil the Five-Year Plan in just four years. Like all good advertising slogans, he thought, these ones stuck in the mind. In a way, they were no less silly or illogical than the posters for Bovril which covered half the walls of London. But of course you wouldn't be arrested and shot for pointing out that Bovril was a swindle – which you certainly would be for criticising the Five-Year Plan. What worried him was where slogans like this might lead. When the cells of the Lubyanka awaited even the mildest expression of non-conformity, and the show-trial judges treated the rules of logic with such disdain, how long could it be until the Party said two and two really did make five – or six or seven – and expected people quite literally to believe it?

He threw the book onto the blankets and lifted the typewriter from the bedside table. He had learnt a new skill since Laurence gave him back his machine: typing on a dinner tray while sitting up in bed. 'The question arises, could anything like this happen in England?'

★

Mid-July. More books about Spain arrived for him to review, but it seemed wrong to waste such a fine day splitting hairs with red duchesses and closet fascists. What he needed was a picnic. It was a second Friday, usually Eileen's visiting day, but she was off to Windermere – he suspected in the car of Laurence's friend Karl Schnetzler, who was in Britain on the run from Hitler's thugs. He could hardly blame her; he was hard enough to love at the best of times, and the sick are such bores. She was still attractive, pretty even, and deserved to be allowed to get on with life. He was the one who had wanted an open marriage, and he had got one, or at least she had. Who was going to touch him in his present state?

He put on his jacket and went outside into the sunshine. It was one of those bright summer days that are so hot you can almost take your clothes off, and he could feel the warm air going deep into his lungs. In no time he was through the flowerbeds and out into the shady tranquillity of a small wood. He stopped to listen to a thrush whistling and clicking its song. For whom was it singing? For him, for a missing partner, for a lost chick? Or for joy, for life, for the few summers it would have before it was found dead on someone's lawn and thrown onto a garden incinerator, its reverie and life noted by no one, except now himself?

At the end of the wood he found a patch of wild chrysanthemums and delphiniums, their blue flowers reaching skywards.

He bent over, without pain, and picked some, thinking to give them to the nurses. He looked up and glanced over the low-hedged boundary of the property. The scene held his gaze. The landscape was somehow familiar, although momentarily he couldn't place it: an old close-bitten pasture, with a footpath wandering across it, and, twenty yards along, a pond covered in duckweed. The Golden Country! The dream! It must have been three years since he'd last had it. I'll bet there are carp in that pool, he thought. What I wouldn't give now for some fishing tackle! Before he knew what he was doing, he was through a gap in the hedge and on his way into Rochester.

He opened his wallet and did some calculations. There wasn't much, but perhaps enough for the bus and some fishing line and hooks of the sort you could get in Woolworths. He wouldn't need a rod – a stick would do for a pond like that. If he caught the bus at Blue Bell Hill rather than in Aylesford, whose line went via Maidstone, it would save him sixpence, meaning he could afford a bun and a cup of tea as well. A proper holiday! So what if it was a mile and a half to the bus stop? So what if Laurence had told him not to exert himself? He was feeling fine, breathing like a bellows. In fact, he felt completely cured. Why hadn't he thought of this weeks ago? These Medway towns may not be as beautiful as the Thames Valley, but they were still something to see.

The bus dropped him in Rochester, the town of Dickens. He took in the cathedral, with its Anglo-Saxon remnants, before walking past the purported model for Miss Havisham's Satis House. While it may have been a forbidding pile, and a symbol of the unnecessary inequalities of the last century, it occurred to him that, given the choice, the workers would still prefer a world with Satis House next to slums to the world of glass and steel and bureaucratically enforced equality being offered by the screeching dictators.

He located the gate where Pip must have met Estella, but found the wall next to it pasted over with a poster. It announced a Left Book Club meeting on 'The Coming Imperialist War', with an address by some visiting speaker with a vaguely Marxist-sounding name, the famous author apparently of *A Philosophy for Modern Man*. He could guess it all already: some thin, sharpfaced man wearing a tweed jacket, woollen tie and disc-like spectacles, haranguing the bored, dumb audience with the usual nonsense about why everyone should disarm, except of course for the Soviet Union. Suddenly hungry, he shook his head and walked back to the High Street.

He found a tea house and sat at a table. Too late, though, he realised just what sort of place it was – one of those mock Tudor 'shoppes' with fake beams, nylon tablecloths and pewter plates nailed to the walls, fitted out to impress the day-trippers brought up by the Southern Railway and the charabanc operators. A waitress eventually came over and took his order, which he had to repeat because she was distracted by a radio tinkling somewhere in the background. Predictably, his tea when it came was so weak that it looked like water until he added the milk. 'Would you like sugar or saccharine, sir?' the girl asked him. The scone, all air, was already sliced in half, coated in some cream that had bubbles in it and smeared with jam in the unmistakeable shape of something squeezed from a tube. Despite his hunger, he pushed it aside, threw a few coins on the table and left.

Walking to the bus stop, he heard a loud, throaty noise and looked up to see a black-bellied bombing plane flying fast and low overhead. Back in Spain he would have run for cover. It was one of the new types endlessly talked up in the newsreels as part of the rearmament drive. You couldn't escape the things nowadays; they were racing about the skies incessantly. From its course he guessed it must be using Rochester Castle as a dummy target, practising for what was inevitably coming. He remembered Laurence's uniform. They're getting ready, he thought. It can't be long now.

At that moment he could feel the war – it was a physical presence in his life already, pressing down on his chest, with its bombing planes and air-raid sirens, its cratered streets and smashed windows, and its loudspeakers bellowing that our troops had taken a hundred thousand prisoners on some front no one had ever heard of. And after that? Dictatorship, just like there would be in Spain, when the fascist noose was finally pulled tight. Yes, it was all going to go – all those things they were now taking for granted: the England of Dickens and Swift, the bum-kissers with their frivolous novels, strong tea and heavy scones, thrushes singing in the woods and dace swimming in their pools. All replaced by Comrade X and his *Philosophy for Modern Man*, goose-stepping armies, enormous posters of the leader's face on every wall, show trials at the Royal Courts of Justice, concentration camps and secret cork-lined cells where the lights burned all night . . . It *could* happen in England; it really could.

He realised with a shudder that the future wasn't something to look forward to, but something to be frightened of. Yes, it was coming alright. His bus turned up and he stepped on and bought his ticket. He was already at the outskirts of town when he saw a billboard advertising Woolworths, and remembered the fishing tackle he hadn't bought.

TWO

– 1 –

London, summer 1941. It was a bright, warm evening in August and the barrage balloons were drifting in the sky. He placed his mug of tea on the crumbling wall surrounding the roof of Langford Court, storing the warmth of the sun in his bones for another hungry, freezing winter of coal shortages and limited rations. Just the year before, the German bomber fleets, now busy in the east, had attempted to blot out the heavens, only to be beaten back, leaving England free, or at least what passed for free nowadays.

He scanned the city, which lay like a brown smudge to the south and east. Here and there, when he looked closely enough, he could see where rows of terraces had been neatly razed by sticks of bombs. In every street stood houses with boarded-up windows, rusty iron sheets in place of missing roof tiles, and long baulks of timber propping up doubtful walls. Near the Thames, large parts of the East End and the docks were completely flattened, just as he'd once imagined. Freedom! The very concept seemed an anachronism in a world such as this. Freedom had taken a holiday and wouldn't be coming back until the war was over. Even then, it all depended on—

The sound of a truck crunching down through its gears on Abbey Road broke his line of thought. He tried to summon it again, but the mental effort was beyond him. Then he remembered what he had planned to do. He crushed his cigarette butt under his shoe, threw the cold tea leaves over the ledge and went through the doorway and down the staircase – the lift of course being out of order. The corridor, as usual, reeked of boiled cabbage, and he hurried through his front door to stop the vile smell from wafting into his apartment behind him. The sun was streaming in through the corner window, which, being on the seventh floor, offered spectacular views.

He spotted the highest building in the city, the University of London's Senate House, still bright and new and stepped curiously like one of those pyramids in Central America. It was the wartime home of the Ministry of Information – MINIFORM in telex jargon – in one of whose many subsections, the BBC, where he now worked. His official title was 'Talks Assistant in the Indian Section of the BBC Eastern Service', but as far as he could make out, the job consisted of writing and broadcasting endless hours of wartime propaganda to a non-existent audience in East Asia. The Ministry of Information had nearly twelve thousand employees pumping out the news, newsreels, posters, music, radio and books needed to keep the Empire fighting in the face of the grey-uniformed fascist enemy. They were all under the direction of Churchill's Irish sidekick Brendan Bracken, whom the staff called 'B.B.' for short. Orwell, though, had never seen B.B. and sometimes doubted whether the fellow actually existed.

In the tiny flat the only place for him to write was an

alcove in the living room. It looked as though originally intended for a bookshelf, but he had managed to squeeze a small writing desk into the empty space, which, because of its orientation, had the effect of cutting him off from the rest of the room, out of view of Eileen or any guests. It was the closest thing a person of his limited means could get to privacy, given the housing shortage, and good prose, he thought, could only be written in solitude.

He had an hour to himself before Home Guard duty, and he turned to the half-filled notebook on the desk. He had discovered it a year ago under a pile of old framed prints in the back of a frowsy little junkshop off the Clerkenwell Road – such necessities as stationery having long since disappeared from the high street. There hadn't been any decent paper on sale since the Luftwaffe had destroyed the printing district around St Paul's; he had found himself scratching his thoughts unhappily on the backs of envelopes or on coarse, fibrous notepaper that he assumed to be made of recycled rags. He wiped his hands on his already grubby trousers, then carefully opened the notebook's marbled cover to the bookmarked page, running his fingers over the creamy paper. Clearly, the book had originally had some special sentimental purpose, although he couldn't tell what. He had been using it to write a wartime diary he hoped would interest Gollancz, or maybe even Fred Warburg, another publisher, who by chance was a private in his Home Guard unit.

Despite his plans to pump out a novel a year, he hadn't now written one for nearly two, the war having instead turned him into a kind of pamphleteer. Pamphlets, he thought, with a sinking feeling. Who would remember pamphlets? It was easy to find excuses for this sort of literary slacking, of course. There was the lack of paper, for a start. Even *The Times* had become little more than a couple of folded sheets, much of which, to his anger, was wasted by advertisements for fraudulent medicines and savings bonds. Then there was the lack of sleep due to the Blitz, the lack of time caused by the endless queues and delays, and of course the squalidness of life itself, with its irritating clamminess and itches and constant tragic news – and all these combined to stop anyone working for more than a few minutes at a time. And now he had had to join the war effort to try to earn a living. Starting a novel in such circumstances would be pointless, even though he had an inkling of what it was he wanted to say. It was the worst thing of all for a writer: knowing *what* he wanted to say, but not *how*.

It was this that, back in 1940, had made the diary seem a good idea. At first the concept of it excited him. Maybe the diary – the only place where one could be totally free of wartime censorship – was the answer he was looking for. If Britain were conquered, the diary – if indeed it survived the inevitable hunting down and destruction – might be discovered and read by some free spirit like himself twenty, thirty or even forty years from now, someone hoping to understand how the world had once been. A sort of secret message to the future. A warning.

He opened it. The simple act of touching the paper stirred in him a feeling that was at once abstract and physically immediate. It was the memory of what life itself was once like – its texture soft, silky almost, as if designed to delight people, not set them on edge like the scream of a dive-bomber. Two years into the war, utility had begun to pervade every aspect of existence, from the rough soap that left your skin red and raw to the synthetic food which tasted vaguely like fishmeal; even books had lost their beauty.

He turned to the start of the diary and began to read.

June 1st, 1940. The B.E.F are falling back on Dunkirk. Borkenau says England is now definitely in the first stage of revolution. According to Connolly, off the coast of France Nazi aeroplanes have machinegunned a ship with refugees on board, mostly children, etc . . .

He flicked forward another page.

June 5th, 1940. Last night to Waterloo and Victoria to see whether I could get any news of Laurence.

Laurence – killed at Dunkirk. He remembered now, watching for day after day following the evacuation, hunting for any news of Laurence's fate as trains packed with half-drowned soldiers and refugees pulled in at Waterloo. When the worst was finally confirmed (as much as any truth could be confirmed in the confusion and veil of secrecy that shrouded the war), his first thought had been that Laurence's fate was somehow connected to his own. After all, he had lost his surgeon, the renowned TB expert, who he knew would do all he could to keep him alive, if only for Eileen's sake. With her bedridden with grief – she was still yet to get over her brother's death a whole year later – it had fallen to him to write the obituary for *The Times*, and he pieced together the expected heroic death: machine-gunned by Nazi aeroplanes while tending the wounded on the beach, an example to everyone, etc., etc. It might have been true – he thought so at the time – but now he wasn't so certain.

He read on.

> June 20th, 1940. If we can only hold out for a few more months, in a year's time we shall see red militia billeted in the Ritz . . .

He winced. How much more wrong could he have been? Caught up in the moment, he had hoped the collapse of 1940 would end in an English socialist revolution, and him part of a revolutionary militia, poised for street fighting, man against tank, to prevent the Quislings in the Tory Party from selling out to the invading Nazis. He had given public lectures in guerrilla warfare, and even now, when walking down a perfectly ordinary street, his mind would sometimes busy itself working out the best place to site a machine gun. A handful of well-positioned men on The Strand could hold up half a division. 'If the gutters have to run with blood, so be it,' he had written.

He could see now, though, it had all been wishful folly. The revolution had ended before it had even begun, and English socialism had been stillborn. He thought it rather a good thing; better for the revolution to have never happened than for it to have been betrayed, as it inevitably would have been. As his eyes drifted down the page, an underlined sentence stood out: 'Thinking always of my island in the Hebrides.' What could it mean? The Hebrides? Some idea of escape? Somewhere safe from the bombs?

A last redoubt against Nazi terror? Somewhere, maybe,

he could write in peace? He tried to recall scribbling these words in the diary, but couldn't.

He flicked forward and could see that it was all rubbish. The entries were little more than a stream of consciousness, recording newspaper reports, gossip and even the newsreels he had seen at the flicks. It was pointless, and its predictions mostly wrong. Street fighting? Revolution? English socialism? Who would believe a word of it, except maybe enemies looking to discredit him? No, the history of this war would be written by the victors, by some dull propagandist, some jumped-up clerk, trying to second-guess which version of events conformed with the current party line. That was to say, someone with a job just like his! What truth did the leader want? That was the only question that mattered. The rantings of people like himself would be ignored. Their diaries would be hunted down and burned. History itself would be as the leader demanded, nothing more.

He chewed over the thought gloomily. Writing a diary was nothing but a conceit: the very idea that under a dictatorial government – Nazi, Tory-Quisling or communist – you could be free *inside*. Ha! That down in the street below, six-foot-wide posters of the leader might glare at you from every hoarding, and the stormtroopers demand to see your papers, but upstairs in a room like this you could record your thoughts freely . . . what rot! Hadn't the NKVD invaded his room in Barcelona and confiscated his diary about Spain? The concentration camps, the cork-lined cells, the torture chambers – that's where the free spirits like him would end up. After the liberation of Europe, if it ever happened, few diaries would be found, of that he was certain. The literature of liberalism was finished, and the literature of totalitarianism was coming to take its place. He knew what it would be like: inhuman, cold, mechanical, ugly words riveted together.

He sucked the nib of his pen to remove the grease and began to write his last entry:

> August 28th, 1941. There is no victory in sight at present. We are now in for a long, dreary, exhausting war, with everyone getting poorer all the time. The quasirevolutionary period which began with Dunkirk is finished and the task now is to prevent the war itself from destroying what it has set out to save. I have therefore decided to wind this diary up.

He read over it. He was right to end it. How could you make an appeal to the future when it was likely that not a trace of your thoughts would survive? There must be a better way, but at the moment it was beyond him.

*

He could pinpoint the cause of his gloom. That morning he had been in the usual meeting room at Broadcasting House, the Eastern Service discussing its program schedule. He dreaded these meetings: the arrival on his desk of the agenda, with its summons to Room 101, with its endless, dreary discussions about which academic should be invited on to discuss Boswell or Keats, induced in him a sense of panic. He was convinced that the whole business of wartime broadcasting was designed simply to soak up the mental energies of people like himself, occupying them with trivia when they might otherwise be questioning the war effort or challenging the government's excesses. Each time the clock ticked down to the meeting, he contemplated all manner of escape: forgetfulness, illness, resignation, lying about having been bombed out of his flat. But there was no escape and life had to be faced up to with a false smile. Keep calm and carry on, as B.B.'s slogan commanded.

This morning during the meeting he had drifted off. He was thinking of his recent meeting with Anthony Powell at the Café Royal, and how splendid he had looked in his father's Brigade of Guards 'blues', with its stiff collar and polished brass buttons and those straps under his trousers. They had talked about Evelyn Waugh – a commando of all things! The Tories got all the luck. Powell and Waugh (he now regretted calling them bum-kissers) were both household names and fabulously wealthy, while he spent his time listening to pompous academic bores, filling a dull post merely to keep himself alive.

'Why not this UCL chap Geoffrey Tillotson?' asked the chairman, Rushbrook Williams. 'Expert on Dryden, I hear.'

The question had been meant for him, but he was staring down at the agenda and doodling as his mind wandered. *Wigan Pier, Homage to Catalonia,* those novels of which he was now ashamed . . . all remaindered or turned to smoke when Gollancz's warehouse went up in the Blitz. And here he was, talking rot about Dryden with these people who were too ill or too old or too gormless to fight, and wasting his evenings square-bashing with the Home Guard. The tightening in his chest he'd been feeling all week became more noticeable.

'Blair, what do you think about Tillotson's suitability? You'll be producing this series. Blair?'

Tillotson? All he could think was that it was another of those Marxist-sounding names. Just the sort of name some comrade academic *would* have. 'Well, you see,' he began in his halting, wheezing voice. As he was trying to think of what to say next – he hadn't bothered to prepare for the meeting – he felt a sudden spasm in his lungs and began a painful coughing fit, his chest convulsing as if it were trying to eject some foreign object from the centre of his body. It wouldn't stop, and the contractions of his chest muscles got deeper and more powerful until it felt like they would eventually snap his spine. He had turned white and his face was running with sweat.

'My God, man, are you alright?' he heard someone say. 'Blair! I say, are you alright?'

One person rushed across with a glass of water, but the others instinctively covered their faces. The coughing continued, but he finally managed to wheeze enough air into his lungs to avoid passing out. They laid him down on the floor, where he remained for some minutes while everyone listened in horror to the frightening rattling of his chest. Eileen was called to take him home. It had been two years, but the disease had returned.

★

He heard a key in the lock. Eileen! He guiltily placed the notebook in the desk drawer and locked it. Exactly why he did this he wasn't sure, except that the diary was in some way connected to Inez. It had been her idea, although the collaboration had soon been dropped: two writers giving alternate perspectives on the progress of the war and the revolution that might follow. *Rubbish!*

Eileen appeared at the door with a basket of food, which she had spent an hour after work queuing to buy. Like everyone in London, she had been worn down by the war. Her luscious figure had become thin, and her thick brunette hair was now noticeably speckled with grey. Her once fine woollen suit, which looked like it hadn't been brushed since the invasion of Poland, was flecked with cigarette ash.

They had been married for five years, but whenever she was out of his presence it was surprising even to him how infrequently he thought of her. It had all started so well, but Spain and the war, and especially Laurence's death, had done something to her. At times she seemed completely spiritless. The rebelliousness, the sexiness, even her sense of irony – all the things that first attracted him – had been burned out of her, leaving in her face a perpetually empty stare. She did everything that marriage required, but with a lack of excess motion, and when not fulfilling necessary duties would sometimes sit or lie immobile for hours on end; everyone noted her silence at parties. They still made love occasionally – but mechanically, as if she were some sort of jointed wooden doll, and out of some unspoken duty to produce from their marriage a child.

'Eric,' she said, putting down the basket, 'Wells will be here soon.'

He had forgotten: H.G. Wells had accepted an invitation for dinner that evening.

– II –

The Wells dinner had been Inez Holden's idea, and came from a chance meeting with the great old man himself. At the height of the Blitz her block of flats copped it, and the ever-generous Wells, who had admired the experimental novel she had written in the synthetic language Basic English, offered her use of the mews apartment above the garage of his sprawling terrace in Regent's Park. The place gave off a residual smell of horse sweat and pigeon dung, but its view over trees provoked an impression of being in the countryside. It was a convenient place for her and Orwell to meet after his Home Guard parade drills, and they had been dozing there in the mews flat one afternoon, curtains closed, when a note was slid under the door inviting them both to afternoon tea before Inez left for her night shift at the aeroplane factory.

Orwell had been highly embarrassed, but Inez was unfazed.

'Don't worry for a moment about old H.G.,' she said. 'He's not a gossip. Very discreet. Anyway, he's in no position to talk: this is where he brings that crazy Russian mistress Gorky passed on to him. He's probably just intrigued about you, that's all; you're starting to gain a reputation.'

Still in awe of Wells, he agreed. First Inez had to get ready. She went to the bathroom and emerged wearing the blue-grey overalls of an airframe assembler. It was standard issue for manual workers in the Ministry of Aircraft Production, dull but emboldened by a bright handkerchief tied around her head, which, she said, was to keep her hair from falling into the machinery. Even the dullest overalls couldn't completely suppress her urge to be different. He noticed she'd put on makeup too.

'How do I look?' she asked.

'Vaguely communist and pure. Like some automaton out of one of H.G.'s novels.'

She did a curtsey and sang in her best Gracie Fields voice: 'It's a ticklish sort of job, making a thing for a thingummybob . . .'

'The thingummybob that's going to win the war!' he sang back, almost automatically. The tune – part of B.B.'s propaganda drive to encourage women into the factories – had become inescapable. One heard women especially humming it endlessly on buses and in the tube.

Soon they were sitting on a sofa in Wells' drawing room, listening to the great man hold forth. Orwell wasn't the type to be in awe, but this was H.G. Wells. In a world of pedants, golfers and sniggering Latin masters, Wells had known before 1900 that the future was not going to be the way respectable people imagined it. And yet he found in front of him not the prophet of the future, but a man clearly in decline. It wasn't just Wells' physical shrinkage – he was now over seventy – but the way he launched into his monologue on the usual rigmarole: the world state and the Sankey Declaration – which, as Wells reminded them, should really have been called the Wells Declaration, as he'd written 'most every word'.

The longer Wells talked, the clearer it became that the had not turned out as he had predicted, and yet he just couldn't see it. Inez, who'd seen the old man in this form before, steered the conversation towards literature instead. 'H.G., George here is one of your biggest fans. Simply adores your books.'

'Is that so, Orwell?' the old man replied. 'Any favourites?'

'The early scientific romances, of course; couldn't split them. Maybe *The Sleeper Wakes*.'

'*Awakes*, Orwell. *Awakes!*' Wells seemed miffed. 'Why?'

'Think of how marvellous it was for us as children, H.G. There we were, bored rigid by dimwitted schoolmasters, but when we got back to the dorm we could pull one of your books from under the covers and read about the inhabitants of planets and the bottom of the sea, and someone waking up in the year 2100 to lead a world revolution. Simply smashing. Did you ever want to do these things yourself? Fly, I mean. Cruise under the ocean, visit the stars?'

A look of disappointment crept across Wells' face. 'Well, yes . . . Once, I suppose.'

'Actually, I recall one morning in summer in Prep sneaking into Cyril Connolly's – you know him, editor of *Horizon* – sneaking into his dorm and stealing his copy of . . . I forget which collection of short stories. They were cracking, all about travel to the stars.'

'Nothing more serious? What about my social novels?'

'Well, if forced to choose, I'd have to say *Mr Polly*. Everyone loves a good antihero. The draper, the clerk, the nobody getting his revenge on the system.'

'Not anything more recent? Not my political tracts? I thought you were a Trotskyist, Orwell. That's what I've been told.'

'Sorry, I haven't read much of them, except your articles in the newspapers. I enjoyed the film of *The Shape of Things to Come*, but that was a few years ago now too.'

'Yes, well, the costumes were good. Come to think of it, I can see how *Mr Polly* would appeal to you, Orwell. One man in a simple room with a woman to love. Your sort of utopia, I guess!'

'Ah, you see, so much to talk about,' said Inez hurriedly. 'I suggest a dinner party so we can discuss literature more fully.'

'Yes,' agreed Wells. 'Alright, I suppose; now, just wait a minute.' He walked over to a bookshelf and rummaged through an opened brown-paper parcel, returning to hand Orwell a paperback. 'Here's my latest: *Guide to the New World*. Perhaps you can tell me what you think of it when we dine.'

★

A month later Wells sat at Orwell's tiny dining table in Langford Court. Given the shortages of food, Inez and William Empson had joined them after the meal. The atmosphere was tense with the expectation of battle. Orwell was shuffling his enormous feet under the table and Eileen was filling the wine glass in front of Wells, whose expression suggested a man spoiling for an argument. A copy of *The Sleeper Awakes* sat in front of him and beside it a pen, both untouched by the great man.

'Bill, darling; Inez,' said Eileen. 'Where have you both been? We've been waiting ages.'

'Connolly treated us all to dinner in Soho,' said Empson. 'Eels and rice, I think it was, but I might be mistaken.'

'Washed down with lots of wine as usual, wasn't it, Billy?'

'Glad to say, yes. How they've managed to preserve such a cellar is a mystery.'

'Well, have some more; H.G. brought plenty.' Eileen pointed them to the divan, which Empson nearly tripped over before easing himself down.

'Must be a good view from up here, Eileen,' Inez said. She went over to the window and peeped through a tiny gap in the blackout curtain. 'Senate House lit up like a beacon as usual. Helping the Luftwaffe aim its bombs. Now, what have you two been talking about?' she said, turning to Orwell and Wells.

Orwell broke an ominous silence. 'Gissing and Huxley. H.G. knew both of them, didn't you?'

'The elder Huxley only. The younger one was too much of a cynic for my liking. Taught Orwell here to be likewise.'

'Personally, I think if Gissing was still alive he'd be a fascist; reckoned the working class were savages.'

'That's because he was another one of your underfed, rebellious clerks, Orwell.'

'Like Kipps and you once were,' Orwell returned.

Wells bristled; a meanness entered his eyes and he pushed the book and pen in front of him down the table. 'So, how *is* Connolly? Because, funnily enough, his magazine recently mentioned me.'

No one replied.

Wells got up, walked over to the coat stand and pulled a rolled-up magazine from the pocket of his jacket, returning to slap it down on the table. It was the latest *Horizon*. He turned to a folded-down page. 'Yes, here it is. "Wells, Hitler and the World State", by George Orwell. My thanks to you, Inez, for procuring it.' The journal bore heavy scorings in blue ink.

Wells began reading aloud. '"If one looks through nearly any book that Wells has written in the last forty years, one finds the same idea constantly recurring: the supposed antithesis between the man of science who is working towards a planned World State and the reactionary who is trying to restore a disorderly past. In novels, Utopias, essays, films, pamphlets, the antithesis crops up, always more or less the same. On the one side science, order, progress, internationalism, aeroplanes, steel, concrete, hygiene: on the other side war, nationalism, religion, monarchy, peasants, Greek professors, poets, horses. History as he sees it is a series of victories won by the scientific man over the romantic man." *So says Orwell.*'

There was nothing to be done but sit there and take it.

Wells turned a few pages and continued, his voice – similar in pitch to Orwell's but noticeably less public school – becoming increasingly dismissive. '"Much of what Wells has imagined and worked for is physically there in Nazi Germany. The order, the planning, the State encouragement of science, the steel, the concrete, the aeroplanes, are all there, but all in the service of ideas appropriate to the Stone Age. Science is fighting on the side of superstition. But obviously it is impossible for Wells to accept this." *So says Orwell.*'

Wells turned a page. They sat, no one daring to move.

'"The singleness of mind, the one-sided imagination that made him seem like an inspired prophet in the Edwardian age, make him a shallow, inadequate thinker now." *This is Orwell.*'

'I did write some decent things among all that criticism . . .' Wells ignored him and flicked more pages, before standing up for the denouement. '"Wells is too sane to understand the modern world. The succession of lower-middle-class novels which are his greatest achievement stopped short at the other war and never really began again . . ."' Wells threw the magazine down on the table and completed the sentence, as if from memory:

'". . . and since 1920 he has squandered his talents in slaying paper dragons." *So says Mr George bloody Orwell!*'

They sat in silence for nearly a full minute.

'Well, Orwell, what have you to say? Damned cheek, don't you think, to invite a man into your home after writing something like that?'

'Actually, you were invited *before* I wrote it,' he replied. 'You *did* give me the book and ask my opinion. Anyway. One must write as one sees it; personal feelings can't come into it. It certainly wasn't my intention to offend—'

'It may not have been your intention, Orwell, but it was your effect. Diplomacy isn't your strength, that's obvious.'

'I'm sorry, H.G., but I have to stand by every word. I'm the greatest admirer there is of your work—'

'Only some of it, it seems.' Wells looked down at the novel and pen and pushed them further away.

'Oh, no. Never stops rereading your books, H.G.,' said Eileen.

'It's like being married to a schoolboy sometimes – he's always flying off to some other world. Hard to get him back usually.'

'I think it's pretty clear the world of science and progress you foretold hasn't quite turned out as we'd all hoped,' Orwell said.

'Nonsense, Orwell. People live incalculably better now.'

'Really? Did you notice the bomb craters on the way here this evening? Half of London lies in ruins thanks to the invention of the aeroplane.'

'As I predicted in *The Shape of Things to Come*. You saw the movie! So don't call me naive. I won't have it.'

'You got it half-right, H.G. But science is in the service of tyranny, not democracy. Freedom won't automatically be the victor. You've been to Russia; you've met Lenin and Stalin. You ought to know.'

'Yes, and I thought them dangerous fools. Reason will win out, Orwell. We must keep urging it. You're a defeatist. A defeatist!'

'You must retract, H.G.,' Empson broke in. 'The chap fought in Spain.'

'With Eileen,' said Inez.

'Bagged a few fascists too, as I read,' said Empson. 'And nearly some communists.'

'It's true. Saw him in the trenches with my own eyes,' Eileen said. 'And smelled him. Squalid business.'

Wells loosened a little. 'Alright, then, I apologise. But tell me, what does *your* future look like, Orwell? I guess we're going to hear about it sooner or later. What's *your* utopia?'

A utopia. As a child he'd been fascinated by the idea –

thanks mainly to Wells himself. Mankind starting all over again, creating a new world, free of human vices, with hope triumphing over human folly. Like every literate child of his generation, he'd harboured a secret desire to write such a book himself, but the juvenile nature of it soon became obvious and he had surrendered the notion along with short trousers. Since then he hadn't given it a moment's thought. Gloominess, not jolly optimism about the future, was his thing.

'There's not going to be a utopia,' he told Wells. 'The future's going to be much like the present, except maybe amplified. Unless—'

'How? *How* like the present?'

'The shabbiness, the food queues, the endless wars, the leader worship, the watery beer and plastic meat we're forced to eat.'

'But why? All that's just the effect of the war. It's temporary. The way for mankind is up.'

'Because emotion, not reason, is what governs men. A world state governed by the wise . . . It's impossible! But if—'

'But *how* does emotion govern us? Why can't we change? Look at the progress man has made.'

'Look, H.G., I'm trying to answer, but every time I explain how, you ask why – and every time I explain why, you ask how. The way I see it, progress is just another bloody swindle.' He paused. 'The past was better. *Infinitely* better.'

Empson belched and began to talk. 'Come on, H.G., don't be so hurt. He's got a point. Saw it myself in China. Bloody mess: communists on the one side, Japanese militarists on the other, both claiming to modernise the place. Absolute shambles. I read George's essay too.'

'It seems the whole of London did.'

'George really did say such nice things about you too. You didn't read *those* passages out.'

Empson picked up Wells' copy of *Horizon* and flicked through it. '"Up to 1914–"' Empson let out another belch – '"Up to 1914 Wells was in the main a true prophet. In physical details his vision of the new world has been fulfilled to a surprising extent." A chap can't be much more generous than that.' Empson turned the pages. 'Yes, here it is. "All sensible men for decades past have been substantially in agreement with what Mr Wells says; but the sensible men have no power, and, in too many cases, no disposition to sacrifice themselves."' Empson set the magazine down. 'You see, he's not saying you're the problem, H.G., but that the rest of us are inadequate. Especially the politicians.'

Wells theatrically surrendered. He reached across the table, seized the book and pen and signed it. 'There you go, Orwell. *The Sleeper Awakes*, autographed copy.'

'And anyway, you must make allowances for George,' Empson went on. 'He's an Etonian, and they're trained as sprogs to be blunt. They don't mean it. Do you, George?'

'Well, I suppose my manners aren't so good on paper.'

'Yes, that's right. You should see what George wrote about Auden and Spender, H.G. Called them pansies.'

'A "gutless Kipling", wasn't it?' said Eileen.

'Yes, but he apologised and now they're all the best of chums. Come on, H.G., have some scotch.' Empson lurched at the decanter and managed to pour everyone a measure without spilling any. Wells drank his down.

'Every thinking person agrees with you, H.G.,' said Orwell.

'It's just that the thinking people are not the ones in charge. You know, we really want the same sort of world – some form of socialism and cooperation. It's our only hope. It's just that I have a different idea about how we'll get there.'

'And what's that?'

'We'll probably need to fight the communists first. Then reinstate a little of the world Polly and Kipps lived in. By which I mean keep the Royal Family, the House of Commons, all the judges in their horsehair wigs and so forth. As well as nationalise the mines, the banks and Eton.'

'You see,' said Empson, 'there's plenty to agree on.' He topped up everyone's glasses again. 'We should all drink to something. What will it be, H.G.?'

'Yes, H.G.,' said Inez, warmly. 'What?'

He thought for a moment, then stood and held up his glass.

'To the future.'

'And to the past,' Orwell added.

- III -

London, June 1942. With Eileen he took an early tube to work, taking care not to disturb the drowsy families who had spent the night on their mattresses on the platforms, sheltering from the Luftwaffe's bombers, even though the raids by now had become little more than a nuisance that interrupted one's sleep.

They emerged from the sandbagged station into the West End and passed the hole in the ground where the John Lewis store had been. He'd begged on this very spot once, when tramping, and recalled how after one of the big raids back in '41 a pile of mannequins rescued from the store had been stacked neatly on the pavement like bleached corpses, and how he had absentmindedly kicked a loose hand into the gutter. At 200 Oxford Street, the old Peter Robinson department store, he kissed Eileen on the cheek and descended the stairs to his office. The army of hideously fat charwomen, one of whom must have been a yard across the hips, was already hard at work, singing in chorus as its members swept the passages with their brooms. It was one of the romantic tunes from an American musical that had become ubiquitous. The only uplifting time of the day to be here, he thought.

In the higher of the two basements he found his office, number 310. It wasn't actually what you'd call an office, but one of around fifty identical cubicles, divided by seven-feet-high lath and plaster walls, which provided minimal privacy and did nothing to deaden the intolerable background noise of conversation, dictation and typing that frayed everyone's tempers and made it all but impossible to do anything creative.

His desk was half smothered in unopened mail and copies of news cables. As he sat down, a mailroom clerk paused with his trolley and upended another batch of papers onto it. Ahead of him lay a dreary morning of drafting letters to pompous literary gents, filling out booking forms for radio talks, and tracking down his guests' missing speaking fees. The sheer pointlessness of it all, with everything having to be produced in triplicate to be rubber-stamped by committees full of bloody fools. He couldn't face it yet, and looked instead at a BBC monitoring report on top of the sea of paper before him.

PRAGUE(CZECH HOME STATIONS)
IN GERMAN FOR PROTECTORATE.
10.6.4 2

Heydrich Revenge: Village Wiped Out: All Men Shot:
ANNOUNCEMENT

He read the report. In retaliation for the assassination of SS leader Reinhard Heydrich, all the male inhabitants of the village of Lidice had been shot, the women sent to concentration camps and the children 'handed over to the appropriate authorities'. He read it again: *handed over to the appropriate authorities*. This was the world in which he now lived. Soon enough, he thought, you would probably be jeered at for suggesting the story of Lidice was true, even though the facts had been announced by the Germans themselves. He thought up a list of atrocities he knew to be true and determined to make a record of them for posterity.

He lit a cigarette and began work. It was his day with his secretary, Mrs Barratt, whom he shared with Empson, relieving him of the burden of typing his programs and correspondence. He reached wearily for his Dictaphone and began composing letters. In the cubicle across the narrow corridor he could hear a colleague talking some nonsense in a loathsome posh voice, and flashed him a hostile look.

At midday he took lunch in the canteen on the lower basement floor. With any luck, he thought, *she* would be there – Stevie Smith, the poet, whom he wanted to bed. He lined up, walking past piles of unwashed plates and chipped mugs on the sideboards. Grim-looking stews and puddings sat in steaming serving bins; one dish looked to be boiled cod and turnip tops. One had to grin and bear it; after all, there was a war on and merchant sailors had drowned to deliver this protein – assuming it wasn't synthetic.

When the queue moved along he saw the chalkboard: 'Today's special is Victory Pie.' He handed over a few coins for his portion and searched for a table, spotting Empson, who unfortunately was sitting with his colleague Sunday Wilshin, a silly blonde former actress who he suspected had eyes for his job.

'Ah, Sunday, Bill – just the people I was looking for,' he lied.

'I'm thinking about recording a program for the Indians on Basic English.'

'Excellent idea,' said Empson. 'Its benefits for teaching English are obvious.' With an opening into his favourite topic, the usually engaging Empson became rather a bore. 'The real beauty of the language lies in its simplicity, and its reductions in the number of words in its vocabulary. Do you know you can fit all the words you need onto a single page? Small type on a rather big page, obviously. The Basic English dictionary contains just a thousand words, aside from people and place names and so forth.'

'Just a thousand?' He knew all this already, of course.

'Yes. Difficult to believe, really. Eight hundred and fifty in the first category – these are the basic vocabulary. Fifty in the second category – international words like *radio* and *gramophone*. And another one hundred to do with applied science. Ogden and Richards think only fifteen per cent of the current Basic vocabulary is now of doubtful use, so the next edition may perhaps be regarded as definitive. Your chum Wells wants it to be the language of the world government after the war.'

'I hadn't realised it was so advanced,' said Wilshin, dumbly.

'The secret is getting rid of the verbs. Ogden leaves just ten verbal operations. None of this *will*, *would* business. Just confuses people. And the number of nouns – slashed. I mean, why say *puppy* when you can just say *young dog*? Or for that matter *bitch* when *female dog* is easier to learn? And so on. As you see, by training your mind like this – an object by time, an object by sex, and so on – you can find words for just about anything with a fraction of the words we use today.'

He listened on, distractedly watching fat ooze out of his Victory Pie and congeal in the coolness of the basement air.

'The food here really is better, don't you think?' said Wilshin, who was watching him.

'One mustn't complain.' He hacked off a portion with his fork and managed to swallow it. 'All very ingenious, of course. But, Bill, here's my reservation. Don't you think narrowing the vocabulary like that could also narrow thought? Our thoughts, after all, are limited by the words we have to express them. That's the sort of thing that probably goes on in Russia.'

'Oh, yes, but that's not entirely a bad thing. As Ogden says, a good language is a machine for thought. Fewer words can actually sharpen our thinking and give our words more precise meaning.'

'Less chance for misunderstanding,' said Wilshin, whose stupidity he was beginning to loathe. 'Between nations, as Wells says.' A childish smile broke out over Empson's face. 'You know, I once had a foreign student who thought the literal meaning of "out of sight, out of mind" was "invisible, insane". The fewer the words the better, in my view.'

'So how would you put it, in Basic English?'

'Simple, really: "not seeable, not thinkable". *Much* more precise. And more poetic, when you consider it.'

'Iambic,' said Wilshin.

'Like Shakespeare.'

Inwardly horrified at the comparison, he washed down the last of the pie with lukewarm synthetic coffee. He considered the student's word, *insanity*. It seemed the sort of concept Basic English would struggle to get across adequately.

Wilshin seemed to have read his thoughts. 'Do you think Basic could handle *Hamlet*?'

While Empson answered, he wondered to himself how the new language might describe someone who was insane: perhaps 'wrong-thinker', which could just as easily mean 'political dissenter' to someone with bad motives. A first step, perhaps, to criminalising thought altogether.

'Tell me, Blair,' Empson asked. 'Are you familiar with my essay on the benefits of translating Wordsworth into Basic? Improves his meaning in a lot of ways, actually. Helps people today really understand the Romantics, instead of just pretending to. I'll get you a copy if you like.'

It suddenly occurred to him that, in some important way, insanity actually explained a lot about intellectuals like Empson.

★

After lunch, two basement floors down in Recording Studio 1, he prepared to record the weekly round-up of wartime news for broadcast to the subcontinent. Unlike his other tasks, with their never-ending boredom and routine, this one called upon all his creativity. He thought of it as a game, the object being to explain the facts of the war in a way that was both truthful and untruthful at the same time. The trick was not to make up positive facts or ignore negative ones, but rather to present them in a way that B.B. would consider 'helpful' to the war effort. One could, for example, report a successful fascist offensive, but only by hinting that it was part of a carefully prepared trap into which the enemy had stupidly stumbled. Deaths from bombing raids could be reported, but only to highlight Nazi inaccuracy or perfidy, or both simultaneously. Subtlety was the important thing.

He had prepared this particular bulletin some days before, but it had only now emerged from the censorship bodies through which every utterance on the BBC had to pass. As he waited for the recording to start, his feet traversed the rim of a large manhole cover, beneath which the remnants of the River Fleet flowed on their subterranean course from Hampstead to the Thames. Everyone at the BBC knew its significance: it was the hole down which they must throw all classified documents should the Nazis invade. He had visions of his BBC Talks booking forms washing up on the riverbank at his childhood home in Shiplake, giving to the Gestapo the names of earnest literary dons who had misinterpreted Kipling. Through the concrete walls he heard the low rumble of a train passing along the Central Line, then the whoosh of its doors opening and closing at Oxford Circus.

He scanned the studio's cheap wartime fit-out: the plywoodfaced office table, with its sound-deadening green baize covering; the long and confusing row of electrical switches and dials that controlled the round Bakelite BBC microphone; the bookshelf with stacks of old scripts and cardboard boxes full of uncatalogued soundtracks. He sighed and looked down at the typescript before him, brushing off the ash that had fallen from his last cigarette. It bore two stamps: PASSED FOR SECURITY and PASSED FOR POLICY. Five lines had been blacked out. Remembering what the now censored passages had contained, the reason for their omission was evident: doubt had unwittingly been cast on the outcome of a current military campaign, the sort of unthinking blunder for which a black mark might be placed against his name. At least, he thought, he had kept their propaganda slightly less disgusting than it might otherwise have been. Not that anyone in India was likely to be listening.

Beyond the glass screen, his producer held up his left hand, his five fingers outstretched, and folded the fingers one-by-one into his palm by way of counting down: five, four, three, two, one. A red light lit up on the control panel in front of him and he began to speak, reading from the altered script.

'A great naval battle has taken place in the Pacific,' he began, then skipped the next line, which the censors had blacked out – obviously it contained something less than glorious for the Allies.

'A week ago we reported that the Japanese fleet had made an unsuccessful attack on Midway Island, and since then the full figures of their losses have come. It is now known that they lost four plane-carriers and a number of other ships. Full figures for the Battle of the Coral Sea have now also been released, and it appears from those that in the two battles the Japanese lost thirty-seven ships of various classes sunk or damaged, including a battleship and five cruisers sunk.'

There was, he noted, no mention of the Allies' losses. He continued reading as steadily as he could – praying an outbreak of coughing wouldn't spoil it and cause them to restart. Heavy fighting was continuing in Eastern China, and the Japanese had been making inroads into Inner Mongolia, cutting a vital trade route into Russia . . . As always, there were rousing accounts of production figures, which he fully expected to be overlaid with uplifting martial music. 'Mr Oliver Lyttelton, British Foreign Minister for Production, has just announced the truly staggering figures of Britain's current war production. He announces, among other things, that Britain is now producing vehicles for war purposes – this of course includes tanks – at the rate of two hundred and fifty thousand a year; big guns at forty thousand a year, and ammunition for those guns at a rate of twenty-five million rounds. He announces also that Britain's aircraft production has made a one hundred per cent increase, while the production of merchant shipping has increased by fifty-seven per cent . . .'

That evening he found himself back at the diary. He had reopened it some weeks before, thinking the war had entered a new and more promising phase. Churchill's grip on power had seemed to be loosening and there was increased talk of a second front. The people, he had thought, were recovering their revolutionary spirit. Perhaps under Cripps something positive could be won from the war. But once again he was wrong. How could he of all people – whose job was to produce propaganda – have fallen victim to such optimistic nonsense? Now that the cheap thrill of invention had passed, he recalled with disgust his own contribution to the propaganda effort that afternoon, with its typical fare of vast strategic manoeuvres, glorious victories, countless enemy aircraft shot down and ships sunk, prodigies of manufacturing output, meaningless statistic after meaningless statistic, the final victory once again within measurable distance – all while a neighbour's son had disappeared into some prison camp in the Far East, the enemy air raids continued nightly, and rationing got tighter and tighter. It was nothing but a record of daily forgeries, and he was sure no one believed a word of it.

Where would it end? The problem, of course, was that after he and everyone else who had lived through the actual events were dead, what he had written would likely pass into history as some sort of reliable source – a set of facts taken as the objective truth. More than any air raid, this thought frightened him. Memory – human memory. That's what had to be preserved.

With a start, he realised that while he had been thinking, he had also been writing furiously, filling page after page of the diary, setting out his horror, his fears, his sense of mental loneliness, above all his incomprehension of the world in which he now lived. It struck him that if the literature of totalitarianism was now triumphing, he was complicit in it. He was overcome by a feeling of disgust. He put a cross through the passages he had just written and wrote a single line on the following page:

'All propaganda is lies, even when one is telling the truth.'

How long, he wondered, could he go on being part of it? As soon as he could escape his job, he would.

– IV –

Kilburn, September 1943. Something in the breakfast news bulletin made him prick up his ears. 'They've just given the weather report for the channel. That's the first time I've heard that –' he was going to say 'since Dunkirk', but remembered Laurence – 'in more than three years.'

Eileen looked at him blankly, sipped her tea and glanced back to *The Times*. 'Surely,' she said, 'they can look out the window like everyone else. Rain, usually.'

'Don't you see? It means they don't care if the Germans know what the channel weather will be. They've conceded there's no risk of an invasion. They're telling us the war is as good as won.'

'The rest of us have known that since the Yanks came in. It's all here in *The Times*. Perhaps the Germans don't read it.'

'It means we can start thinking about the future.'

He finished his tea, saw her off to the bus stop and headed for the tube. It was his day off and he was on the scrounge. They had all put up with scarcity for years, some grumbling, others not, but the war's grittiness and privations had a way of hitting you with a series of unexpected blows. Just as you'd got used to the state of things, the soles of your boots started leaking, your bootlace snapped, soap became even coarser and more reminiscent of sandpaper. That morning it had been razor blades. His last remaining blade had become so blunt that his attempts to hack his stubble off had left his face red and raw. He'd heard that supplies were back in the shops, another convoy having got through, and was determined to get his share. There was no point in trying the high street stores, or the usual black market sites, which were under the thorough watch of the authorities, so he headed for the most likely place: Islington.

The morning was hot and the stench of the tube nauseating. He emerged at The Angel, crossed the main road and descended into the sunken alley of Camden Passage. Before him stood a curved row of smoked-dunned three-storey houses with front doors that opened onto the street. Uniformed sailors and soldiers, probably home on leave, stood in the doorways, smoking and talking, waiting for the pubs to open, some keeping an eye on prams parked out front. At number thirty-one stood a junk shop, although not a promising one. Through the dusty window he could see nothing but rubbishy fragments of old metal, worn-out tools and lengths of lead piping, some of which he knew had been there for years.

He left, noticing the grimy exterior of the Camden Head pub and the bomb site opposite. He crossed the main road again to Chapel Market. The stalls were selling dreary winter vegetables, tins of corned beef, packets of 'coffee' that smelled more of chicory, and varieties of oily fish, unknown before the war, which had been dredged up from the floor of the North Sea. He stopped and used some coupons to redeem a tin of orange juice with the word

'California' printed on it, and realised that he could barely remember what an actual orange looked like.

At one stall a group of women were jostling noisily for new pots and pans, which had become almost unprocurable since vast supplies had been melted down to make tin helmets back in 1940. The stock had just run out and he could hear some of the unlucky women shouting abuse at the stallholder, accusing him of favouritism and of holding some of the wretched items back for friends. If only the damned workers would get angry about something more important. They were, he surmised, like ants: able only to see the little things, not the big ones. Another stall looked promising – it had a row of shaving soap and other men's toiletries, a few combs and even boot polish. He selected some items and put them on the makeshift counter.

'Do you have any razor blades?' he asked the shopkeeper, who had oily hair and was in a collarless shirt.

'Any *what*, sir?'

'Razor blades. Do you have some, by any chance?'

'Well, razor blades,' he said. 'I might have. I guess it depends how desperate you was after 'em, sir.'

It was always like this nowadays: the underdogs had become the upper dogs. As a socialist, he was aware he should be happy about this fact, but he wasn't. He took off his hat – the instinctive action of the mendicant – and opened his wallet, pulling out a sum that pre-war would have bought him half a gross.

'I can see from the state of your chin, sir, that you're a needy gent indeed.' The stallholder reached below the stall to a box hidden under a canvas tarpaulin and pulled out a small packet of twelve blades – American, most likely pilfered. 'Most obliged, sir.' No change was offered.

The swine, he thought. All shopkeepers were fascists. Moving away from the stall, he looked up to see three heavily tarnished gilded balls. Ah, this place was always promising. He entered and looked about. The shopkeeper wasn't to be seen, as usual, although he could hear the setting down of a tea cup and the turning of a newspaper behind a curtain in the shop's rear. Rows of picture frames clogged the floors, and above them the shelves were crammed with items of indeterminate value: conch shells, Jubilee mugs, a rusty muzzle-loading pistol, ships in bottles and a collection of glass paperweights, one of which contained a piece of coral. These were rare and fantastically expensive. He picked it up, weighing it in his hand.

'Anything take your fancy, sir?' said an elderly, thin man with longish grey hair, who emerged from the rear. 'I see you've taken a fancy to that paperweight. That's a fine old piece, that is. South Pacific, from the time of Cook, I should think.' The man looked more closely at him. 'I remember you – you bought that young lady's keepsake book from me. Back during the Blitz, wasn't it?'

The diary. He remembered. 'Yes,' he said.

'Can't find its like now.'

Like most second-hand shop dealers, the man seemed somehow too refined to be in such a place. His common accent was inconsistent and obviously fake. A defrocked clergyman, he guessed. 'Any bootlaces?' he asked. 'Bed sheets? Pyjamas?'

'Well, no, alas. No one's giving them up nowadays, what with the shortages and everything. But I might just have another nice writing book. Came in last week, from some blitzed house in Chelsea, I think it was. Now, let me see . . . Just here, it was.' The old man began pawing about on a messy shelf, pushing aside a sad little collection of children's toys, including a few broken bits of Meccano that couldn't make anything and a rather crudelooking set of Snakes and Ladders – constructed, it appeared, from a recipe of cardboard and glue. 'Got it!' The book had a maroon cover and marbled edges. 'Not as grand as the last one I sold you, but feel that paper.'

He hesitated. It was bound to be ridiculously over-priced.

'Go on, sir.'

He took it in his hands. It was certainly too good for scribbling notes in or using for accounts.

'From before the Great War, I imagine. Quality, that is. I remember the things you could buy back then. Books . . . they were beautiful, not like now. There was this one book I had, you should have seen the binding. Stitched by hand, I reckon . . .'

He had stopped listening, recalling the news report from that morning. The war was petering out – things would soon free up. Life would get back to something resembling normal. It meant only one thing: a novel. He interrupted the man mid-sentence.

'I'll take it.'

'That will be nine shillings and eightpence, sir. And a further ten shillings for the glass weight.'

He left the shop with the feeling of having been hit over the head with a rubber club.

★

Arriving home, he went immediately to his study, sat at his desk and, pushing the diary aside, set the new notebook in its place. He opened to the first page and wrote a title decisively: 'For *The Quick and the Dead* '. He settled in for an afternoon of creative work, in a state of excitement he hadn't experienced for as long as he could recall. He would be taking his holidays soon – a whole three weeks – and he could make a decent start in that time.

The story had been brewing in his head since 1940. It was to be a 'proper' novel, the sort every writer needed on his list, with its 'proper' subject of England in decline. Over a pot of tea, which he stewed several times, he worked up the themes: the fading pull of the Church; the men marching off in 1914, only to return on stretchers four years later; the coming of modernity, with its tractors replacing carthorses; the pointlessness of moneyless middle-class life; the protagonist's death in Spain; Dunkirk. It would make him the novelist he'd always wanted to be, a sort of Galsworthy of the left.

After several hours' work he read the notes over. Something was wrong. It could have been the script of *In Which We Serve*, which he'd recently seen at the movies. He knew the problem: it was a novel for 1940, and as outdated in 1943 as a 1914 recruitment elegy had been after Passchendaele. Something about the war – *this* war – had got inside people's brains, changed them, threatening to make even the victors less free and their lives more squalid. That's what any book about it had to explain.

By now his high spirits had faded, and a familiar feeling of failure enveloped him. He was *still* a journeyman hack, *still* chained to his Remington beneath his handpainted shingle − 'Reviews and essays £5' − and *still* earning no more than a prole at his lathe. Little more than a drab clerk. The war had used him up and left him with less to show for his efforts than the wounds a soldier brings home from a campaign.

His mind wandered once more, so much so that he barely noticed what he did next. Turning a dozen or so pages, he wrote five words, underlining them to make them into a title: The Last Man in Europe. He knew what it had to be about: the revolution betrayed, man betrayed, the end of the utopia! That was the only story that mattered right now. Understand the great betrayal of human hopes over the previous decade and you understood everything; even the war could somehow be explained by it. Everything else he was writing had to be pushed aside.

He turned the page and kept writing. Ideas gushed out like water from an unblocked pipe, and it took him barely an hour to get the outline clear. Newspeak − rectification − the position of the proles − dual standards of thought − the ideologies of Bakerism and Ingsoc − the party slogans (War is peace. Ignorance is strength. Freedom is slavery.) − the Two Minutes Hate − war with Eastasia in 1974 and with Eurasia in 1978 − A, B & C present at a conference in 1976 − the disappearance of objective truth − the love affair − the rebellion of the individual − torture, confession and the recognition of insanity.

It was a nightmare world, to be sure, but would people think it too nightmarish, too fantastical to be taken seriously? Doubts began to crowd out his positive thoughts. No one would be interested in a story such as that . . . After all the people's sacrifices, they want to be told things are going to get better . . . No publisher will touch it . . .

He was back where he had started. But something stopped him from ripping the notes out and returning to his previous idea. It was a conviction, which he could feel in his belly, that he was right. Life *had* changed for the worse, and if life had once been better, it could be better again. The future could be altered.

He went to the cupboard and rummaged around. Soon he found it: a box that had once contained expensive handmade chocolates, the sort of thing that could only have come from before the war, and which he vaguely remembered had been a wedding gift. He took it back to his desk, opened it and tipped out the clippings he had stored in it. Leafing through, he found what he had been looking for: the reports of the 1938 show trials. There they were, the photographs of Yagoda, Rykoff and Bukharin. No doubt the three of them had been written out of Soviet history books by now, but there they were, in *The Times*. He was right: the past *had* been altered. The revolution *had* promised so much more but had been betrayed. The past still existed, though, and its existence could be proved.

He read over his notes. It was all very rudimentary but he knew what he had to do: resign from his job and get writing straight away. In two months' time he would be free.

★

BBC recording studio, 200 Oxford Street, October. He was sitting next to the sound engineer, cigarette in hand, a pair of earphones on his head, helping with the flash cues at the recording of a radio play he had adapted from Ignazio Silone's short story 'The Fox'. He presumed the audience for these plays to be tiny, but it was better than producing propaganda.

A light came on and the recording began. The script before him said 'PIG EFFECTS' and the engineer added in the sound of several pigs snorting and squealing. When it stopped, he pushed a button to cue the actors, several of whom were poised behind the studio's glass partition. One of them, playing the narrator, his hand over his left headphone, began reading from the script held in his right.

'The birth started well and three little pigs hardly bigger than rats had already come into the world. There was practically nothing for Agostino to do than find a suitable name for each little pig as it appeared. There was some trouble with the fourth one, but after that it went well and there were seven altogether. Agostino held up the fourth pig, the one which had not wanted to be born.' A second, more handsome, actor leaned into the microphone and began to read. 'That's a very poor pig. We'll call this one Benito Mussolini.'

The sound engineer inserted an extra loud squeal and waited for him to hit the flash cue button again, but he was too slow. He had been distracted by a new idea.

★

Kilburn, December. He was sitting on the sluttish armchair beneath the lamp, reading to Eileen, who was wrapped in a blanket on the couch.

'So, Snowball is Trotsky, right?' she asked.

'Right.'

'And the chickens who've just confessed to working for him – they're in the Show Trials?'

'Yes.'

'About to be slaughtered?'

'*Pour encourager les autres.*'

'How very sad.' She took another drag of her cigarette. 'The hens . . . Why haven't they got names? You named all the others. Even the goat! Which, by the way, you should change to Muriel.'

'After that fussy old dam of ours.'

'She wasn't fussy at all. Just intelligent; she had your measure completely. You know, for some reason I always picture goats wearing glasses.'

'Yes, that's a good point.'

'Anyway, the hens?'

'Best not to give hens names; makes it harder to eat them.'

'We ate our old cockerel, Ford.'

'We were hungry, remember? Anyway, he was a right bastard, as I recall.'

'This book – it's going to be your most successful yet, I can just tell. Even children will like it.' She took another drag.

'Although I suspect parents might have to censor it for the really little ones.'

'Especially when I kill off the carthorse.'

'Oh, poor Boxer! Say you won't! There'll be tears at bedtime.'

'Revolutions never have happy endings – that's the whole point.'

'When I read it to our little boy or girl – if we can ever find one to adopt – I shall say Boxer joined the circus to give rides to children.'

'Believe me, darling, upbeat endings never work.'

- V -

Greenwich, July 1944. The sirens sounded once more, and the drum roll of the distant barrages resumed, getting louder as the firing crept closer and closer. When its moment in the symphony arrived, the battery of 3.7s in the park opposite opened up, rattling the walls and windows and sending little showers of plaster dust falling to the floor. Incredibly, the new baby slept through it. Orwell turned to Eileen and whispered, 'They're conditioned to it in the womb nowadays.'

They had named him Ricky, short for Richard Horatio Blair. The first name after his friend Sir Richard Rees, the middle one after the only English hero not automatically taken for a Tory. He'd always secretly admired old Nelson up on that plinth in Trafalgar Square, facing down Britain's enemies. If only, he thought, Churchill had been a socialist. The boy was a war orphan, left to some unfortunate girl by a Canadian soldier now presumably trembling in a foxhole in Normandy.

He got up and stuck his head out the open window. It was a foolish act, certainly, but if a doodlebug were to hit the house, what would it matter? The rapid-fire flashes of the anti-aircraft battery lit up the streetscape. Here was the world the boy would inherit, with its bomb-chipped footpaths, boarded windows, empty lots and hastily filled craters. His mind went to Wells' glittering, antiseptic world of glass, steel and snow-white concrete. Yes, he had been right about H.G.

Through the blasts and the whining of night-fighters they could hear the terrifying purring of a pulse-jet engine. Around fifty of the rocket bombs were being launched every day, with about half making it through the coastal defences to drop on the city's terrified people. 'Don't let it stop,' he prayed. 'Let the engine die out only when it's well past.' When it did go silent, Eileen hugged him tightly and braced for the explosion, which was nearer than any they had experienced before.

'Always going clean over us,' he whispered, conscious the baby was still sleeping.

'How do you know?'

'Oh, I can tell. When they're getting really close, your heart beats faster. Never fails.'

'Superstition.'

'Like the Cockneys say, at least you can hear doodlebugs coming and dive under the table before they hit.'

'We didn't dive anywhere.'

'No, but we'll be looking back fondly on the old doodlebug one day. The next weapon won't give as much warning.'

Shrapnel from spent anti-aircraft rounds tinkled onto the roof above their bed. Ricky began to cry.

'The class of '64 has woken up,' Eileen said. They weren't going to get back to sleep in a hurry.

He got up and brought Ricky back to her, picking up the

bottle of milk that was still warm from the summer heat. It had been a trial trying to find a plastic teat – anything made from war materials like rubber was impossible to buy. The ack-ack started rolling towards London again.

'Darling, what sort of world is our little boy going to inherit?' She pressed the baby to her chest and began feeding while he tenderly rubbed the boy's cheek with the back of his index finger, putting his other arm around her back as they sat up in bed. Richard's arrival had brought them closer together, and his affairs had stopped, especially after the frightful row over his secretary Sally McEwan. And as far as he could tell, she too was no longer straying.

'That depends, I suppose, on us. What we do and what sort of world we leave him.'

'He won't be our age until the 1980s. Seems like forever. At least this war will be well over by then, I suppose.'

'He deserves a better life than we've had, doesn't he?' He thought of the shabbiness and drudgery of their lives. This far into the war, all but the wealthiest Londoners had taken to patching their clothes and eating cabbage. He thought he could see ceiling dust in the pores of Eileen's skin. Somewhere across London another doodlebug hit the ground with a dull thud.

'We should take him to the country. A little farm cottage, with a wood fire and a vegetable garden and roses growing across the veranda. We could live off almost nothing – the way we used to in Wallington. Send Ricky to the village school. Be a proper little family.'

'Like the proles; they know how to live.' He pulled her and Ricky closer.

'You could even escape from the stupid literary life and

get back to writing novels, now that you've broken your drought with the fairy story.'

The fairy story. He'd pushed the frustrations of not being able to find a publisher for it out of his mind. Stupidly, he had allowed this to stop him from starting his other planned novel, and now it seemed that might come to nothing. More time wasted! 'Talking of farms . . . David Astor's told me about a place on Jura that might be available for rent.'

'Jura? Where's that?'

'Scottish Hebrides. Inner. Apparently the laird is a decent sort who went to Eton with him. I can't imagine the Germans or the Russians wasting their doodlebugs on a place like that.'

'Sounds a long way away from anywhere.'

'Precisely.'

Across London the rain of rocket bombs continued as all three of them drifted off to sleep.

★

He rose early, leaving Eileen and the baby sleeping peacefully in bed, and breakfasted with Gwen, Laurence's widow, in the kitchen downstairs. Gwen, like Laurence a doctor, who had arranged for Ricky's adoption, had thought it better for them to be close by in the early days, and like everyone else believed Greenwich to be safer from V-1s than Kilburn. A rumour had got around that Churchill was using false news reports to trick the Germans into aiming their missiles at the working-class suburbs. The BBC was playing the morning exercise program that was part of its wartime fitness drive. The instructress's voice was exhorting the listeners to bend over and touch their toes – a task he knew would leave him battling for his next breath, even though he was only forty-one, an age at which fit men were still expected to be on the front line. To escape the wretched babbling, he polished off his meagre breakfast and went out.

Returning home to collect the mail, he found the Kilburn flat a ruin. A near miss by a doodlebug had taken out the windows and brought down part of the ceiling. Maybe, he thought, the rumours were right. Through a crack in the wall he could see the world outside. Their furniture was covered by a thick layer of plaster fragments, and his books lay scattered across the space that was once his study. Then he remembered what he had come back for. Getting down on his hands and knees, he scrabbled through a pile of letters that had been pushed through the door, spotting a large brown envelope. He picked it up, brushing off fragments of brick and glass.

He was hoping for just a letter but it was the manuscript, returned again. First Gollancz, then Deutsch, and now Cape. He read the letter enclosed with it:

I mentioned the reaction that I had had from an important official in the Ministry of Information with regard to *ANIMAL FARM*. I must confess that this expression of opinion has given me seriously to think. My reading of the manuscript gave me considerable personal enjoyment and satisfaction but I can see now that it might be regarded as something which it was highly ill-advised to publish at the present time. I think the choice of pigs as the ruling caste will no doubt give

offense to many people, and particularly to anyone who
is a bit touchy, as undoubtedly the Russians are . . .

He guessed immediately what had happened: the Ministry
of Information had been penetrated by the communists.
Everyone knew the literary world was full of silent
party members who were as good as Soviet agents, their
ultimate allegiance being to Russia. This racket of writers
worshipping Stalin had been going on since at least the
early 'thirties, and now even the Tories were too gormless
to insult him. It wasn't that long ago they wouldn't insult
Hitler. He seethed. To hell with them! Why not publish
the story himself, as Swift would have done? His anarchist
friends would have some paper hidden away for the
revolution. He collected everything of value he could fit
into two suitcases; the rest would have to wait.

The summer had turned baking hot, and his journey
across London was sapping. The war was as good as won,
everyone thought, with the fascists in retreat on all fronts
and the church bells ringing out victory after victory. Yet
he had a strange feeling that the fighting would never end.
Each advance brought fresh horrors: new weapons to cower
from, and new stories of atrocities in the east that would
whip the British population to new heights of patriotic
indignation.

At a Lyons tea house he sat down to rest, pulled out the
typescript and wrote a fresh covering letter by hand.

This MS has been blitzed which accounts for my delay
in delivering it. If you read this MS yourself you will
see its meaning is not an acceptable one at the moment,

but I could not agree to make any alterations. Cape or the M.O.I., I am not certain which from the wording of his letter, made the imbecile suggestion that some other animal than the pigs might be made to represent the Bolsheviks. I could not of course make any change of that description.

He stopped at the post office, bought an envelope and posted it to T.S. Eliot, c/o Faber & Faber, 24 Russell Square, Bloomsbury, London, WC1.

★

Four weeks passed. He opened the mid-morning post before heading out to *Tribune*, where he had a new job as literary editor. There was a letter from Faber:

> We have no conviction that this is the right point of view from which to criticise the political situation at the present time . . . After all, your pigs are far more intelligent than the other animals, and therefore best qualified to run the farm – in fact, there couldn't have been an *Animal Farm* at all without them; so that what was needed, (someone might argue), was not more communism but more public-spirited pigs . . . I am very sorry, because whoever publishes this will naturally have the opportunity of publishing your future work: and I have a regard for your work, because it is good writing of fundamental integrity. Miss Shelden will be sending you the script under separate cover.

So much for the judgement of the great T.S. Eliot! At the start of the war, he'd accused Eliot of having a soft preference for fascism, and now here he was, in thrall to the Reds. Circus dogs jump when the trainer cracks his whip, he thought, but the really well-trained dog is the one that somersaults before the whip appears. He had one more publisher on his list. He made for the city.

★

He entered the crush of the main bar of the Bodega in Bedford Street, just off the Strand, and was hit by the sour smell of beer and sweat from the draymen drinking there. He was in time to catch Fredric Warburg, who had just finished his lunch. He looked at Warburg: tall, heavy-set and expensively dressed, with Brylcreemed hair and a cigarette holder clamped between his canines. It seemed a strange place for a successful publisher to eat, and he guessed he was trying to avoid the legions of journeyman poets who swarmed like blackbeetles around Fitzrovia.

'Sergeant Orwell, what brings you here? You should have made an appointment; we could have eaten together.'

'I need to talk to you, Fred. I went to the office but they told me you were here. I've only got a minute.'

They went over to the bar and sat down. Warburg ordered two half-pints of dark ale, which they downed immediately.

'Don't tell me you've been bombed out again, Orwell? These damned doodlebugs.'

'I have, actually, but that's not what I'm here about. The commos at the MOI have blacklisted my latest book.

Harmful to the war effort, damaging to Anglo–Soviet relations, nonsense like that. That coughdrop Eliot has fallen for the same line. Well, it's yours now if you're interested.' He unbuckled his dispatch case and pulled out the slim typescript, now marked by additional sets of grubby fingerprints. 'Here's the bally manuscript. You get last dibs on it, Fred, if you can find some paper to print it on. If you don't want it I'll publish it myself, underground, with Astor's money.'

'What's it called?'

'*Animal Farm.*'

'Unusual!'

'It's about a lot of animals that rebel against their farmer – and it's very anti-Russian. Too anti-Russian even for you, I'm afraid.' He knew, though, that Warburg, who had published *Homage to Catalonia* when no one else would touch it – and lost money doing so – was the most courageous publisher in England.

'You're thinking of my wife, Orwell. Pamela's as pro-Russian as it gets. Thinks Stalin morally infallible.'

After leaving the Bodega they walked eastward down the Strand, their ears alert to buzz-bombs. They halted near the bombdamaged Royal Courts of Justice, opposite the burnt-out ruins of St Clement Danes, which had been destroyed in an air raid three years before. Orwell looked again at the ruined church, which seemed forgotten on its lonely traffic island, with its blackened walls and its steeple sprouting branches and weeds. 'Oranges and lemons,' he mumbled. 'Have I ever told you, Fred, that I'd like one day to produce a book of nursery rhymes?'

'There's actually a jolly good market for that sort of

thing, you know. I should be interested, Orwell . . . if ever the paper could be found.'

They looked up to find themselves beneath the statue of Samuel Johnson reading from his dictionary.

'They say it's a poor likeness,' Orwell said.

'Eight years that dictionary took him, Orwell. Did it all himself.'

'It'd be a committee job now. And much shorter.'

'Why do you think the old boy bothered? Money? Ego?'

'It's a celebration, Fred. Of words.'

'One hundred and forty-two thousand of them, apparently.'

'Nowadays people want to destroy words.' Orwell paused. 'Or at least their meaning. In Johnson's day governments were too disorganised to do such things. You know, they actually gave him a royal pension for creating that dictionary. Wouldn't happen now.'

'No, not now.' Warburg slapped the burnt ruins. 'The same raid that destroyed this church sent my warehouse up in flames. Hundreds of thousands of volumes, turned into smoke. Including some of yours, as I recall.'

'Destroy literature, Fred, and it becomes easier to destroy people. You're even allowed to commit murder these days as long as you call it something else.'

Warburg looked at the bomb-battered street and cocked his head. 'Area bombing.'

'Yes.'

Warburg's usually placid face hardened. 'Solving the Jewish problem.' He turned back to the statue. 'I suppose you've heard the stories too.'

'Sadly, yes.'

'What sort of world have we created? Women, children . . .'

'One can only guess at the horrors, Fred.'

'The bastards! The bloody bastards!'

Orwell touched his shoulder. 'Old Johnson's a man for our times.'

'He certainly is that.' Warburg turned back around. 'This new book, Orwell. You say it's anti-communist?'

'And anti-Nazi.'

'I've got a feeling Pamela's going to be very unhappy with me indeed.'

They shook hands. 'Until next time we meet.'

Before setting off down Fleet Street, Orwell looked again at the gutted St Clement's. *When words lose their meaning, we bomb the past into the ground.* It sent his mind back to that ruined church in Barcelona where he had spent the night hiding from Stalin's agents. He tried to remember the rest of the rhyme, but could only recall the ending:

> *Here comes a candle to light you to bed,*
> *Here comes a chopper to chop off your head.*
> *Chop, chop, chop, chop,*
> *The last man's dead.*

– VI –

He walked another thirty yards down the Strand, entered the front door of the Outer Temple and went through to the headquarters of *Tribune*. It was a tiny office that had once been a barrister's chambers but now was crammed with an assortment of furniture, which gave the place an air of impermanence that reminded him of lodging houses he had endured ten years before. He poked distractedly at review copies of books piled on his desk, noting only *The Road to Serfdom* by that Austrian economist with the Nazi-sounding name of F.A. von Hayek. He couldn't face reading any unsolicited poems and essays, so he collected them up and slid them into an already stuffed drawer, pressing them down with a wooden ruler so he could push it shut.

At the top of his correspondence pile was an angry letter from James Burnham, taking exception to something he had written in *Tribune*. Burnham had started the war predicting first a Nazi victory, then a Soviet one, and he now believed the postwar world would be dominated by three different power blocs, led by the Soviet Union, Japan and the United States, which would coexist in a kind of stasis maintained by continual low-level war. Each would be totalitarian in its own way, ruled by a self-selecting oligarchy of managers. Burnham, he could see, was nothing but a naked power worshipper, and one of those annoying writers, typical of Marxists and former Marxists, who kept half a dozen directly contradictory ideas active at all times, sustaining the complex trick by means of subtle adjustments of his earlier definitions and prophesies. Dialectics, they called it; but he had coined his own term for it: doublethink. We could all be geniuses, he thought, if we could invent our own logic and adjust our predictions *after* the fact. He detested Burnham, but had to admit the man had a point about the way the world was heading. He decided he would write that week's column about this new and sinister theory.

Scarcely an hour later he was searching for a suitably dismissive conclusion when it occurred to him that for all Burnham's self-deception and dissimulation, he had done the world a service. He had shed the camouflage and exposed the single objective of modern politics for all to see: power for its own sake. All else was flummery. Whether they were called commissars, gauleiters or capitalist managers, the essential philosophy of Burnham's rulers was the same: control, manipulation, coordination – the crushing flat of whatever joy life promised, under the guise of efficiency, productivity and rationality. It would be a world in which true human feelings had no value or place. The end of man. Managerialism, Burnham called it, but a subtle form of totalitarianism would be a more accurate description. Here was the real threat to future freedom, the one people had to fight against or succumb to, perhaps forever. Here was the boot stamping on humanity which he'd first witnessed in Spain.

He started typing, racing to capture the clarity of his thoughts before another argument popped into his mind to cloud them.

'Where Burnham and his fellow-thinkers are wrong,' he wrote, 'is in trying to spread the idea that totalitarianism is unavoidable, and that we must therefore do nothing to oppose it . . .'

He pulled the article from his typewriter and passed it to Sally. 'Give this to Kimche, will you, Sal?'

She placed another letter in front of him. 'It's that genius Walter again.'

'Let's see what he's complaining about this time,' he said eagerly, leaning back in his chair, cigarette in his left hand. He opened the letter to discover a note inside in Sally's handwriting: *This afternoon, my apartment?* He shook his head, mouthing, *Sorry*. He had arranged lunch with Muggeridge and Powell. It could easily be put off, and in the past he would have done so, but now, with Ricky in his life, it didn't seem right.

Martin Walter – the self-styled 'Controller of the British Institute of Fiction-Writing Science Ltd' – had been laying siege to the letter pages for months, ever since Orwell had started using his *As I Please* column to ridicule his claim to have 'solved the problem of fiction writing'.

'Walter, everyone,' he said loudly, flourishing the letter above his head. He started reading so the rest of the tiny office could hear. '"I have established that the nature of the 'plot' is strictly scientific, and have evolved a Scientific Plot Formula according to which all successful novels are constructed. By sending one guinea to the Institute, you can obtain the secret to novel and story-writing success.

Numerous well-known authors can testify to the soundness of the Institute's methods.'"

'Do you think we could ask him to name one of these wellknown authors?' Jon Kimche, *Tribune*'s editor, asked. 'After all, who'd buy a hair tonic from a bald man?'

'The man's certifiable!' yelled out another.

'On the contrary,' Orwell said. 'He's a swindler, of course. But the swindle only has a chance because he's smart enough to be onto something.'

'Go on, George, give us your theory,' Kimche laughed. 'What's Walter onto?'

'Why, the coordination of the arts by the state. Look at this pile of books on my desk. I'd be willing to bet I could predict, within certain reasonable limits of accuracy, the arguments and evidence in each.'

'Including the fiction?'

'Especially the fiction. The plots, characters, language – all totally predictable.'

'Keep going!'

'Our current methods are too inefficient. Books could quite easily be mass-produced on a production line – a sort of conveyor belt process that follows some algebraic formula. Keep human initiative to a minimum.'

Everyone in the office was listening now, and chuckling.

'All it would take would be a directive from above and a bit of a touch-up at the end by a squad of tired hacks – like you lot – who've been trained to subordinate their own style to the needs of the publisher or party or whoever's in control. Isn't that how Disney films are made? And Ford motorcars. Same principle, when you think about it.'

They waited, amused, for him to go on.

'The parameters would be easy to set. Just dial in the relevant party ideology, the events of the time, the style – romance, mystery or tragedy – pull a lever, and there you have it, a book at least as readable as all this garbage in front of me. Authors? No need of them. We could even automate reviewing. Which of course I've been known to do myself, mentally.'

'George, really! What a cynical view for a literary editor to hold.'

'I'm serious. No doubt books are already being produced in Russia like that. That chap Gleb Struve reckons that hardly a single decent piece of literature has been produced there for about twenty years. This explains it.'

'You should write a column on it, George.'

'Oh, I will. Don't worry.'

★

Nye Bevan had an unexpectedly high-pitched voice, which he raised as the buzz of the approaching doodlebug got louder. With perfect timing, he finished outlining the following week's leader on nationalising coal just as the pulsing noise abruptly stopped – worryingly, *before* passing overhead. The other members of the *Tribune* editorial committee sat silent and still, anticipating the explosion. Foolishly, no one ducked under the heavy oak table, which would at least have protected them from flying glass and bricks, but they instinctively braced their hands against it, waiting, waiting . . . Orwell could see they were all thinking the usual thing: *God, please let it fall on someone else.* He shuffled a pile of typescripts in front of him, trying to appear unperturbed and looked up, through the facing window, to see the small black flying bomb, resembling a torpedo with wings, plunge inelegantly beneath the near horizon of already blitzed roofs and broken church steeples to land with a *crump* somewhere across the river.

'Looked like Stepney,' he said. 'East End copping it again.' The workers, he thought; at least the workers could take it.

'Closer than usual,' Bevan said. It broke the tension, and they continued. 'George, what's the topic of your column this week?'

'In a word, Nye, Warsaw.' For the past few weeks the Red Army had waited on the eastern bank of the Vistula, watching the Nazis exterminate the Polish Home Army, which Stalin had encouraged to rise up on the supposed eve of their liberation.

'Not exactly a *literary* theme, George. Clem Attlee's not going to be happy with me if we reopen that wound. But I suppose there's no changing your mind. I'm guessing more angry letters and cancelled subscriptions can be expected?'

'Yes, most likely.'

'We've covered Warsaw at length already, and rather strongly, I thought.'

'Not strongly enough.'

'So what have you written? Can you give us a taste? Forewarned and all that.'

'Simply the truth. That the response of the press here in Britain has been cowardly. The brave Poles have taken the fight to Hitler with nothing but pistols and the odd captured rifle, and we're treating them like naughty schoolchildren who won't behave themselves.'

'Some of which we have already stated, repeatedly, in our editorials.'

'But not all, Comrade Chairman.'

'No, you're right, George, not all. Mr Editor, what do you think?'

Kimche spoke. 'We're planning an editorial for the next edition which will outline what we know has unfolded in the past fortnight. In my opinion, it was unwise of the Poles to have acted so precipitously, knowing the Russians' policy towards the Home Army.'

'Knowing the Russians would allow the Nazis to exterminate them, you mean,' Orwell said. 'Why shilly-shally, Jon? Let's cut out the abstractions and state what will happen.'

'I wasn't suggesting the costs wouldn't be great.'

'Costs? Sounds like an accounting exercise. What do you think will happen when the uprising is crushed, as it will be without Russian help?'

He looked around.

'Alright, I'll tell you. The SS will execute every man they can lay their hands on. The women and children will no doubt be treated in the usual fashion. *Resettled*, I think, is the term they're currently using. It's going to make Lidice two years ago seem like a picnic.'

'There are two sides, George,' said Bevan. 'It's obvious the Polish government in exile wants to liberate Warsaw before the Red Army arrives, as a bargaining chip. They're playing the power game too.'

'Two sides? Bargaining chips? How can one be even-handed about Stalin?' He had remained cool but spoke insistently. The room went silent. He continued, slowly and deliberately. 'Dishonesty and cowardice towards dictators like this have to be paid for eventually. You can't one day be a boot-licking propagandist for the Soviet regime, or any other murdering regime, and suddenly return to mental decency the next. Once a whore, always a whore.'

'Let me guess who you're calling a whore, George,' said Bevan, amused. 'Kingsley Martin.'

'The *News Chronicle* and the *New Statesman*, of course.'

'Kingsley will doubtless be after us again in the courts,' he said, smiling. 'This is going to cost me another good bottle of claret at El Vinos to talk him down.'

'I'll remind you that the Soviet Union has suffered enormously too in this war, and that they are our allies,' Kimche said.

'And supposedly the allies of the Poles!' Orwell said. 'There can be no real future alliance on the basis that Stalin is always right, Jon. The world has to drop its gutless illusions about the communists, just as it eventually had to about the Nazis. And faster this time.'

'The Poles will lose support here if the reactionary elements in their government persist in trying to exploit the suffering of their people.'

Orwell groaned inside. How mechanical people sound, he thought, when they're covering up some unpleasant truth. 'Reactionary? Exploit the suffering of their people? How easy it is to justify killing hundreds of thousands of innocent people just by giving them a label! "You're a reactionary – here's a bullet. You're a Jew – here's a gas oven." How can we call ourselves socialists and democrats while excusing a bloodbath?'

Bevan glanced across the table. 'I'm not going to take

the feeling of the room, George, because I'm not sure it will be with you. I believe we have been strong on the issue already, and probably tested the tolerance of our readers. But I won't stop you from publishing it.'

'No, you won't. Because I think you know I'm right. We have to show the world that socialism means more than pyramids of corpses and secret police cells.'

'Yes, comrade, we know.' They had all heard him on this subject before. 'Anyway, what other columns are coming up? Any chance we can get back to the usual fare your readers like so much? It would be nice to attract more subscribers instead of scaring them away. You know, about how to make a nice cup of tea or grow roses, and why the price of second-hand alarm clocks is so outrageous?'

'Yes – something you'll like, Nye. Why people should be nicer to taxi drivers.'

'Ah, good. Anything else – of a slightly *literary* nature perhaps? It is the literary pages you edit, isn't it?'

'I do have something, as it happens. How to write a novel using a machine.'

'Splendid.'

– VII –

Islington, February 1945. Eileen had somehow managed to find them a permanent flat to replace the one the doodlebug had wrecked. It was just as he liked it – up high, in the roof, where one could at least put out incendiaries – but as others told him, it was vacant precisely because it was in the roof, and therefore a death-trap in a raid. On the way downstairs, through a partly open door he heard his neighbour, a broken-down drudge of just thirty, whose husband had disappeared into some prisoner-of-war camp in the Far East, hard at work at the kitchen sink he last week had helped her unblock. His lungs weren't feeling strong. Thank God I'm going down instead of up, he thought.

He reached the ground floor, opened the door and let in a swirl of chilling, late winter air that disturbed the dusty entrance parlour and set his chest off. He wrapped his scarf tighter and did up the top buttons of his greatcoat, which covered the captain's uniform he was wearing. He had taken up Astor's offer to become a war correspondent and was on his way to the airport and Paris. It was an indulgence, he knew.

The book! He should have been getting on with the book, but how often did a writer get a chance to see the front? Anyway, to see totalitarianism close up, to find out what it was really like – that was the thing.

He threw his duffel bag over his shoulder and tramped around Canonbury Square, its Georgian terraces once smart but now the borderlands of the East End. The district hadn't had an easy war – everywhere the pavements and walls were cracked, some held up by large wooden beams, and possibly a quarter of the windows in the street were smashed and boarded up. He walked past Kopp's flat. Kopp had somehow found his way out of both communist and fascist gaols, ending up uncomfortably – and suspiciously, he sometimes thought – close to Eileen. A moment later he was into the prole quarter of Upper Street.

Instantly he rounded the corner the street was in upheaval, with people sprinting for cover. He heard a curious double crack, followed by a sudden rushing sound. 'Gas pipe, bang overhead,' said a passing workman in filthy overalls, who grabbed his arm and pulled him into a doorway. Immediately there was a wallop, unbelievably loud, which shook the pavement and the remaining windows of the shopfront, even though the rising column of smoke and debris suggested it had landed a mile or more away. 'Gas pipe' was the name Londoners had given to the Germans' new and more deadly rocket bomb, officially known as the V-2.

'Blimey, what's the next war going to be like?' the man said. Orwell thanked him, noticing how, after hearing his voice, the man seemed to regard him as a sort of exotic species, not often sighted in this part of London. He walked off and turned south towards the Angel, marvelling at how quickly people resumed their normal activities, although not a suburb away some poor souls had likely just been wiped out.

★

Paris, March 1945. It was the lonely hour of three p.m. in Closerie des Lilas. He looked around the near-empty room. The afternoon sun was warming him feebly through the front window. It was the same yellow light he recalled here from the twenties.

Back then, the café still had some of the glamour and disreputability of its glory days, when the likes of Hemingway and Fitzgerald would gather each afternoon to write and to drink themselves into oblivion and insanity. Even by 1929 such men had begun to seem relics, the last great figures from a time before literature had been conscripted into political struggles. It was a more innocent world, he mused, with a buoyant freedom that you could feel in your belly – a spirit almost impossible to conjure up now. Today there were no writers in the café, just a group of chess players silently engaged in battle, the waiter quickly refilling their glasses when they were empty.

He looked up at the clock. In wartime, no one ever managed to arrive on time. The waiter was watching him. '*Encore du café, s'il vous plait,*' he said.

As he waited for his coffee, he reached into the pocket of his greatcoat and absentmindedly fingered the loaded pistol – a Colt .32 – which Hemingway, whom he had interviewed the previous day, had chosen for him from the armoury of weapons he kept in his suite at the Ritz. With the Nazis gone, rumour had it, Stalin's French agents were at large, assassinating the party's opponents whenever an opportunity presented. Suspected Trotskyists like him were still the enemy. He kept his right hand on the gun. One could never be too certain, especially in a café like this, which seemed for some reason the sort of place they would shoot you. A figure approached and he gripped the gun tighter.

'Monsieur Orwell.' It was a man perhaps half a dozen years older than himself, tall and thin, with thick blond hair brushed back from a noticeably care-worn face. His faded grey suit, along with his pale features, gave him a ghostly appearance. 'Józef Czapski.' The man gave a slight bow.

'Monsieur Czapski. Delighted.' They conversed in French.

'Koestler tells me you are the one Englishman who can help tell the truth about Poland. He sent me your articles from *Tribune*.'

The waiter came over and took Czapski's order, Orwell noticing the hint of contempt on the man's face on hearing a Polish accent.

Czapski outlined his story. A soldier in one of the elite Polish regiments, he had been taken prisoner by the Soviets in 1939, and held first at a prisoner-of-war camp in a place called Starobilsk, but subsequently moved on to another at Gryazovets.

'You have lived in a Soviet concentration camp?' Orwell desperately wanted to know what it was like.

'For two years, yes.' When the German invasion of the Soviet Union began in 1941, Czapski continued, he had been freed and sent to find eight thousand officer comrades, who were to be the nucleus of a new anti-Nazi fighting force. 'I found them eventually: shot in the back of the head and dumped in a mass grave outside the village of Katyn. The graves of even greater numbers of civilians – bureaucrats, lawyers, teachers, the educated – are now being discovered in other places.'

'The Soviet newsreels said they were shot by the Germans.'

'Just as the German ones said they were shot by the Soviets.' The truth, it seemed, depended on whose newsreel cameras were passing over the mass graves at any given time.

'They were shot in the back of the head,' Czapski said, as if to settle the matter. 'The Germans favour less personal methods.'

He remembered what Arthur Koestler had told him: the NKVD always shot their victims in the back of the head. So it was true. They really did live in an age when such things were possible – the leadership of a whole nation exterminated in the name of human equality and brotherhood. 'Do you have evidence?'

'Evidence? That depends what you mean. You won't find a single document in the whole of Poland or the Soviet Union to prove anything. It has all been destroyed or hidden or rewritten.'

'A cover-up.'

'There is a giant hole in the world where the Soviets bury the truth. One day it will be uncovered, but for now it is sufficient to know that the dead don't speak.'

'I was in Barcelona.'

'Koestler told me. It's one of the reasons I knew I could trust you with this.' Czapski reached into his shabby briefcase. 'You asked for evidence. Here it is.' He handed over a book written in French. 'Just small traces of the truth; scattered facts that have survived. I need you to help me get it published in England and America.'

It was more a pamphlet than a book, thin and poorly printed. The glue holding the pages together had long ago dried up and crumbled away, though enough of the spine remained for him to see the book's title: *Souvenirs de Starobielsk*. He scanned it while Czapski talked. Thumbing through dates, lists and eyewitness accounts of terrible atrocities, he recognised immediately its supreme importance. The survival of inconvenient facts meant everything.

'I will do all I can.'

They talked for another hour, then Czapski prepared to leave.

'One more thing, Monsieur Czapski.'

'Anything.'

'You met officials in Moscow. Did you ever meet Stalin?' At the mention of the name, Czapski flinched.

'No.'

'A pity. Everyone else I know who has met him has turned out to be a fool.'

'I will tell you, though, without him in 1941, the Germans would have taken Moscow. I'm certain of it.'

'A generous admission.'

'It is the truth. That is enough.'

They shook hands and Czapski left. Orwell observed him as he walked out onto the street and merged into the crowd. It was a strange sensation, like watching a visitor from the grave, the bearer of a memory they had forgotten to destroy.

Hotel Scribe, Paris, 30 March. He was lying on his bed, smoking idly, trying to recall for his dispatches the events of the past week. He had pursued totalitarianism beyond the Rhine, *into the lair of the fascist beast*, where he had collapsed while artillery bombarded a village in which a detachment of the SS was making a suicidal stand. Feverish, sweating, gasping for breath, coughing blood, he had reached a makeshift military hospital in the rubble of Cologne – where the doctors once again diagnosed bronchitis – and then made his way back to Paris.

The halting, uncomfortable journey had reminded him of something from his childhood, and now he remembered what: the rout of mankind from *The War of the Worlds*. From the window of the truck in which he had cadged a lift, he had seen millions of people on the move: ragged displaced persons seeking revenge on their tormentors; miserably dressed prisoners of war – dirty, bearded, exhausted, gathered into vast barbed-wire holding pens, from which, he presumed, many would eventually be chosen and submerged in the great slave labour camps in the east. Here and there he saw groupings of graves where Jews and Russian prisoners had dropped on their death marches. In villages the locals would turn away from the pitiful refugees; some would jeer and spit. Everywhere were roadblocks and traffic jams and rubble-strewn roads littered with burnt-out tanks and vehicles; he surmised there wasn't a bridge left standing between the Rhine and the Marne, and hardly a town or city between Stalingrad and Brussels whose centre hadn't been pounded into a pile of dust. London, he could now see, had got off lightly. It occurred to him that if he had predicted in 1925 that peaceful and civilised Europe would be laid to waste like this – to become a set of ruins governed by resentment, distrust and revenge – he would likely have been labelled a lunatic.

On reaching the Hotel Scribe, he had taken out his typewriter to record his dispatch for Astor. 'To walk through the ruined cities of Germany is to feel an actual doubt about the continuity of civilisation,' he typed. For the first time, he was no longer certain he would live to see the world rebuilt. And even if it was rebuilt, maybe it would all happen again, people's memories being so short.

He had stopped coughing blood, but the fever had not subsided. His illness, seemingly defeated four years earlier, was massing, once again, for an assault. He pulled from his rucksack the document he had prepared before leaving England, 'Notes for My Literary Executor', against the possibility that a fascist sniper wouldn't miss him a second time. But now he knew the real enemy was somewhere inside himself. He made a handful of corrections, then threw the pages down. It was a poor list of books to be remembered by, especially as it wouldn't be added to unless Warburg could find some paper for *Animal Farm*.

Animal Farm! While in Europe, he'd almost forgotten about the little book, so long was it taking to get published. The thought of it bucked him up. After years of trying, he had finally found the style he wanted – for the first time he had managed to write about politics without sacrificing his artistic purpose. It was bound to succeed. He couldn't allow himself to die now, with success so close.

He forced himself over to the sink, counted out eight

M&B tablets (he would blitz the bacteria into submission!) and washed them down with a glass of water, refusing to look in the mirror.

As he stood, shakily, there was a knock on the door. He opened it, holding onto the lip of the sink to be safe, to find the bellboy, who passed over a tarnished plate containing a telegram. It was from the *Observer* – no doubt Ivor Brown, the editor, wondering what had become of his dispatches.

He opened the telegram carefully, putting the envelope aside to reuse. It was from Brown, but not about work. In his feeble condition, he had to read it three times to be sure he comprehended its simple but terrible message: EILEEN IS DEAD.

That night he drifted in and out of a feverish sleep. His mind worked its way through the single fact he had got from the short telegram: she had died on the operating table, probably of a heart attack in reaction to anaesthetic. She had been just thirty-nine. As he tossed and turned in the stuffy room, he saw Eileen, lying on a trolley bed, rolling down a hospital corridor a mile long, smiling peacefully at him. Then she was trapped in a sinking ship, slipping deeper under the green water, looking up at him, but he was doing nothing to help her. She had no reproach in her eyes, but they both knew she was down there because he was up here . . .

*

It took him two days to get to Newcastle and the funeral, and now, back in Islington, having dropped Ricky off to be looked after by the Kopps, he turned, finally, to the letters Gwen had collected from Eileen's hospital room.

'Dearest, your letter came this morning . . . I am typing in the garden. Isn't that wonderful? Richard is sitting up in his new pram, naked from the nappy down, talking to a doll. I have bought him a playpen and a high chair and a truck too, the latter for an appalling amount of money. I had to forget the price quickly but I think it's important he should have one . . .'

He began to cry, but then steeled himself and read on. Facing the truth – one had to do it, always.

'Gwen rang up the surgeon Harvey Evers and they want me to go in for this operation at once. You see, they've found a grwoth (no one could object to a "grwoth", could they?). This is a bit difficult. It's going to cost a terrible lot of money. What worries me is that I really don't think I'm worth the expense, but this thing will take a longish time to kill me if left alone, costing money all the time.'

The only thought he could rouse to stop himself breaking down completely was that she had been oblivious to what lay ahead.

'You may never get this letter, but there's something I want to impress on you, which I have expressed to you before. Please stop living the "literary life" and become a writer once more. This will mean getting out of London. From my point of view, I would infinitely rather live in the country on £200 a year than in London on any money at all. Everything would be better for Richard too, so you need have no conflicts about it. To this end, I have been in contact with Astor's man on Jura, about the empty farmhouse, Barnhill. He tells me it is quite grand, with five bedrooms and all else we need in order to live there twelve months of the year . . .'

He finished the letter, but at the end of the packet found another, brief and handwritten.

'Dearest, I'm just going to have the operation, already enema'd, injected (with morphia in the *right* arm which is a nuisance), cleaned & packed up like a precious image in cotton wool and bandages. When it's over I'll add a note to this and get it off quickly. This is a nice room – ground floor so one can see the garden. Not much in it except daffodils & I think arabis, but a nice little lawn. My bed isn't next to the window, but it faces the right way. I can also see the fire and the clock . . .'

He turned over the page, looking for more. Two tears trickled down the sides of his nose. He remembered what they had said to each other in Barcelona: to remain true to each other, to stay human in spite of everything, that was all that mattered.

Stop living the literary life and become a writer once more. He wiped his tears on a handkerchief, folded her letters and placed them back into the envelope.

He opened the bottom drawer of his desk, pushing aside a mass of typed notes to find the old chocolate box. Inside it, beneath the glass paperweight, were the yellowed clippings from the late 1930s, and underneath them, two hardback notebooks. The first was the old keepsake book he had used as a diary; he set it aside. The second, with its maroon cover – the one he had purchased two years ago, just before he'd had the idea for *Animal Farm* – was the one he was after. He flicked through the pages until he came to the title *The Last Man in Europe*.

– VIII –

London, January 1946. The island farmhouse wasn't yet ready, so he filled part of his days searching the now familiar junk shops and black market haunts for various hard-to-find items he knew he would need there. Wandering through Islington, he found himself drawn into a bookshop. *Animal Farm* had sold out its first edition within weeks, and Warburg assured him a second printing was now on sale. He entered and looked around. He pawed through the 'new arrivals', then the literature section, but without result. The sight of Waugh's *Brideshead Revisited* gave him a pang of envy. His book was nowhere to be seen. Surely it hadn't already begun its gravitational journey from the eye-level shelves to the shoe-level ones, or from there to the remainders pile?

'Can I *help* you with anything?' It was the shop attendant, a schoolmistress type, whose tone suggested she was onto a likely book-pincher.

'*Animal Farm?*'

'Children's section, just behind you. I've heard the kiddies love it.'

She remained between him and the door, monitoring, and he had no alternative but to go to the rear of the shop and pretend to look through his book. He examined its cover: *Animal Farm: A Fairy Story*. Hard to blame her. He flicked it open to the first page, only to be reminded that Warburg had pulled the preface, with its attack on the self-censorship that intellectuals reflexively practised towards anything Soviet. Typically, Warburg had done it at the last minute, so that he couldn't object. 'No point in narrowing the sales to political types,' he had said. 'Let the readers see in it what they want.' Maybe Warburg had been right, but the fact it was in the children's section told him he might not have been.

The manager became distracted by another customer and walked to another room in the shop. He picked up the two shallow piles of *Animal Farm*, placing one on the table in front of the section labelled 'Literature', and the other beneath the label 'Politics', having pushed aside Wells' latest appalling effort, which he had recently reviewed as gently as he could; the man was dying, after all. With a glance back, he opened the door and left.

★

That evening, Susan – the young nanny he had found to move in and look after Ricky – was awakened by cries for help. She discovered him lying on his back in the corridor. The only evidence that he was still alive were the bubbles forming in the blood coming from his mouth, which trickled slowly down a trenchlike groove in his chin, spilling onto his ragged pyjamas.

'What can I do?'

'Get a block of ice and a jug of cold water,' he gasped.

Despite her lame leg – the result of cerebral palsy in childhood – she managed somehow to get him back to bed, then she wrapped the ice in a threadbare towel and applied it to his forehead. He had a roaring fever. 'I don't expect to live much longer,' he told her, breathing heavily as he waited for the bleeding to stop. Eventually he fell asleep while she held his hand.

When he awoke next morning, she forbade him to get out of bed. She made him stay there for a fortnight, and sent delaying telegrams to all the editors who were harassing him for reviews and essays. He had suddenly become one of the most in-demand writers in the world; *Animal Farm* was a bestseller. After a week, she called a doctor – on the pretext that Ricky was sick. The doctor proved dim, believing his usual palaver, and diagnosed pleurisy.

*

He spent the rest of the winter indoors, venturing out only to purchase equipment for Jura. With his coal supply almost out and the gas pressure so low the heater would hardly light, it seemed the miseries of that dreadful season would never end. He achieved nothing; the book had not advanced a word.

Then, at the start of April, the miracle of spring. A mass of warm air hit London, along with what seemed a brighter sun. He threw open the partly boarded windows and surveyed the square below. The sooty privets had turned bright green, the leaves were thickening in the chestnut trees, and the daffodils in the neighbouring window boxes were out. Even the patrolling bobbies' tunics looked a deeper shade of blue. A sparrow ducked in a terracotta pot of recently melted ice, having its first bath since September. They had yet to finish packing for Jura, where they were headed in just a few days' time, but as he drank in the crisp, warm air, he decided to take Ricky and Susan out for lunch.

The pram was stored in the entry hall at the bottom of the rear stairs. He'd wanted Eileen and the baby to have something grand – the sort of mini-carriage that nannies to titled families had pushed around Hyde Park back in the twenties – but all he'd been able to find was this strange contraption, which looked like a cross between a bath chair and an office trolley. They went through the back gate and crossed Alwyne Villas to Canonbury Tower, then cut through the adjoining garden. He stopped the pram to show Susan and Richard the tree supposedly planted by Sir Thomas Cromwell or Sir Francis Bacon, he couldn't remember which. From a rain-filled bomb crater came the croaking of a toad. He listened hard and combed through the grass to find the creature sitting on a clump of soil beneath a crocus, its shrunken body supporting a pair of enormous eyes like the gold-coloured semi-precious stones you sometimes saw in signet rings. It had an almost spiritual air about it, reminding him somewhat of a strict Anglo-Catholic towards the end of Lent. A part of nature Hitler and Stalin and the managers had failed to eradicate.

They walked another hundred yards to his favourite pub, the Canonbury. It was just minutes from Upper Street, yet always free of drunks or rowdies, and with all the solid comfortable ugliness of the nineteenth century – no glass-topped tables, sham roof beams or plastic masquerading as oak. They entered the saloon bar and ordered.

'Hello, dear,' said the barmaid. 'What will you be wanting?' All the barmaids, who were middle-aged and unflashy apart from occasionally lurid hair colouring and strong scent, knew him as Mr Blair, the widower with the posh voice, who wrote books and was some sort of famous socialist. He and Susan chose roast beef with potatoes and peas and a boiled jam roll, which he decided to leave for Ricky; not bad for six shillings in total. There being none of his favourite draught stout, he asked for a pint of dark brown ale, getting Susan a half of the milder wallop.

Despite the warm weather, a fire burned reassuringly in the grate, and they chose a table near it and talked of their move to their Scottish island. Susan would look after Ricky while he wrote; his younger sister Avril would look after the household. 'We'll be safe from the inevitable atom bombs,' he said cheerily. 'Everyone these days dreams of escape from atomic war, but we will actually do it. Up there, a bomb could drop on London, or even Glasgow, and we'd be none the wiser.'

As they ate they heard snatches of the conversations going on among the regulars – the football pools, grandchildren, aching joints, incontinence. Not once since the end of the war could he recall hearing anyone in a pub talking about politics. Not since the thirties had he heard any member of the working class call another 'comrade', or indeed say much of anything that would be considered 'ideologically sound'. Bevan's fight to create a socialist medical system, the Attlee government's plans to nationalise coal and steel and the railways, the return of servicemen to full employment – none of it seemed to matter to the people in whose name it was all being done, and in whom the socialist movement had invested so much hope. And yet it was they who had won the war. And it was only they who could stop the intellectuals making the peace inhuman and unbearable. Without them as ballast, the struggles and sacrifices of the war would be wasted – they'd be organised and modernised into something cold and intolerable.

There were swings and slides in the beer garden, and after their meal Susan took Richard to play on them before they went home for his afternoon nap. Alone, he ordered another pint and then went out into the sunshine to watch them and have a smoke. Sitting around little green tables under the shade of plane trees, whole families – some with three generations present – were making the most of the weather, delighting in the joyful squeals of the children playing in the sandpit. He watched as young mothers, girls of eighteen or nineteen, handed their babies over to other girls just thirteen or fourteen, who played with them as if they were dolls. Another set, sixteen or seventeen and heavily made-up, were drinking pop and making eyes over the fence at a group of tough-looking boys in the street. That was their life, he thought: to be born, to blossom in a brief period of beauty and sexual desire, to reach middle age at thirty, and then to end up bloated grandmothers in their mid-forties, obsessed with gossip and gambling.

It struck him, though, that for all that, they didn't need Laski or Von Hayek to tell them how to live. They didn't need books from Gollancz to make them miserable in order to bring the revolution and its day of eternal happiness closer. Their love for each other, the enjoyment they took in life's simple pleasures, their natural wariness of authority – all the things the revolutionaries had been promising, but dressed up in catchwords like brotherhood and equality and democracy – came to them naturally. They pursued happiness the way a flower pushed towards the light, and a miner sought the surface at the end of each shift.

In Wigan he'd seen this as weakness, as a cause of political inertia. If only they could be made conscious, he thought. Only now did he grasp how wrong he had been. Only now did he see what they represented. It was the workers – not the managers or the intellectuals – who carried the true human spirit in their bones. They had merely to survive, just as they were, to pass that spirit on to a better time. If there was hope for the future, here it was.

He downed his pint, stood and called out to Susan. They had packing to do. His island was waiting.

THREE

- I -

Jura, May, 1946. The journey was nearly over. It had taken almost two full days: tube from Islington to Paddington, loaded with luggage and rations; sleeper to Glasgow; that ancient Scottish Airways Rapide from Prestwick to Islay; car and ferry to Craighouse; then twenty miles bouncing over the boggy, unsealed roads in the mail van, which also served as Jura's taxi service. Getting out of the vehicle proved far more difficult than getting in. By turns he had to tilt his head downwards, twist sideways, plant his left foot followed by his right onto the puddled gravel of the Fletchers' farmyard, then use his elbows to lever himself free, like a contortionist escaping from a box. Resting to fill his lungs with the island's clean air, he heard the crunching of footsteps on the ground, and turned to find his new landlady, Margaret Fletcher, standing close behind him.

The woman made an involuntary half-step backwards, and, as if instinctively, covered her mouth with her hand. 'Surely,' she said, 'someone told you the situation here?'

He looked at her blankly, noticing that her accent was English, not Scottish. She was tall and rather too fine to be living in such a remote place, even for a laird's wife.

'The nearest doctor is on Islay,' she continued. 'We don't even have a telephone.'

'Mrs Fletcher? Eric Blair. How do you do?' His voice came feebly. 'I've had a terrible case of the 'flu, which I'm just over.' He could see she didn't believe him.

'A difficult trip for someone who is unwell.'

'At least I'm almost there.'

'Well, you've made it to Ardlussa. Barnhill is still seven more miles down that track, I'm afraid,' she said, pointing to the bleak, treeless hills beyond. 'Come and have tea and we'll sort it out. One of the farmhands can give you a lift.'

'I'd prefer not to be of trouble to anyone.'

'It's not possible to live here, Mr Blair, without troubling one's neighbours.'

A misty rain began to fall. By the time they'd collected his possessions from the rear of the van, paid the driver and made it inside, the rain had become heavier and was slanting into the house almost horizontally.

★

Late July. His plan had been to complete a rough draft of the book by the end of autumn, but once he arrived on the island he knew it was impossible. The war, Eileen's death, Ricky's care and the debauch of journalism into which he had dived to drown the pain of 1945 had left him capable of little more than absorbing energy and keeping himself alive, like a jellyfish.

When his strength did return, the delights of the perfect summer and the company of the many guests he had invited consumed him in what seemed like a second, glorious childhood. He felt like Gulliver on his island, fishing, planting crops, shooting rabbits, cutting peat and spending hours a day reading to and playing games with Ricky. He dreamt it would go on forever. Then, one morning over breakfast, the ra   dio announced that Wells was dead.

In a purely intellectual way, it was like losing a father. At his actual father's funeral, he had placed pennies over the old man's eyes, later throwing the coins into the sea. He hadn't really known why; it was pointless but something about the tradition of it appealed to him. It was only when he wrote the obituary for Wells that he realised what the custom meant: the old man's vision was spent.

He had been asked to write the obituary in advance the previous November – 'something to have on file, just in case'. He had bashed it out at speed, giving it little thought, the clichés queuing up obediently like bowler hats at a bus stop. He could now barely recall the thrust of what he had said. From memory, it was something about every writer being at the height of his creative powers for just fifteen years, which for H.G. meant 1895 to 1910, and that only once in that time – in *The Sleeper Awakes,* with its picture of a totalitarian society based on slave labour – had the old man got it nearly right.

Fifteen years, he thought. *Down and Out* had been published in 1933, and therefore by his own reckoning in just two years he too would be on the downhill slope – at the same age, forty-five, as Wells had been in 1910. No one could foretell when he would die, and, as Wells had shown, it was possible to live too long for one's own good, but with the old man dead, the task of explaining the future now fell to others. It was time for the holiday to end.

He turned to Susan and Avril, who were both fussing over Ricky, and said, 'I have to write.'

He headed to the stairs. Halfway up, the wheezing began. It wasn't as severe as when he first arrived on the island, but bad enough to make him pause at the landing and notice how much water from the overnight summer storm had dripped from the ceiling into a rusty bucket. His breath back, he continued up the second flight, along the passage, its walls grubby from human contact, and into his writing room.

It was small and, like all the rooms in the farmhouse, in desperate need of painting, but it had a view of the sea. He sat at the narrow desk in front of the window and lit a cigarette. Before him was the black case containing his portable typewriter. He put his hand to the brass latch at the front, pulled it up and slid the small sprung lever from right to left. He felt the mechanism click and the lid detach from its base.

Carefully he set the lid down at his feet, and looked at the shiny black Remington with its worn, glass-topped keys, relieved it had survived the journey. How many words must it have typed? Eight books – all but *Animal Farm* complete failures. Some seven hundred reviews, mostly of pure tripe for obscure socialist and anarchist journals, but they'd kept him alive. Around two hundred and fifty essays – including a few he could actually feel proud of. And hundreds upon hundreds of letters. Four million words at the very least.

On the right-hand side of the typewriter was a rounded metal knob; he pulled it out, then guided it along its curved track, raising the typefaces and lowering the keys to their starting positions. He ignored the dull pain in his side – one got used to persistent pain, he had found – and picked out a sheet of paper from a packet on the desk, rolled it onto the platen and pushed the cylinder to the start of its carriage. He then sat there, dumbly.

I have to write. It was easy to say, but in the process of resting his mind, he'd emptied it almost entirely. His mind sought distraction.

Hearing a door opening downstairs, he looked out to the yard and saw Susan and her boyfriend, a writer called David Holbrook, who had recently arrived on the island, make for somewhere secluded to do the obvious. He wouldn't have begrudged her the simple pleasure of making love in the open if it hadn't involved Holbrook, who was a communist – something he had only discovered after the man's arrival on the island. A member of the party under his own roof? It was too big a coincidence. He thought of Trotsky, assassinated by a guest at *his* farmhouse. Surveillance, even on Jura! Fortunately, he had remembered to bring his Luger. It wasn't as good a weapon as the Colt, but at least you could conceal it on your body, which you couldn't do with a hunting rifle. As he watched them disappear over the hill, he pulled the gun out, checked that it was properly oiled and loaded, saw that the safety catch was on, and slipped it into his jacket pocket.

He had to make a start, if for no other reason than so he could return to London with a settled mind. Starting the novel there, with all the pressures of working and surviving through another winter of rationing, was unthinkable. But apart from his notes of a few years before, he had little to go on. The nuances of plot, the names of characters, even the year in which it would be set – he hadn't got that far. It was difficult to make serious progress in any novel without these things, but at present such creativity was beyond him. Starting had to involve something more prosaic. He would start with the theory.

Every political novel needed a theoretical core, but the tricky thing was how to present it in a naturalistic work. Jack London had mucked it up badly in *Leon Trotsky – My Life*, with all that clunky philosophical dialogue that made the protagonists sound like Marxist gramophones. Wells – he had been as terrible at that sort of thing as he had been at predicting the future.

He could put it all in an appendix, but that would be an admission of failure – and who would read it? An inkling of an idea came to him from an unexpected source. Letters had started arriving from Ukrainians and Poles working in displaced-persons camps in the western zone asking for permission to translate *Animal Farm*. They had hit upon the same idea independently: to smuggle copies of the translated story into the east for underground distribution among enemies of the communist regime. The Ukrainian request came from a man called Szewczenko, whose readings of the story to his homeless countrymen had met with the most extraordinary response.

He plucked one of Szewczenko's letters from the pile on his desk. The Ukrainian peasants, it reported, were taking the fate of Manor Farm almost literally – Lenin having given them farms, only for Stalin to take them away again – and Szewczenko's public readings of the book were creating pathetic, emotional scenes the like of which the man had never before witnessed.

He had immediately assented to the publication request,

refusing any royalties. It was almost too good to be true! He had written his little story to awaken the world to what a betrayed revolution meant, and now it was going to be published in clandestinely printed editions and passed from hand to hand, to be read in attics and secret hiding places, wherever the party's secret police couldn't reach. It would be like a depth charge dropped into the totalitarian sea, and it gave him the idea he was looking for. That's how the rebellion in this new novel would begin – with a secret book, circulated among a dissenting few.

Like *Animal Farm*, it would have to be a caricature of the Stalinist system. Fortunately, Bolshevik theory wasn't difficult to spoof. He crossed the small room and took a volume from the warped bookshelf. Unlike any book printed after 1940, it was heavy and impressive, expensively made, with a red hardback cover and a dust jacket showing the author's portrait beneath the bold lettering of the title: *Leon Trotsky – My Life*. It struck him that, east of the Elbe, the price for being caught with such a book would be death. He looked at Trotsky, with his unruly mane of greying hair, goatee beard and pince-nez; the man certainly looked clever, but had not been clever enough to evade the ruthless manoeuvrings of Stalin. He opened it and flicked through to find a passage he had marked, explaining the logic behind Lenin and Trotsky's decision to seize power.

Marxism considers itself the conscious expression of the unconscious historical process. But the 'unconscious' process, in the historico-philosophical sense of the term – not in the psychological – coincides with its conscious expression only at its highest point, when the masses, by sheer elemental pressure, break through the social routine and give various expression to the deepest needs of historical development . . .

What on earth could it mean? He read on.

And at such moments the highest theoretical consciousness of the epoch merges with the immediate action of the oppressed masses who are furthest away from theory. The creative union of the conscious with the unconscious is what one usually calls 'inspiration'. Revolution is the inspired frenzy of history.

As far as he could make out, it was some sort of justification for dictatorship, some flatly contradictory assertion that the proles were simultaneously a revolutionary force and a dumb, inert mass. But who could be sure? Doublethink! Such nonsense could only lead to disaster. He remembered that he'd fallen for a version of it himself, back in 1940. Red militias billeted in the Ritz, the gutters running with capitalist blood, English socialism . . .

He put the book down and remembered an interesting term coined by his old friend Franz Borkenau, who'd seen through the whole totalitarian swindle before just about anyone: 'oligarchical collectivism'. Yes, that's almost certainly how it would have ended, had Dunkirk led to the revolution he had wanted: with a collective run by an oligarchy, a democracy run by an elite, the workers betrayed by psychopaths. He typed.

THE THEORY AND PRACTICE OF
OLIGARCHICAL COLLECTIVISM
by
Emmanuel Goldstein
<u>Chapter 1.</u>
<u>The Genesis of Ingsoc</u>

The words began to pour out of him, and within a week he had finished the first draft of Goldstein's secret book, with its mingling of Marx and Burnham, its world divided into the constantly warring superstates of Eastasia, Eurasia and Oceania, with Airstrip One under the terrible thrall of Ingsoc.

He was exhilarated by his success in creating this alternative world – which he had decided to set in the year 1980 – but still didn't feel ready to tackle the story proper. To maintain momentum, he decided to write a series of disconnected scenes, based on experiences plucked from the recesses of his memory and the many diaries he kept. He didn't yet know how they would fit into the narrative, but he would find a place for them once the story had worked itself out fully in his mind. There was that train journey to Kent with four generations of proles to pick hops for the summer holidays, and the packed prison cell in Bethnal Green, with its revolting toilet that inmates were, disgustingly, forced to use in front of each other.

There were also other scenes – dark, sometimes shameful episodes from his life that he recalled with embarrassment, like the bitterly cold, moonless night he'd had that prostitute for sixpence on a patch of grass behind the Guards' parade ground, only to see her afterwards in the light of that all-night café in St Martin's Lane – toothless, greying, fifty, with make-up plastered so thick on her face that it threatened to crack. Writing such scenes made him feel soiled and humiliated, and he would have torn them up immediately if they hadn't matched perfectly the squalid atmosphere he wanted to evoke – where people expended their short, timorous lives in foetid tenements with damp walls, peeling wallpaper and broken furniture, crawling like beetles through the filth and grime that invaded their skin and left them feeling polluted and vile.

By the time he had written himself out, he had a pile of some fifty pages – not enough to meet his promise to Warburg of completing it by the end of the year, but enough at least to have made the summer on Jura worthwhile. He took some days off and rested.

*

Late August. He was reading through the pile of completed pages when he noticed something. It was a hair. It was too short to be either Avril's or Susan's, and the wrong colour to be his own. It was lighter, without any grey, belonging to a much younger man. Holbrook! He must have sneaked in while he was away on the other side of the island, fishing with Avril and Ricky.

He opened the desk, took out the pistol, which in his complacency he had stopped wearing, put it into his jacket pocket and went downstairs, the manuscript pages in his hand. He found Holbrook alone in the kitchen, listening to some political lecture on the radio, despite his request that the batteries be saved for the evening news. He walked over and switched it off. Holbrook didn't protest, but made to stand up and leave without saying anything.

He motioned for him to sit down. 'What have you to say for yourself, Holbrook?'

'What do you mean?'

'Spying.'

'Spying? Really! You *are* paranoid. Just as I thought.'

Orwell held up the wad of papers, then threw it onto the kitchen table. 'Had a good read, did you?'

Holbrook said nothing but looked at him contemptuously.

'Going to report back to Comrade Pollitt, are we?'

'Pah!'

'Well?' Orwell said, letting seconds pass by. 'I'm waiting.' Holbrook, who was only twenty-three but a former tank commander, showed no fear. He merely leaned back in his chair and lit a cigarette. 'I was just wondering what you were doing up there at all hours, keeping us awake until three in the morning with your constant typing. We can hear every bloody tap! So I decided to find out.'

'Did you just?'

'Yes, and now I know. A lot of gloomy drivel about the future. Who do you think will ever want to read such depressing rubbish?'

'You'd be surprised.'

'It's a bunch of anti-Soviet propaganda, nothing more,' Holbrook said. He reached over and picked up the papers, shuffling through them. He held up a typed sheet and began reading, imitating his host's voice, each sentence drawn out, with long wheezes in between. It was clearly something he had practised. '"The citizens of 1980 no longer expected comfort, leisure or freedom,"' he read. '"Cut off from foreign contacts and from knowledge of the past, they had no standards of comparison, and the poverty and harshness of their lives appeared to them as something natural and unalterable. Efficiency, even the type of efficiency that produces good roads and germ-free milk, had ceased to be necessary. Nothing in Oceania was efficient except the Thought Police." You're a reactionary, Orwell. You call yourself a socialist, but you write what the Tories want to read.'

'You didn't recognise anything of the Soviet Union in there?'

'Actually, I thought it sounded more like this place. The disgusting food your sister cooks. The way she treats Susan like some sort of slave. The constant mess. It seems everything you touch, Orwell, immediately disintegrates. Is there anything in this dump that works?'

'Only the Thought Police, it seems.'

'Do you really think you're important enough to be spied on? You know what, I might just pay Pollitt a visit after all. I'll tell him you're nothing more than a mouldering old crank.'

'As I suspected. Off you go, report to your masters.'

'I noticed you've got some sexual hang-ups too. All those prostitutes and Asian brothels and cutting some girl's throat at the moment of climax. Very interesting.'

'You can clear off. The ferry's that way,' he said, jerking his thumb to the south.

Holbrook got up and moved towards the stairs. 'I was told you were a great writer, Orwell, and a genuine left-winger. It's rubbish. You offer no hope to anyone whatsoever. None!'

'Not to the likes of you.'

Later, he watched as Holbrook – and Susan too – walked down the goat track towards Ardlussa, carrying their suitcases. Beside him Ricky, being restrained by Avril, cried out, 'Susie, Susie,' as if somehow aware that this was the last he would see of his nanny.

– 11 –

Barnhill, Jura, April 1947. *Animal Farm* had succeeded beyond everyone's hopes, and he could feel Fred Warburg's impatience for a follow-up radiating all the way from London. He somehow had to hold him at bay – to write under such pressure was intolerable. He stared at the letter he was writing his publisher. *Finishing the rough draft . . . breaking its back . . . hoping to finish in early 1948, barring illness . . .* he too had begun to resort to imprecisions. The truth was his lungs had worsened over the winter; what he needed more than anything, if he was going to finish the book, was for his health to hold.

He had spent the winter and early spring in London, expecting to find it rejuvenated after its second summer of peace, but the buildings were unrepaired, the trains still packed and the food as spare and revolting as ever. Even bread, which had remained white and unrationed throughout the war, had become dark-coloured and required coupons to obtain – all to help feed starving Germany, which overnight had become Britain's ally. With coal in short supply, he had been forced to break up old furniture and even Ricky's wooden toys to use as firewood. Heating water for washing had been out of the question, and he recalled with particular displeasure peeling off sticky socks and underwear to be replaced with others slightly less adhesive. Only the absence of rocket bombs and the blackout reminded him that the war was actually over.

Compared to the sun-touched country people on his island, Londoners were dark and ill-favoured, short and sickly. The heroes of the war had vanished, replaced by a race of beetles scurrying around under the sideboard, competing for crumbs. Churchill, Cripps, the airmen who had nightly flown to Berlin, those who had kept watch for fires, even the women who had made the thingummybobs – all had lost the war's nobility but not its privations. The war-winning statesmen had become statistic-generating bureaucrats; the aircrew were now factory hands; the firemen now clerks; the Stakhanovite women of the aircraft industries, now widowed kitchen drudges with hungry, screaming children and dust in the creases of their skin. Winston, Julia, O'Brien, Mr Charrington, Parsons and the workers at the ministries, even the proles in their pubs – all now entered his mind like ghosts emerging from the smoking ruins of the London left behind by the failed revolution and the war.

Being in London had brought back something else: the dream. Working on the novel in the horror of the city had been impossible; instead his mind sought out the origins of his nocturnal vision. He began writing about his days at preparatory school.

His mind had started doing this sort of thing regularly of late. The older a man got, he found, the greater the proportion of time he spent living in the past. For hours on end, sitting at his desk, pen in hand, he found himself walking through the world of his childhood. It was a period he couldn't think about without a certain feeling of terror – of the sort a goldfish might feel if flung into a tank of pike. He remembered from prep the inedible food, the forbidden books which he and Connolly had somehow managed to smuggle into their dorms, the fearsome beatings and forced confessions of misbehaviour, but mostly the constant feeling of being under surveillance. He had associated this with those giant posters of Kitchener, whose eyes and finger appeared to follow you in every direction. It had given him a feeling of being imprisoned; of being denied happiness; of feeling that no matter how hard he wanted something, it would always be snatched away at the last moment.

★

Eton College Chapel, June 1918. 'Abbey, N.R., Lieutenant, Grenadier Guards, killed France, 12th April. Acland-Troyte, H.L., Lieutenant-Colonel, Devonshire Regiment, killed Mesopotamia, 17th April. Arnott, J., Military Cross, Captain 15th Hussars, killed France, 30th March . . .' The list, which the provost, M.R. James, was sombrely reading, seemed interminable.

'Lascelles, G.E., Second Lieutenant, Rifle Brigade, killed France, 28th March.'

A murmur went through the packed stalls. Cyril Connolly nudged him and said in a low voice, 'Lascelles – he was in Sixth last year. Fine oar.'

He hazily pictured Lascelles' face, but the memory faded as fast as it had appeared.

The war! He thought of the parade ground last week,

packed with a thousand inattentive pupils and masters. After nearly four years, the Eton Rifles had turned into a ragged affair, it having become fashionable to treat all things military as a bore and to put in the minimum effort. Some of the more advanced thinkers of the senior elections had taken to booing lowly whenever the chaplain, wearing khaki and army boots under his cassock, invoked God to urge them to greater exertions on the range. The war had already been won, several times over – they had been told variations of this regularly since 1914.

But that day something had changed. The commanding officer of the Officers' Training Corps, a small, greying man of indeterminate age, flourished a piece of paper and read out General Haig's Special Order of the Day: 'With our backs to the wall and believing in the justice of our cause, each one of us must fight it out to the end.' A wave of understanding rippled through the ranks: Britain was in danger of losing. There was a straightening of backs and weapons. Even among the worst slackers, he sensed a transformation, an instant removal of doubt. Even he, the most notorious rejecter of orthodoxy, felt it.

Just before, he and the others had thought that the war was futile, that conscripted eighteen-year-old Germans were just cannon-fodder like themselves, and that they, the young, were being hurled into a giant pit by stupid old men for no good reason. Yet now he found it impossible to resist the same nationalistic fever that infected the others. His secret loathing of 'them' – the dim-witted, the unthinking, the schoolmasters and even the King himself – was, he found, suddenly turned onto Krupps, U-boats, Hindenburg, Ludendorff and the Kaiser. He felt a sudden impulse to pick up his rifle and smash its butt into the nearest enemy, and knew with a certainty that should a German soldier suddenly walk into the school, that is what he would do. Hate, he realised, is one of the hardest of all emotions to resist, especially when in a crowd. A spontaneous rendition of 'God Save the King' rang out and, unconsciously, he'd joined in, singing at the top of his voice.

He dragged himself back to today's chapel service. The list of names finally ended.

Old James seemed on the verge of tears. 'Boys, those fifty-four boys whose names I have just read out, who have fallen in just the last term, take to more than one thousand the number of Etonians lost in the service of the King since August 1914.' James closed his book and nodded to Bobbie Longden, the most admired boy of their election, who marched up and replaced him at the pulpit.

Longden's loud voice boomed through the chapel: 'In Flanders fields the poppies blow . . .'

A not her elegy, he thought, barely listening. Clichéd rubbish.

A few moments later, Longden's voice became savage. 'We are the dead.'

Blair snapped to, as if violently kicked. A tremor ran through his bowels. A similar sensation struck the pews of teenagers, the oldest of whom were seventeen and just months from becoming infantry subalterns or airmen. They were corpses waiting to be sent to the grave.

For effect, he suspected, the rebellious Longden paused and repeated the line.

We are the dead. Short days ago
We lived, felt dawn, saw sunset glow,
Loved and were loved, and now we lie
In Flanders fields.

One by one the war would consume them. As they filed out past the roll of honour, one of the college workmen was already adding the new names to the wall.

'This war's never going to end, is it?' said Connolly. 'It will be our turn soon. We are the dead.'

'We're not dead yet,' he replied.

★

Something distracted him out of the corner of his eye, ending his reverie: a large brown rat. It must have crept in while he had been motionless, gazing out the window towards the sunny field and the calm sea. With the coming of spring they had multiplied like bacilli in a dish; the farmhouse was crawling with the filthy brutes. He had seen them devouring a dead stag on the path down to the beach and was revolted. Another time he saw a buzzard carrying one off in its claws. Now they were laying siege to Barnhill, drawn by the calving livestock and the food he had stockpiled. He could corner and beat the house's many mice to death quite easily, but these monsters were too big and too numerous.

He tried to keep perfectly still, looking for something to throw. He inched his hand towards a glass paperweight on his desk, then flung it, but the creature was too fast, slipping through a gap in the wainscoting, and the missile bounced harmlessly off the wall and rolled under the bed.

He completed his letter to Warburg, slid it into an envelope and took it downstairs to the pile in the hallway. Avril was in the kitchen, reading the local newspaper. Along with Richard, they were alone now, apart from holidaying visitors.

'Eric,' his sister said, 'apparently there's a plague of rats on all the islands hereabouts. Something to do with the dead cattle and the bad spring keeping the hunting birds down.'

'No surprise there. The swine are everywhere, even upstairs.' She flinched. 'Not in the bedrooms?'

'Afraid so.'

'It says the medical bods are telling parents to be wary of leaving babies and young children unattended,' she continued.

'Two children at Ardlussa have been bitten on their faces while sleeping in their prams.' She looked up from the paper. 'Can you believe it?'

'Oh, yes. In Spain I saw one chew the leather off a man's boot while he was sleeping.'

'Ooh! It gives me the shivers.'

'Rats took over the hostel where I lived in the war. You'd get up for breakfast and the kitchen would be swarming with them, licking the unwashed bowls and cutlery. Revolting.'

She threw the paper down. 'The bedrooms! We have to do something to protect Ricky.'

He took what remained of the morning off from writing and set to work. Determining the rats' many routes into the house from their droppings, he blocked up holes and set a number of traps along the run they had established into the larder. He set a number more in the byre. The ancient traps, which he had discovered on a shelf in the barn, were a slightly sinister-looking French type: flat-bottomed cylindrical cages, shaped like hourglasses. They were divided into two chambers, the second of which was entered through a funnel-like opening, ingeniously designed to spring shut once the doomed creature was inside.

The next morning, he entered the byre to the sound of highpitched squeals and the rattling of metal. One of the disgusting creatures was leaping about in a state of frenzy in its cage. He pictured the floor of the barn crawling with them in the middle of the night, like a moving carpet, and the vision caused him to shudder. It was a massive specimen – one of the largest he had ever seen – and it stood against the wire of its prison and eyed him, baring its teeth in a show of defiance. It seemed to be trying to claw its way towards him through the ancient, rusted wire, alternately scratching and biting the thin iron bars. He had no doubt that, if freed, the creature would attack.

Grimacing, he lifted the cage by its handle, and, holding it as far from his own body as possible, carried it to a barrel of water and dropped it in. The creature thrashed about but the commotion soon stopped. He raised the cage and the drowned body floated to the surface, belly-up, with bloated fleas swimming away from it. He walked outside, clicked the lever that opened the rear of the cage and threw the carcass onto the waiting bonfire heap.

− III −

August 1947. The warm air of high summer was wafting through the farmhouse, filling it with holiday optimism and dosing his lungs with what seemed a life-giving force. Even his violent morning coughing fits had stopped. In the previous weeks more guests had arrived, including several children, and they had spilled out into a large army-surplus tent he had rigged up on the lawn. He had joined them occasionally on picnics and fishing expeditions by the beach at Glengarrisdale and Loch nan Eilean, but the book had taken on a new urgency, and for days on end the only evidence of his existence had been the thumping of his typewriter keys and his infrequent appearances at mealtimes. Here on the island, in the midst of that glorious season, he felt a sense of security from his illness, a feeling that his life could go on forever, that his lungs would continue to work as long as there was air to fill them.

As he worked, he became aware of a slackness in his prose; often, reading over what he had just written, he winced at the superfluous clauses and even whole passages. But these could be tightened up later, like the rigging wires on an aeroplane, and weren't the problem. What concerned him was fulfilling the image of the story he had first held some four years before. What he wanted to get across was how present-day politics made life *feel*: how it changed the sensation of a razor blade on your skin, the meaning of a knock on the door, your capacity for love and loyalty. The ideologists and the managerialists couldn't tell you those things, especially the last. Love and loyalty could never be understood through statistics, only through experience. The doomed love affair would explain everything; he had to get it right.

He tossed aside the pages he had read and braced himself to start again. Sonia: if only she'd kept her word and come to the island, escaping with him even for a short while. He'd written to her time and again, but it was no use. No one could push her from any path she had chosen. At first he had resented her independence, but now he could see its sense. She was loyal, not necessarily to others, but to the conception of life she'd developed for herself. She didn't challenge the system but instead flouted its conventions covertly, sexually. It was this determination to live as one chose, he now realised, that was the very basis of freedom.

*

Cyril Connolly's flat, Bedford Square, December 1945. His first thought was that she might be a spy. At the very least, she might be a low-level informer of some sort, swapping gossip with the Soviet ambassador for a meal at some swanky restaurant. 'George, old thing,' said Connolly, handing him a drink made with some vile gin he had found on the black market, 'I can see you've noticed our Venus.'

She was Sonia Brownell – known as 'the Euston Road Venus' or 'Buttocks Brownell', depending on whether or not people liked her, and many did not. The nicknames came from her time as an artists' model, when she'd posed nude for a variety of painters, with whom she had sometimes conducted affairs if she considered them famous enough.

'Impossible not to,' he replied.

She was a tall, fair-haired girl, with a full figure and a graceful way of holding her cocktail. She had a correct posture and a face with aquiline features, which he suspected fronted a mind not wholly noble, although this was something that did not concern him greatly.

'Well, she simply adores famous authors. Even living ones. And is *very* nice to them.'

He could see her looking over, giving him an up-and-down sidelong glance that was thrilling, but also slightly terrifying. Her beauty and reputation induced in him a nervousness, a sort of black terror that at the ultimate moment, should it ever arrive, he might not be able to perform. After all, she could have anyone, and frequently did, if the rumours were to be believed. She was looking again in his direction, flicking her golden locks like a Hollywood actress. Connolly summoned her with a waggle of his finger and she came mincing over, pausing instantaneously, he noticed, to catch her own perfect reflection in an ornamental mirror.

'George, this is Sonia, my editorial assistant. She's responsible for the mechanics of the journal – everything from retyping manuscripts to checking proofs and occasionally wrestling with t he aut horities to procure more paper. Physical wrestling, I mean.'

'Not in the Greek fashion,' she replied. 'At *Horizon* we leave that sort of thing to Cyril. He was good at it at school, I hear. You were there with him, weren't you?'

'We also studied the goings on of the inhabitants of Lesbos,' Connolly added, before Orwell could answer. Obviously, she had refused to sleep with him.

He shook her hand. '*Enchanté.*' Her grasp lingered, just long enough to convey interest. While she was close, he noticed her expensive-smelling scent, unusual among women in left-wing circles. 'Do you write too, in addition to doing all Cyril's other jobs for him?'

'Oh, no. I leave the writing to Cyril. Have to let him do something. But I know what I like in writers.'

'She certainly does, George. Best judge of an author's quality in our office, apart from my girl Lys, of course.' Connolly excused himself to attend to his other guests.

Now here, he thought, was the sort of girl he had always wanted to sleep with.

★

The only question was how. As a widower for barely half a year, anything too public would have been social folly, so they met again, secretly, in little-known restaurants, far from the gossipy circles of Soho and Fitzrovia. Four, five, six – maybe seven – times they met before she agreed to go back to his flat.

He made love to her in a rush, like a fumbling schoolboy or someone far too familiar with prostitutes, and they lay in bed smoking. He watched her taking in the room – with its grubby walls, the slatternly armchair by the fireplace and even the antique bed with its ragged blankets and coverless bolster – noticing how she seemed to shrink back into her own skin to minimise her contact with her surroundings.

'Tell me, you've done this before, haven't you?' he asked her.

'Many times.'

'Dozens?'

'Perhaps scores.'

'I'm glad.'

'There's a change,' she smiled. 'Most men think I'm wicked.'

'I like people who violate conventions, especially the marriage convention.'

'That's me, then.'

'You know that my wife died earlier this year?'

'Yes, Cyril told me. Terribly sad, especially with the little boy and everything. What's his name?'

'Richard. We had a ruddy marriage, you know. From about 1940 she became rather withdrawn. Her brother died, you see. Dunkirk. She never quite got over it. Became somewhat frigid. But she was a good old stick, I suppose.'

He noticed the faint look of shock on her face.

'It's like living in a prison, being in a marriage like that,' he said.

'I imagine so.'

'When she died I was upset, but I'll admit there were times in our marriage when I secretly hoped she were dead. You know, that a bomb would drop on her while I was out of the house, or a ship she was on would be torpedoed. It's the sort of thing you immediately disown, of course, totally unworthy, disgraceful in fact, but there you have it. But by the time of her death I loved her again.'

'Why?'

'We'd been through so much, you see. We'd planned to escape together. From London and this vile life.'

'All that sounds achingly average,' she said, trying to lighten the mood. 'I expect every married person feels that way at times.'

'If I married again, I would never expect my wife to be completely faithful. I wasn't to Eileen, nor she to me.'

'I suppose that's just being realistic.'

'No, I'm not referring to realism. I believe there's a natural human longing for freedom, and there's too much constraint in marriage. Marriages should be open, to some extent anyway, if they are to be happy.'

'Like the anarchists' marriages in Spain?' The topic had fascinated and scandalised London a decade earlier.

'Yes, I suppose so.'

'Then why marry at all?'

He could tell she didn't like where the conversation was heading. Had Koestler's sister-in-law, Celia Paget, told her how he'd proposed to her and others?

'There's something unnatural about living alone, I suppose,' he went on. 'The idea of absolute loyalty to another person, not sexually but emotionally, rather than to the state or a party or an ideology, is the foundation of freedom in my view. If the state can't tell you whom to love, its power isn't absolute, is it? The first thing an omnipotent dictator would do is ban the orgasm, followed by marriage and parenthood; perhaps even stop people living together. I expect that, under torture, the first thing they'd do is get you to denounce your wife. They routinely get children to denounce their parents. Makes you think.'

'I suppose so. But surely people still love each other in Russia. You can't suppress such things completely.'

'Tell me, would you consider marrying someone like me, under those sorts of terms?'

'I could never be in a loveless marriage, just for sake of convenience,' she replied immediately. 'I'd rather wait.'

Clearly, he realised, men asked her this all the time.

★

His mind returned to the task at hand. He'd conceived of the affair with Julia long before he had met Sonia, but there was something about her that suited Winston: an unwillingness to think too far beyond the present, an obstinacy and a crude defiance that was liberating but must eventually lead to pain, misery and downfall, but never surrender. The romance now took shape on the page. He threw himself into the task with an energy that he suspected he was stealing from some future time, like a hungry farmer eating his seeds. It was only when Winston and Julia were arrested that he took a holiday.

★

Glengarrisdale Bay, 19 August. The western side of the island was the freest place in Britain – a haven saturated by soft sunlight, bounded by the sea and the hills and the blue sky, safer even than Barnhill from the commissars and the managers with their snoops and atom bombs. Even in

Airstrip One, he reckoned, the Thought Police wouldn't have bothered putting hidden cameras or microphones somewhere so remote.

He had brought Avril and Ricky and his late sister Marjorie's children – Lucy, Henry and Jane – for two nights' camping. They slept in an abandoned hut, and spent the days swimming and hiking and fishing. He felt he had escaped, and – perhaps more completely than at any other moment of his adulthood – that he was living inside his dream. He wanted to stay like this forever, spinning out a present that had no future, drawing strength from the air and the sun and the land to continue writing his books as long as he could.

The boat journey back to Barnhill was proceeding smoothly. Avril and Jane had decided to hike, leaving the four of them to take in the majestic views of Mull and Scarba.

'Look what the girls are missing out on,' he shouted over the noise of the outboard engine and the water smoothly splitting from the prow. They were all insanely happy. He felt invincible.

As they rounded the point to enter the sound near Corryvreckan, they hit a swell. He decided to power through it. After all, the engine was driving strongly and the boat was well caulked. He had checked the tidal charts and there was nothing to worry about – the whirlpool wouldn't be a problem for hours yet. Just then the boat dropped alarmingly, and at the bottom of the swell they were hit with a violent spray. Water sloshed over the gunwales and the boat dipped again. Ricky squeezed Lucy tighter and put his fingers in his mouth.

'I'm taking her around,' he said. But before he could turn, they clipped the edge of one of the whirlpools and the boat started to spin. The engine wrenched off its mount and plummeted down, still revving furiously.

'Henry, take the oars,' he said calmly. 'I'll handle the tiller.' They steadied the boat, which was running straight on with the current, but he could see more swirling whitewater to the east. 'The island – make for the island,' he shouted. It was no more than a rocky outcrop a hundred yards or so long, but it lay between them and another whirlpool, which could be yet more turbulent, and was their only chance.

Jinking up and down, they reached the rocks, but the waves, rising and falling twelve or so feet, made getting out of the boat almost impossible. Henry readied himself to leap, hoping to pull the boat safely to shore by the rope, but just as he leapt, holding onto the painter, the boat overturned. They were all dunked and as they came to the surface, Lucy lost her grip on Ricky, who disappeared under the vessel. She screamed. Orwell dived down and plucked the boy from the boiling waters under the upturned hull. Then he followed the others in a struggle to the shore, the jagged rocks making the going painful. Sopping wet, scratched and grazed, they scrambled to the high point of the tiny islet, which was home to thousands of nesting birds.

It was three hours before a lobster boat happened by and they caught its attention. One by one they were dragged by rope to safety, he with Ricky on his back, and deposited on dry land for a long walk home, barefoot. Their boots had gone under with their blankets and other supplies.

Days later, his temperature increased and he was confined to indoors.

Barnhill, October. 'What about Driberg? A communist, surely?' Behind the easel, his old friend Rees was shaking his head. Rees, who had sunk money into Barnhill in the hope of turning it into a going concern, had become a frequent visitor, using it as a base for his new career as a landscape painter. 'No.'

'An underground party member; has to be. Also homose—' He stopped in deference to Rees.

'No. Not a party member. My close friends would know about him. Trust me.'

Orwell crossed out the asterisk next to Driberg's name in the small notebook on his lap. He was sitting up in bed, having been stuck there for a few weeks. 'Priestley?'

Rees shook his head. 'Too English, surely.'

'I've heard he gets Moscow gold. He's certainly richer than most artists and writers.'

'If that were the case, I'd be a commo, which I'm not.'

'Not convinced. I'm keeping the asterisk against him. How about Michael Redgrave? The actor chap.'

'Scraping the bottom there, George. Fellow traveller at the very outside.'

'Smollett? Ah! I'm keeping him no matter what you say, Rees. He's the swine at the MOI who blackballed *Animal Farm*. Just a matter of time before he's exposed.' He tossed the notebook onto the bed and picked up the packet of mail Rees had brought. There was yet another letter from Warburg; he put it aside and opened one from his accountant.

Rees leant back and surveyed his picture, which was

nearly done. He was portraying the scene after Van Gogh's room in the yellow house: bare and sloping floorboards, a threadbare rug, a simple wooden chair, and an austere metal-framed cot that resembled a camp bed. He was trying to capture the griminess of the walls, yellowed by Orwell's incessant smoking and the fumes given off by the paraffin heater, which now had to be on, the summer having completely vanished.

'I'm wealthy,' Orwell said, wheezing, waving the opened letter at Rees. 'The Yanks are buying *Animal Farm*.' He stared at the accounts disbelievingly. Earnings for the year past: £7826 8s 7d. It wasn't that long ago he was scraping by on two hundred a year. Even as a civil servant at the BBC, with Eileen working, they had lived on barely a tenth of that. But stuck in bed on this remote island, where there was nothing to buy, and with Britain still in the grip of rationing in any case, the money was like so much fairy gold. 'I'd trade it all for a steady thousand a year and no filthy journalism to worry about.'

'True indeed.'

Orwell looked at the boots beside his bed. They were the only pair he had left now, after the boating accident; they were five years old and falling to pieces. He saw Rees looking at them too.

'I've asked Warburg to buy me a new pair; at least my American dollars will come in handy for something. It seems shameful, really, to deal on the free market like this when half the country is almost barefoot and everyone is scraping together clothing coupons, but there it is.' He stared at the letter from Warburg and held it up, contemplating whether or not to open it. 'From my publisher, again.'

'Ah! So how is progress with the novel, then?'

'I've got the main character Winston in the basement of the Ministry of Love now, poor sod, and I'm going to give him hell.'

'Ministry of Love – doesn't sound all that bad.'

'Huh! It's not what you think. It's the place where all love and all hope gets cut out of you.'

'So nearly done, then?'

'By the end of October, I hope. At least that's what I've told Warburg. Still very much a first draft, I think, and it usually takes me a good half a year to bash a rough cut like this into something worth publishing. It's a beastly mess.'

★

November. The pain that was twisting through the left side of his torso was so terrible it woke him up, drenched and gasping for breath, like a whale breaching the surface from five hundred fathoms down. He rolled onto his back and tried to fill his lungs with air. Shallower breaths, deepening them gradually – that usually did the job in the morning. This time, though, it didn't work. Pain like the thrust of a bayonet continued with each breath for some minutes. He could get his lungs about two-thirds full before it returned, but that was all. It was terrifying, like drowning on dry land.

Every morning since his dunking by the whirlpool it had been the same. And every morning he repeated his mental trick, eventually kidding himself that he'd torn a muscle in his chest while rowing or digging for peat. Yesterday he had overexerted himself again, pruning the fruit trees in front of the farmhouse, taking advantage of the clear weather, although it had been dreadfully cold. This, he figured, is what getting old is like – a continual narrowing of one's physical possibilities, each constriction becoming the new normal measure of health, then narrowing once again until . . . well, nothing.

The pain had ripped him from a dream. The Golden Country had been replaced by variations on a nightmare. This time he had been walking through a pitch-dark room to face a wall of blackness, behind which there was something too terrible to contemplate. He knew what lay beyond: the infinite itself. But he wouldn't allow his mind to interrogate it further.

He was only middle-aged, yet the blackness was already entering his life. It was like having an assassin on his trail. As well as being chronically short of breath, he had started losing weight. Most annoyingly of all, the pain was making it harder to write. At present it was almost impossible. Just sitting up and using a pen felt like lifting a dumbbell. He consoled himself with the idea that thinking about the novel was akin to actually writing it, but he knew he had to get well enough if he was ever to manage a second draft.

The bones were all there. Winston had committed thoughtcrimes, begun his doomed love affair with Julia, joined the Brotherhood, discovered the true manner of the Revolution's betrayal and the Party's manipulation of thought, language and history, then endured the horror of the Ministry of Love. It was an obvious parody of Stalinism and of Burnham's power worship, but such was the insanity of the world around him, he could imagine people taking it literally. It struck him that parody could easily descend into comedy, and while he wasn't against the book being funny, too much would rob it of the horror he wanted to convey. He had drawn a world of political horror, but now realised you couldn't fully convey horror in a line-sketch. Horror lay in the shadows, and if Winston's thoughtcrimes meant death, in the rewrite he had to make the reader understand what living in that shadow of death was really like.

He had just a few hundred words of the first draft to go, after which he would rest, before getting back to London for the winter. Once there he could see a decent specialist – that chap Morland, perhaps, who had worked on D.H. Lawrence, and about whom everyone spoke so highly.

He took his breakfast in bed – porridge and tea as usual, followed by a cigarette – dressed himself with discomfort, and went to his desk. He'd write until lunch, after which, if he was feeling better, there were the eggs to collect, the paraffin and Calor gas levels to check, and work to begin on a new greenhouse for the tomatoes.

He wrote on. Winston, now a tortured shade, was in the Chestnut Tree Café, listening to the telescreen, awaiting his final trial and the inevitable bullet. He might just finish it in the next few days, he thought. He came to the end of the page and turned to another. Just then, the movement of his arm sent a fearful sharp pain scything across his chest, causing him to double over in agony. He wheezed, trying to fill his lungs with air, but the exertion began an uncontrollable cough, which continued for a full minute, each contraction of his lungs bringing the feeling of being kicked viciously in the ribs.

When at last it had stopped, he could hear someone, probably Rees, running up the stairs. Sweating and shaking slightly, he opened his eyes to see the page before him sprayed with red ink. The splotches grew as the ink was absorbed by the miserable postwar stock. He presumed that in the panic of the coughing fit he must have broken one of his pens, and noticed that his right hand was also splashed with the stuff; it was surprisingly warm. As he stared, a large drop of the dark red liquid fell from his face onto the page. He had the taste of blood in his mouth.

★

The chest specialist from Glasgow could hardly be asked to make the last seven miles of the journey to the cold and uncomfortable farmhouse, the goat track being almost impassable to vehicles due to the onset of the winter rains. The Fletchers had therefore prepared a room for Orwell at their house, where the examination had taken place. The hosts were having tea with Rees when the diagnosis was delivered, although not to Orwell, who was still in bed, nearby. Normally, with such dire news, the specialist would tell the patient first, but they had to know – for their own safety.

'He can't be allowed to return to Barnhill,' the doctor said.

'Jolting up and down again on that track may cause a haemorrhage. How he got here alive, I don't know.'

They didn't understand. Orwell had assured them it was only recurrent bronchitis.

'His case is fibrotic, and old, and on both lungs; they're like dried-out old leather. You need to keep him here until an ambulance can be brought across to the island to take him to hospital. I should let you know, his sputum is positive, so he's infectious.'

The Fletchers looked at each other, but neither spoke.

'It's reasonably safe if you keep him isolated, especially from the little ones. I can leave these behind.' The man held out some surgical masks. 'Make sure they cover your nose and mouth. Oh, and you'll have to destroy his bedding; anyway, it is bloody.'

'He's not the sort of man who likes to impose on anyone,' Margaret Fletcher said. 'He'll almost certainly want to go back to the farmhouse.'

The doctor was looking out the window over the sodden fields; the rain hadn't stopped since he had arrived. 'Well, he's a fool if he goes back down that goat track in his state. He should never have been all the way out here like this in the first place; it's insanity, sheer insanity. If he'd been in care for the past year we might have been able to help him. As it is, well . . .'

'I'm sure he knows what's wrong,' Robin Fletcher said.

'If he doesn't, he's a madman. He's extremely advanced. Someone should be held responsible. How did he manage to deceive his doctors for so long?'

'By deceiving himself,' said Rees.

'Pardon?' said the doctor.

'He fooled everyone because first he deceived himself. All he wants is to complete his novel. I doubt anything else is as important to him.'

'Not as important as living? Believe me, when confronted with dying, he'll change his priorities. How close is he to finishing this novel of his?'

'He says six months.'

'That long?' There was a terrible tone to the doctor's voice. It was met with silence. 'Well, I'd better go and tell him.'

The doctor entered Orwell's room to find him in bed, smoking and reading Gissing. The first thing Orwell noticed was that this doctor fellow was wearing a surgeon's mask.

– IV –

Hairmyres Hospital, January 1948. He had always known it would come to this: the operating theatre where the bright lights always burned, the hard faces around his bed, the indignities and humiliations forced upon him by his treatment, the inevitability of pain. There was no point any longer in deceiving himself. His being there, he now knew, was a logical progression, a working through of decisions he had made long before. He finally acknowledged his illness, confessing it in letters to his friends, admitting he had been foolish in putting off treatment to finish the book.

He was lying flat on his back, looking up at the ceiling. It didn't seem like a purpose-built operating theatre, more like a large bedroom in a seaside resort, suitably modified. Like all hospitals, he considered this one, despite its relative modernity, to be just another place of torture and death, a sort of antechamber to the tomb. In his boredom, he started counting the white tiles on the walls (it occurred to him that blood was easier to remove from porcelain than from painted walls and floorboards), but in his perpetually tired state he soon lost count. He had the sensation of having counted wall tiles like this before, but when?

For some minutes, which seemed like an hour, he lay there, ignored by the nurses. Entering a hospital, in his experience, meant forfeiting your rights, your identity even, to become a number, a collection of organs to be manipulated as the overseers saw fit. He listened to them discuss what they were about to do to him, behaving as if he weren't there. Unlike other Greek and Latinate words, medical ones got to the point. There was no hiding the unpleasant meaning of *lobotomy* or *appendectomy*, for instance. He certainly didn't like the sound of the procedure they were about to perform: *artificial pneumothorax*, which one of the nurses rather ominously mentioned required something called a *phrenic crush*.

He watched the surgeon – a thickset Scotsman in his mid-forties called Bruce Dick – as he entered the room and began presiding over the white-clad operating theatre staff, who were busying themselves with various dials and instruments. In his day Dick must have resembled a boxer, but his muscles had now begun their inevitable gravitational descent, like a tightly packed sack of potatoes shaken about in a bouncing cart. He had heard somewhere the man was a Catholic and had fought with the Francoists in Spain, but he couldn't be certain that was true. Anyway, even if he had been a fascist at some stage, there was something about him that was appealing: a gruff pragmatism mixed with an obvious independence of mind that suggested one could have a decent conversation with him, as long as one wasn't on the operating table. He looked at the walls and suddenly remembered where he had counted tiles before: in the Bethnal Green lockup back in '31 or '32, when he had stupidly got himself arrested as research for one of his tramping stories.

Placing him under a local anaesthetic, the surgeon made an incision just above the collarbone on his left-hand side, and peeled back the skin and muscle to expose the phrenic nerve. One of the nurses was holding his head steady, so the only things visible to him were the shiny metal instruments Dick was wielding. The operation had been explained earlier. It was this nerve – in fact there were two, one on each side of the upper torso – that controlled the movements of the diaphragm, and with the left or right side of the diaphragm immobilised, the corresponding lung could rest, drawing in less of the oxygen on which the tubercule bacilli thrived, and without which they would more easily succumb to the body's natural defences. That was what the medical books said anyway, but to a layman it seemed like a product of the Victorian belief that anything that caused pain and discomfort must somehow do you good.

He realised he was wriggling involuntarily on the table, wondering how they intended to crush this so-called phrenic nerve of his; no one had told him, which he guessed was because the contemplation of it was alarming. There was pain coming, definitely, but from where?

'Please stay absolutely still,' said Dick, who he now saw was holding a surgical clamp. 'And . . . now!' the surgeon said, decisively, prodding the clamp inside him and closing it suddenly.

There was an explosion, or what seemed like an explosion. His vision was overcome by a blinding yellow light, which radiated outwards from the point the clamp had been fixed. The pain's severity left him gasping for air, but it was momentary, the nerve having just been put out of action. It was over. The clamp was removed, and a wave of relief washed over him. He relaxed his body and his involuntary wriggling stopped.

But it wasn't over. A nurse in a white coat was breaking an ampoule and drawing back the plunger of another syringe, which she placed in a metal kidney dish and offered to the surgeon. Orwell noted, unhappily, that there were more syringes on a bench nearby.

'This is just another local anaesthetic,' said Dick, settling his glasses on his nose before pulling back the sheet covering his lower torso and sliding the needle in. Some other new form of pain must be coming.

A tide of numbness started to spread disconcertingly across his middle. As the anaesthetic was doing its job, the nurses turned him onto his right side, wedged a cushion under his pelvis, and placed his left arm over his head – a position that made him feel totally helpless and once again unable to see what was being done to him. Then Dick picked up another syringe. 'A little deeper this time.' Orwell winced as it went in.

Immediately after that was done, the surgeon began fiddling with yet another instrument. It too was a syringe – one big enough to disconcert a cow or a horse. Its needle was attached by a rubber hose to what looked like a bicycle pump with a pressure gauge attached. It looked savage and straight out of one of the Gothic horror stories he had so loved as a child. This syringe too was slid into him just below the lungs. He felt a stinging somewhere deep inside his abdomen, even with the anaesthetic.

'There is blood,' said Dick. 'Let's try again.'

He watched with horror as the needle was removed

from his side, drained of blood into a dish and once again poked into him, sliding its way deep. A sudden tremor of pain caused his legs to kick out. 'Pleural cavity breached,' the surgeon said coolly. 'No blood this time. Let's stay in.'

What in God's name were they doing to him? To have this gruesome machine connected to you, in fact buried deep inside your body, was at once terrifying and humiliating.

Dick began pumping the top of the tube up and down. 'It's just nitrogen; nothing to be worried about.'

He felt like a specimen laid on a slab for the surgeon's sadistic pleasure. 'Can you please tell me what you are doing?' he gasped.

'We are filling your diaphragm with air, which will cause the lung to collapse and remain still and free of oxygen. Best if you don't talk.'

The knowledge didn't make him feel any better. The procedure seemed to go on forever. Peering towards his belly, he could see the space between it and his chest, which had sunken on the left side, start to rise like a balloon. All he could do was lie there mute as they continued to work on him.

The nurse, who he assumed was looking at the gauge of the pumping device, read its progress to the surgeon. 'Fifty . . . seventy-five . . . one hundred.' His eyes turned involuntarily towards the dial.

'Remain still, please.' The pumping continued. 'Two hundred.'

To calm himself he breathed as steadily as he could manage, trying to think of anything other than the terrible thing that was happening to him, but found his mind wandering back to Spain and the electro-shock treatment they had given him to stimulate his larynx after he had been shot.

'Three hundred.' It kept going. 'Four hundred . . . five hundred.'

'That will do,' Dick said. 'Better not push it.' He sounded almost disappointed.

The large needle was removed from his side, stinging again as it emerged, and the wound was cleansed with antiseptic and covered with a sticking plaster. Again, a wave of relief washed over him and a sweat broke out on his forehead. Everything was alright; there was to be no more pain.

'That's you done for the day, Mr Blair. Nurse, let's mark down seven-fifty for the next time. Perhaps a thousand subsequently.'

'For the day?'

'We shall have to build you up slowly, of course. The nitrogen is absorbed slowly. By your body.'

'Oh?'

'Yes, every few days or so to begin with.' The thought of the giant syringe . . .

Dick must have been reading his mind. 'After a while it's only once a week. Eventually just monthly, if we're lucky.'

'For how long?'

'Weeks, months, Mr Blair. However long it takes. We intend to cure you.'

He writhed under the sheet. Was this what the rest of his treatment – his life – was to consist of: being squeezed dry and filled up again by other people?

'It gets easier.'

During the weeks that followed, he lived in some sort of sleep or stupor as his body tried to adjust to relying on one lung. Periodically he would be wheeled back into the tiled room for what they euphemistically called 'refills', where the dial would reach eight hundred, nine hundred and a thousand; how many times it occurred he could hardly remember, and it took all his public school resolve to keep himself from grovelling pathetically and begging for it to stop. Almost daily, white-coated medical staff would take his temperature and his pulse, tap his joints, peer down his throat and remove samples of blood. Between times, he was regularly shaved and his hair was cut. They even removed his teeth and gave him a set of dentures, his natural teeth having succumbed to the relentless assault of the drugs they had given him, and the clenching of his jaws under the intense pain.

He wanted to live, of course, but felt himself governed by some urge to resist all the good they were doing to him, so he could get back to the novel. They assured him that what he needed was *complete rest*. Sitting up, wriggling around, reaching over to grab fresh sheets of paper, moving his arms up and down to type in his two-fingered fashion – it all deepened his respiration, which encouraged the bacilli. But even after it was explained to him, he felt powerless to resist the compulsion to write. Dick responded by getting the nurses to take away his typewriter, but could see there was no stopping him.

'Writing with a pen now?'

Orwell, who was so absorbed in his prose that he hadn't

noticed Dick enter the room, looked up and smiled a hello. 'Actually, one of those new biros. It's easier to use in bed – no ink bottles – but less pleasant. You have to scratch the ink into the paper rather than writing upon it. Completely different.' He saw the look of schoolmasterly disapproval on Dick's face. He should have been flat on his back, but here he was, propped up by pillows like some kind of sultan.

'Something important?'

'A review. Pompous book about India. For the *Observer*.'

'Do you find it difficult, reviewing books?'

'It's a game, really. The idea is to say as much as you can about a book by reading as little of it as possible. Passes the time. And anyway, it pays well. This illness is becoming an expensive habit.'

'I couldn't think of anything more difficult than sitting down to write a thousand words.'

'Oh, it's easy. Bread and jam. It's writing novels that kills you.' Dick took another drag on his cigarette, turning as he saw a Rolls-Royce pulling up to the car space outside the ward.

'Horrible and exhausting business, a novel,' Orwell went on.

'A bit like having a painful illness you just can't throw.'

'One could always just stop.'

'One could always just stop breathing.'

'Try it, Mr Blair. Put away the pen, listen to the radio for a few months, read, but not too much. You can be cured, if you want to be, but it's going to take a bit of effort. Perhaps some sacrifices you haven't been prepared to make yet.'

But the patient just chuckled, as if to say, 'Not a chance.' Dick looked at the mess of the room, with the full ashtrays, the piles of books on the floor, the basket filled with discarded paper. He noticed a framed photograph. It showed his patient, seated in front of a set of sagging bookcases, a young boy propped on his lap. Both were caught in a moment of sublime tenderness, the shot being perfectly framed. Dick's eyes were drawn to the missing buttons on the man's lapels, suggesting some privation or loss – a dead wife, or maybe just a general lack of care for himself.

'Tell me, Blair, do you *want* to live? If not for yourself, then for someone else? Someone who needs you.'

Orwell glanced at the photograph and smiled. 'Of course I want to live. If I'm not alive, I can't write.'

'Couldn't all that wait a year? Books will still be published in the 1950s.'

'A year? Now that's a long time.'

'So tell me, then, what's this novel of yours about? What makes it so important and urgent?'

'They tell me you were in Spain, Mr Dick, on Franco's side.' He saw surprise in the surgeon's eyes.

'I was younger then.'

'How do you feel about it *now*?'

'Well, I never thought it would lead to Hitler or the war we've just had, if that's what you mean. I did it for Catholic reasons, you see, not political ones. Anyway, I was a doctor. I didn't go to kill anyone.'

'I did, with a grenade. Are you still? Catholic, I mean?'

'Not as much. The war! Are you still a socialist?'

'More so. Although in a different way. I'm less naive too. That's one of the things my book is about, you see: the dangers of extremism. Anyone can fall for it.'

'*One* of the things? What else?'

He took a moment to order his thoughts. 'All the things worth saving. You know . . . democracy, a full belly, the freedom to think and say as you like, the laws of logic, the countryside, the right to love others and not to live alone but in a family . . . human things.'

'Time to take a short break from it, Mr Blair. You'll do a better job when you're fully recovered.'

'Oh, I can work just fine on it from here. It's not like I'm out digging ditches.'

'Do you understand what tuberculosis is, and how it kills people?'

'You could say I'm something of an expert. Anyway, I have a good idea for the next one, and you can't pop the cork when you've got another book inside you.' Orwell turned his eyes to his writing pad.

'Good day, then,' Dick said, and left the room.

In the corridor, he summoned the head nurse and instructed her to put Blair's arm in plaster the following morning. 'Tell him it's something to do with that arm pain he's been suffering, and that it's caused by the TB spreading to his elbow. I don't think the man's prepared to admit how much he has to live for.'

Dick turned to see a man standing at the nurses' station, holding a box filled with foods that hardly anyone had seen in a decade. It was obvious this was the owner of the Rolls-Royce.

'David Astor for Mr Orwell,' the man said, in a soft voice whose fineness was reflected in the clothes he was wearing.

'You mean Mr Blair, of course,' Dick said, approaching.

'Over there.' He pointed to the room he had just left. 'Mr Astor, when you've finished your visit, would you mind stopping by my office? I'm Mr Blair's surgeon.'

'Not at all.'

'The nurses will direct you.' They shook hands.

★

Later, Astor sat in Dick's office, drinking tea. 'How can I help you, Mr Dick?'

'As you will have guessed, it's about Mr Blair – Mr Orwell. I wanted to apprise you of the seriousness of his condition.'

'Certainly.'

'Normally I wouldn't betray the confidence of a patient, but you may be in a position to help.'

'My discretion is assured, Mr Dick, and I want you to understand from the outset that I will do anything to help my old friend.'

'Well, his condition is rather more serious than we thought. He had an old lesion – TB – in his right lung. We've discovered through X-ray a new cavity in his left lobe.'

'So, both lungs, not good.'

'No. He may recover with complete rest. I have to emphasise that means no work, not even writing.'

Astor put down his teacup. 'My God, I've just given him another commission. I thought I was helping him out, keeping up his spirits.'

'Indeed, perfectly understandable.'

'I won't give him any more.'

'That would help, but there's actually another way you may be able to assist.'

'Any way I can.'

'There's a new anti-TB drug the Americans are having great success with. It's not yet available in England. The Medical Research Council is conducting tests, which won't help us here at Hairmyres, but the drug can be purchased directly from the Americans. Only it takes American dollars, which we don't have. In fact the Board of Trade wouldn't permit it even if we had them.'

'I have an office and funds in New York. Consider it done.'

'It's called streptomycin.' The surgeon handed over a typed note. 'We'll need seventy milligrams for a full course of treatment, I think. I'm afraid it will cost around three hundred American dollars.'

'I shall wire New York.'

'There's one other thing. The health ministry may object. They usually put restrictions on imported medicines, especially those under trial. Undue officious-ness sometimes gets in the way of sound treatment. But I read the *Observer* and I assume you know the health minister?'

'Don't worry about that. Mr Bevan is one of George's greatest admirers. Leave it to me.'

The two men shook hands and Astor made to leave. At the doorway he turned and spoke. 'You have probably worked out by now that Orwell is a highly adamant character and far too principled for his own safety. He won't accept charity or queue jumping. So I want you to deal directly with me about the amount and cost of the treatment he requires, and generally not tell him too much. Such decisions must under no circumstances be left to him.'

- V -

Hairmyres Hospital, February. In the hospital ward the lights burned all night. He had been awakened for his midnight injection: half a milligram, three times a day. The task was performed by nurses, but he suspected it was Dick directing his pain. He seldom saw him, except on his weekly rounds, but always there was the feeling he was lurking just out of sight, making all the important decisions: when he could sleep, when he should wake, when he could work – always Dick, his oppressor, his rescuer, the reminder of his mortality.

He couldn't get back to sleep so he switched on the bedside lamp, thinking he may as well do his correspondence while Dick wasn't around to tell him to stop; the nurses knew not to deal with him alone. He opened a letter from Warburg. *Cheered that you're writing for Astor . . . nothing to really consult you about . . . but when are you likely to be out of hospital?* He could just as well have telegrammed WHERE IS MY BLOODY NOVEL? Where indeed? Orwell contemplated the manuscript – a large, unruly wad which he could see sitting on top of the wardrobe – but he knew that beginning it again right now was impossible.

He reached over with his left hand and took up the tablet

of paper from the bedside table, an effort that pained him, and the new biro that Astor had brought him as a gift. Both of them he placed on the meal tray he used as a writing desk. He arranged the tablet so that it lay under the fingers of his plastered right arm, and was able to write legibly enough.

Fred,
Thanks so much for your letter. As you inferred, my beginning to do articles in the *Observer* is a sign of partial revival, though even that is an effort, especially as I now have my right arm in plaster. I can't attempt any serious work while I am like this (1½ stone underweight) but I like to do a little to keep my hand in & incidentally earn some money. I've been definitely ill since about October, and really, I think, since the beginning of 1947. I believe that frightful winter in London started it off. I didn't really feel well at all last year except during that hot period in the summer. Before taking to my bed I had finished the rough draft of my novel all save the last few hundred words, and if I had been well I might have finished it about May. If I'm well and out of here by June I might just finish the novel by the end of the year – I don't know. It's just a ghastly mess as it stands, but the idea is so good that I could not possibly abandon it.

That would have to do to keep Warburg at bay while the streptomycin was doing its magic. It seemed to be working, as he felt slightly better, although his throat was painfully sore. Dick had even told him his latest sputum sample had come up negative. Making an effort, finally, to lie flat on his back and keep movement to a minimum, he drifted off to sleep, regaining consciousness only when a blue-uniformed nurse arrived at his bedside to give him his next dose of the drug.

He woke with blood on his lips. In fact, the blood, which had been appearing for some days in tiny blisters on his lips and inside his mouth, had increased dramatically in the night and dried in his sleep, gluing his mouth shut. He found the development vaguely terrifying, as did the staff, who had never seen such a thing before. The nurse gently drizzled his lips with warm water to prise them apart. Something was going wrong. They summoned Dick.

'It's just a mild allergic reaction,' the surgeon assured him, not wholly convincingly. 'Nothing that should stop us continuing the treatment.'

'Rather like sinking the ship to kill the rats, don't you think?' His voice was rasp-like, his throat now frightfully painful.

He watched as the nurse broke a fresh ampoule and drew back the plunger of a syringe. The injections had to be intramuscular, and as the needle jerked into his arm and plunged deep into his wasting flesh, he had the alarming sensation of it scraping his bone.

As the agonising procedure continued, Dick talked to him as a form of distraction. 'Do you have any questions? You can ask me anything you like.'

'When is my next diaphragm refill?'

'Tomorrow.'

'When can I get out of bed?'

'Probably not for some time yet.'

'Can I have my typewriter back?'

'If you keep showing improvement.'

'How long have I got to live?'

There was a hesitation – not a long one, but long enough for him to know Dick was dissembling. The nurse flinched perceptibly, and chose that moment to withdraw the needle from his arm and place it, with its bloodied tip, in a kidney dish held by a colleague. 'Everything depends on you,' the doctor said. 'You could go on for years and years, although it might be that this treatment has to be repeated once or even twice more before you are fully cured. The possibilities are dictated by several factors, none of which can be calculated with any accuracy.'

These were meaningless imprecisions, which Orwell knew to be the same thing as lies. The only conclusion he could draw was that the end might come suddenly and unexpectedly.

'What I can say with certainty is that with reduced respiratory capacity you're likely to be what we call "a good chronic". No more running around the Scottish Isles.'

'Will I be able to write, as a good chronic?'

'Certainly.'

★

Being a 'good chronic' – what would it mean? A lie-in every morning, *The Times* crossword over his morning coffee, and two to three hours of gentle writing after lunch. Perhaps a short stroll around the garden, before whiling away the late afternoon drinking gin and playing chess with Rees, or Snakes and Ladders with Ricky.

Different visions, though, began to enter his night-time thoughts. The gentle, natural dreams of his past had been replaced by hallucinatory affairs that took place in some indefinable moment in the future. In these, he had been made right again and was writing the novel out in his mind, with incredible lucidity. So real had it seemed that he could almost remember it word-for-word when he woke, but could never raise the energy to write it all down. Later he saw that his thoughts had been nothing but the useless expenditure of mental energy. It was only when some pleasant but impossible element added itself into his dreams – being reunited with an older, greyer, thicker-set Eileen, or watching Ricky take his own son fishing in the Golden Country – that his mind realised it was fantasising. He would awake to find an ampoule of the drug next to its syringe in the metal kidney dish sitting coldly beside him.

Each morning he found that the small blisters in his mouth and on his lips had spread even further down his throat, some becoming painful ulcers that prevented him from eating normal food. Annoyingly, his fingernails had become brittle, splitting on the slightest impact and making it difficult to write, even though Dick had removed his arm from the plaster cast. They were letting him smoke, which Dick thought helped him cough the phlegm out of his airways.

This morning, unusually, Dick had come to supervise the nurse giving his injection. It had become a tricky business. His withered muscles needed careful selecting before the needle could be inserted, and it seemed not a square inch of him had been left un-jabbed. Dick asked Orwell to hold out his palm, and must have been considering injecting him there, when he seemed to reach a decision. 'I think the strepto's done its job.'

'Do you think I'm cured?'

Dick turned to the patient, his manner becoming less severe; friendly, even. 'Well, we've given the bacilli a decent knock, that's for sure. The rest is up to nature.' He guessed the next question.

'I think you can begin to write again, but start gently. Finishing your novel is as good a goal as any. Having something to occupy you in your recovery may do you good.'

Orwell smiled.

'By the way,' Dick said. 'We've got a bit of the drug left over. Do you mind if we give it to some younger patients? They're the wives of three of my colleagues – young mothers.'

'Go ahead.'

★

He tried to fill the following days with writing, but it was useless. It was as if his treatment had induced a deterioration inside his skull, making the act of inventing prose irksome. Maybe it was another lingering side effect of the drug. His mind seemed normal but revealed its helplessness whenever he tried to put anything down on paper; whatever he attempted to write came out sounding stupid and obvious, despite the good ideas behind it. Even when he could pound out a decent sentence, stringing more than two or three together seemed impossible.

The pumping of nitrogen into his diaphragm continued,

but not as often; it was interesting what one found normal after a while. The secret to making it bearable was acceptance – an act of self-deception that convinced you that you could endure it. It was rather like drifting with a current instead of swimming against it in some self-defeating gesture of defiance.

A few days later he resolved to try again. The pen felt fat and clumsy in his fingers, the ends of which had become soft and spongy because of his deteriorated nails. People underestimated the importance of fingernails, he thought; perhaps that was why torturers always pulled them out. He didn't know quite where to begin, and instead of purposeful work found that after half an hour all he had done was jot down in large capitals some random slogans from the book that had come into his head:

BIG BROTHER IS WATCHING YOU

Underneath it:

FREEDOM IS SLAVERY

Then beneath that:

TWO AND TWO MAKE FIVE

And after that:

WHO CONTROLS THE PAST CONTROLS
THE FUTURE; WHO CONTROLS THE
PRESENT CONTROLS THE PAST

It occurred to him that he was good at slogans, remembering SOME ANIMALS ARE MORE EQUAL THAN OTHERS. He could have had a decent career in advertising, rattling the spoon in a swill bucket for a good salary and a nice house in the suburbs – the choice Gordon and Rosemary had made in *Keep the Aspidistra Flying*. If he had, he figured, there would have been no Wigan, no Spain and possibly no illness . . . But the very thought filled him with the urge to rebel. He started scribbling compulsively, almost unthinkingly –

DOWN WITH BIG BROTHER
DOWN WITH BIG BROTHER
DOWN WITH BIG BROTHER

– hoping that something else would come into his mind, but nothing did. He calmed down and tried to begin again.

Reading it over, he saw that large chunks of the book were little more than notes; the scenes seemed like disparate episodes, political ideas, rather than parts of a coherent story. The torture scenes, the concluding chapter in the Chestnut Tree Café, even Goldstein's Testament – they were all terribly underdone. Clearly, he had made a hash of it. Even should he live, how could he ever make it as good as he wanted, given how addled his mind was? If only he hadn't got sick, how much better it would have been.

He put down the typescript, picked up his writing tablet and jotted down a note to Rees, his literary executor, instructing him to destroy the novel should anything happen to him before he could complete it. He sank back onto the bed and lit another cigarette, which induced an immediate coughing fit.

★

May. How many days had he been at the hospital? One hundred and twenty? One hundred and fifty perhaps. And how long since they had finished the painful injections of streptomycin? Twenty or thirty days, he thought. His throat and mouth had cleared and the keenness of his mind was slowly returning. They had even given him back his typewriter, although using it was still beyond him; but, his fingernails having partially grown back and the dexterity having returned to his fingers, he could manipulate a pen sufficiently well to complete whole pages. He felt his physical and mental recovery was almost complete.

Lying propped up in bed, pen and manuscript in hand, he heard a familiar heavy tramp of feet in the corridor. Dick entered, followed by a white-coated male attendant who was wheeling an unusually high-backed bath chair. 'Get up, Mr Blair,' the doctor said. 'It's time to see if we've really cured you.'

Once he was sitting upright, Dick bent down to him. 'How's your throat feeling?'

'Completely healed, I think. No soreness at all.'

Dick produced a small wooden paddle and a tiny medical torch, and held down Orwell's tongue while he peered down his throat. 'Say ah.'

He did so, feebly.

'Yes, looks back to normal.' Dick nodded to the assistant.

'Theatre,' he said.

The room was white-tiled, like the one in which he had his refills, but smaller; it was a place, he figured, for messy procedures not possible in a normal hospital room. The nature of the chair now became apparent. A nurse produced a leather cap attached to a strap, which clamped his head tight to the high headrest at an angle that left him looking at the ceiling. 'We have to keep your head entirely still, Mr Blair,' she said, seeing a look of terror emerging on his face.

'We just need to get a steady look,' Dick added. 'And keep your air passages open.'

The nurse put a wide bit between his teeth to stop him from closing his jaws. Unable to swivel his head, he could only see as much as his peripheral vision would allow. It was similar to how they arranged him for his refills, but as he was not lying on an operating table, it seemed somehow more chilling. Out of the corner of his right eye he could see Dick fiddling with a polished metal instrument about two feet long. It had an eyepiece at one end and a lens at the other; it looked like a cross between a microscope and a cattle prod. He quickly grasped its purpose: they were going to insert it down his throat and look inside his lungs. He had never in his life – not even in Spain when caught unexpectedly that morning by the sun rising in no-man's-land – felt so hopeless and so exposed.

The attendant held his head tightly from behind, while the nurse stood by with a large swab and another of the hated kidney dishes – he always associated the evil objects with pain. 'In case you need to vomit,' she said.

'Open,' said Dick.

The simple act of opening his mouth at this angle

forced him to gag. It was a horror of horrors. Until then he had submitted to every treatment they had forced upon him, but now he had to struggle against his own body. As the probe entered his mouth and began sliding down his throat, he began screaming inside, a sort of silent rage against everything that had brought him to this point: the obtuseness that had seen him go out tramping, the curiosity that led him to those unsanitary lodging houses in the north, the ambition that sent him to the freezing dugouts of the Catalonian front line. He would go back, undo it all, betray the causes they had served, anything, anything, just to escape this horror and be cured.

He could feel the cold metal against the insides of his throat, and rivulets of sweat running down from the now slimy leather cap and dripping from his jaw. Slowly, the probe was now drawn upwards, but the relief he felt at its emergence was crushed straight away by the feeling of it descending into his other lung. Would it never end?

When the probe finally emerged to be wiped on a towel, Dick turned to him again. 'Not perfect, Mr Blair, but the lesions seem to be healing. With luck you may indeed be cured.'

★

June. He was lying awake, listening to the general hum of the hospital. Simultaneously he could hear the following: the blaring of a radio, the tinkling of a gramophone, a vacuum cleaner, an orderly singing, someone hammering, the usual clatter of boots and trolleys, running taps, people coughing and the opening and shutting of doors. Outside were the cries of rooks and the cackling of hens. In the same way a song could conjure up ancient memories, the noises of the hospital reminded him of those photographs in *The Times* of Yagoda, Rykoff and Bukharin. It stimulated an urge to write.

His life had become like this: an alternating round of drifting sleep followed by periods of lucidity in which he was able to rework the novel decisively, filling the margins with changes, sometimes adding whole new pages. He would wake in the middle of the night and happily read or work, then find himself sleeping half the day under the full glare of sunlight – something he was capable of doing for the first time in his life.

This morning, although wide awake, he found it impossible to concentrate. He needed a wash and a shave, and had had enough of the disgusting bedpan; he resolved to get up and use a proper bathroom, which the doctor had finally given him permission to do. He hadn't been out of his room for weeks, his greatest exertion being to sit in the bedside chair and read the newspapers. Pyjamas were still rationed after all these years, and the ones he had on, which had been endlessly patched by Avril, now sported a variety of buttons; the pants were held up by an ill-matching length of cord. Carefully he bent down to put on his well-worn slippers, and noticed the slowness and stiffness of his movements.

Shuffling out of his room, he made the short distance to the bathroom, pushed the swing-door open with moderate difficulty and entered the space, which was cooler for its tiled floor and profusion of metal and porcelain fittings. The cubicle he wanted, which offered greater privacy, was at the end. Making his way towards it, he noticed that someone else was in the room, and moving towards him slowly. He then realised he had left on his new reading glasses, and after a few moments registered that he was in fact approaching a full-length mirror.

He stopped and removed the spectacles. The image ahead frightened him, for it was almost unrecognisable as himself. A once tall figure, now bowed and stooping, stood shakily and looked directly at him through watery eyes, scanning him up and down. There was sweat on the man's forehead, from which skin was flaking off. A streak of obscenely grey hair ran across the top of his scalp. He had never had more than the odd grey hair before – neither for that matter had Eileen – and he raised his hand to touch it. Could it be his own? It certainly hadn't been there a few weeks before. He tugged gently and was shocked when a tuft of it came out easily in his hand, like a ball of fluff plucked from the surface of an old blanket; disgusted, he dropped it and watched it waft to the floor.

He looked back to the mirror. From his gaunt face, scarred around the mouth from the recent blistering, protruded the only part of him that had been improved: his teeth. Perhaps the most horrible thing of all was the emaciation of his body, parts of which poked through his thin pyjamas at sharp angles, making him look like one of those anatomy class skeletons they had once dressed in the master's gown and mortar at school. He could make out that his knees were wider than his thighs, and, further up, that his stomach – now pumped up after his recent refill – protruded well beyond the caved-in barrel of his chest. It struck him that, in his prime, he could have snapped this new version of himself in two with little effort.

Here, then, stood the body of what looked like a sixty-yearold man suffering from some malignant disease. He found it hard to believe that this scarecrow was having the same thoughts that were now running through his own mind. He was just a month or two shy of his forty-fifth birthday. How long he had left to live he didn't know, but he knew now with certainty that time was running out.

He returned to bed and threw himself into amending the typescript. As with any book, it was only when you were well through it that you knew what it was really about. There was so much he had yet to get clear in his mind. For whom was he writing it? The future, certainly; he'd known that from the start. But whose future? He turned to the page where Winston started his diary.

April 4th, 1980.

He now felt unsure about the date. Too far into the future and it would be science fiction, like Wells' stories, and of literary interest only; too close to today and it would be dismissed as propaganda. It wasn't so simple, this business of communicating with the future; a possible future, as opposed to a fantastic one, had to be pitched carefully.

He had originally planned for Winston, who had been born in 1940 – the year of the battle of Airstrip One and the seizure of power by Ingsoc – to be thirty-nine or forty years old at the novel's opening. It was the age he had been when he conceived of it – the age at which one was still young enough to have hope for the future, but realistic enough to accept that one's fate was already largely settled. But now

1980 seemed too close. It was just thirty-two years into the future, and he could remember that far back – when he was still at Eton – as if it were yesterday. It wasn't far enough.

He roused himself, sat up straighter, picked up the biro and changed it:

April 4th, 1982.

That sounded better. But no sooner had he written the new date than a sense of complete helplessness overcame him. The date meant nothing. He had lost his train of thought. Perhaps the treatment hadn't just tired him out but had made something happen inside his head; sometimes it felt like there was a large patch of emptiness, as though a piece had been taken out of his brain.

Defeated, he looked at the framed picture of his son in Islington, taken when the boy was just two years old. For some months now they had stopped Richard from seeing him, as a precautionary measure, and before that he'd had to push the boy away when he tried to climb on the bed and show him his toys, including the children's typewriter he had got for Christmas.

What sort of life, he wondered, could the boy look forward to? Certainly a better life than those living under Stalin's gaze could ever expect. Britain may have ended the war more measured and regimented than before, but there were no torture cellars, no rubber truncheons, no goose-stepping political armies stamping on people's faces, no June purges, no holding camps full of desperate, fearful refugees, no mass graves. In Britain, basic freedoms seemed safe for now, but their survival had been a close-run thing. How long, he wondered, could they last?

He looked at Richard's photograph again. Would the boy, who like Winston Smith was born in 1944, know what freedom meant when he too turned forty? Would Richard's generation know how their parents had taken a passably human world and turned it into a nightmare? Would they recognise the danger signs if ever they returned?

Orwell picked up the biro again. His mind hovered for a moment around the doubtful date on the page, before he scratched over it:

April 4th, 1984.

- VI -

The MV *Lochiel*, 28 July 1948. The green and treeless hills rose up on either side of the dark waters of the Western Isles. He had never been on the ferry on a day so calm; instead of pitching and rolling its way forward, the ship seemed to be sucked onwards by some silent force moving beneath the sea's surface. The weather was so warm and the wind so slight that he sat on the deck, enjoying the unusual sensations.

Dick had finally let him leave, but with strict orders not to exert himself. Work sparely, he had told him; even if the bacilli were now dormant, his lungs were terribly scarred, the blood veins exposed and brittle, and only time and relaxation could heal them. He would follow the advice, he decided, as it offered his best hope. Convalesce or die: Dick could hardly have been clearer. But Dick had said a lot more than that. He had told him to keep somewhere dry and warm, somewhere near a hospital, somewhere like Glasgow, where Dick himself could monitor his progress. The surgeon may as well have stamped 'ANYWHERE BUT JURA' across his discharge letter. But there was only so far he was willing to submit.

He scanned the draft of the novel, which was held

together by a tarnished bulldog clip. The clean typescript he had taken with him to the hospital nearly eight months before was now a ragged collection of different sizes and types of paper, some lined, some not, covered in deletions and additions. This, he thought, was all he had to show for two years of work, and indeed every serious thought he had had since Spain. It would be too easy to blame the mess that lay before him on his illness, though he was certain that with more energy he could have done a proper job of it. He could remove the bulldog clip, fling the pages overboard and start again, but he knew he wouldn't. Every book was the product of its time – not just its era, but the days and the circumstances in which it was physically created; it had to reflect that or not get written at all. Afterwards, a writer always looked back, thinking what could have been done better, but always knowing that once the book was set in type and cast in metal, it was unalterable.

He put the manuscript back into his briefcase and pulled out the letter from Warburg which had arrived just as he was leaving Hairmyres. He had feared opening it, suspecting another missive of the 'where is it?' type.

Dear George
This is to tell you that the literary world simply can't get enough of your writing. I have just received news that some fifty Japanese publishers bid for the translation rights for *Animal Farm*, which topped the list for publishing interest from seventy-five titles the Americans submitted to them. Unfortunately, the yen is blocked, so you can only access the money by heading to Japan. Perhaps a trip one spring in cherry blossom time might

be practicable for you, if and when the world clears up.

Michael Kennard reported to me how well you looked. I was of course especially pleased to learn that you have done quite a substantial amount of revision on the new novel. From our point of view, and I should say also from your point of view, a revision of this is far and away the most important single undertaking to which you could apply yourself when the vitality is there. It should not be put aside for reviews or miscellaneous work, however tempting, and I am certain that sooner rather than later it will bring in more money than you could expect from any other activity. If you do succeed in finishing the revision by the end of the year this would be pretty satisfactory, and we should publish in the autumn of 1949, but it really is rather important from the point of view of your literary career to get it done by the end of the year, and indeed earlier if at all possible.

He knew publishers well enough to see the subtle subterfuge of flattery and urgency, yet Warburg had a point. Until this moment of the homeward journey, Dick's parting words had been ringing in his ears. He had resolved that the book would have to wait; he could finish it slowly and still get it done, instead of trying to knock it off by Christmas as planned. The amount of work required to get it right was frightful. It might take a year, but it would be better for it. But here he was, the toast of the literary world. It was the moment to strike; he was certain.

An iron grate lifted somewhere in his mind, and Dick's careful instructions were dropped down to some fiery place and forgotten.

Jura, September 1948. His biro gave out. He pushed harder, hoping to get the ink to flow, but succeeded only in scratching empty trenches between the lines of the typescript and the cheap paper. He threw the hated instrument down on the desk in disgust, then poked about in a shoebox for a fountain pen. As he sucked a nib to get the grease off, he looked out the window, seeing the remains of the flattened henhouse, which hadn't lasted even one serious storm. To the rear of the farmhouse stood a broken truck, and inside the barn a motorbike that no longer started, meaning that he was almost completely cut off. It had been a fine late summer, but the autumn weather had been filthy, and it had been a week since he'd been in the garden. Even pulling up a weed robbed him of energy, and the colder weather had made going outside impossible.

He looked down at the desktop to see Warburg's latest letter, which had arrived that morning. 'Not having heard from your remote fastness for many weeks, I hope it means you have been making steady progress . . .' A wave of pain shot through his chest but the spasm soon passed. Along with the worsening pains, his temperature had returned.

He reached for an enamelled metal cup – glasses would never have survived the trip, given the island's rough roads – and the bottle of brandy next to it, poured his daily ration, a double, and knocked it back in one gulp. The immediate burning sensation in his stomach quickly gave way to a cheerfulness that put him in the right frame of mind for the day's most important task.

Keeping on his dressing-gown, he slipped into bed,

carrying the much-altered typescript with him. It felt somehow safer to work there. The horizons of his world were narrowing as the daylight shortened. Including the revisions he had done at Hairmyres, he was two-thirds through.

Now, working in bed, he couldn't remember any beginnings or ends to his prolonged writing sessions. He drifted in and out of sleep, succumbing mid-thought, then picking it up again upon awakening. One moment he might be grappling with a particularly thorny question involving the story, and in another it might be something minor and obvious, but which his weakened mind found frustratingly difficult to resolve, like whether to include commas before or after parentheses. Then, before fully resolving either, he was dreaming or thinking, his body tired but his mind still working at full screws. The thoughts were seemingly unconnected. He was playing games as a child with his mother and Avril; at prep being flogged by the headmistress's cruel husband, Sambo; in a dank room with an ancient, hideous prostitute whose years were concealed by layers of make-up; watching the rocket bombs falling on the East End; and once again strolling across the Golden Country, the sun at his back.

One dream stuck in his mind. He had been walking in almost total darkness – it must have been in Barcelona after his final return from the front – when he felt a voluptuousness press against his arm. It was Eileen. She looked younger and full-figured, her thick brown hair sticking out in waves from under a fetching black beret, and her painted red lips beckoning him to kiss her. The dream was like a delirium, with a weird, hallucinatory quality, possibly caused by the painkilling drugs he was taking. He sniffed her to make sure it wasn't a dream; she had put on perfume, and he had an over-whelming desire to take her to his hideaway in the ruined church and make love to her on the ground. Yet despite her loveliness, which reminded him of why he had immediately wanted to marry her, she had the unmistakeable look of someone living under a regime of terror: the edgy sideward glance, the controlled facial expressions, the determination to be invisible.

She had taken a foolish risk and followed him. In the black of night, they may have gone unnoticed, or been taken for any other amorous Spanish couple, but the problem would come if they were stopped by the patrols: 'Comrades, your papers . . .' For this reason, they could talk only in a whisper.

'I've broken my first rule, not to take risks,' she said, as she tugged him into a shadowed doorway and kissed him hard on the lips. He felt warm tears on his cheeks. Then, as quickly as she had appeared, she disappeared, whether into the night or from his consciousness, he couldn't tell. Although she hadn't said it directly, he could sense what she intended to say, knowing he would figure it out the way lovers do: 'I betrayed you and I'm sorry,' but also: 'I love you.' He found himself running down the street in search of her, but she had vanished.

The intensity of the dream woke him, and he felt himself floating up to the surface of a pool, all the while trying to sink back down into the depths of unconsciousness. Tears welled in his eyes. At that moment he loved her more than ever before. He finally understood the risk she had taken. In going back to the Hotel Continental, she had acted as a decoy to make the communists believe he was still at the front. They could easily have arrested her and maybe even tortured her; after all, her administrative knowledge made her more valuable to them than he could ever have been. It was a protective act, a gesture that was futile – and yet because of its futility gloriously human. The book. He had to finish it, as an act of fidelity.

With an effort, he picked up the pen that had dropped to the floor when he had fallen asleep, and began writing a version of the encounter into the story. He had found this sort of thing happening again and again as his mind slipped between the parallel grooves created by fever, drugs and sleep. It was as if time was so precious now that not even his unconscious moments could be wasted.

Upon finishing the scene, he read it over. Immediately he saw that the accretion of these deliriums was ruining his story. He crossed the scene out and cursed the time he had wasted on it. Flicking back through the manuscript, he could see that what had started as a naturalistic novel had descended gradually into a hallucinatory nightmare. Everything he had added since entering the hospital seemed infused with a savage, unhinged quality that made his earlier storyline seem almost schoolboy-like. Winston's shocking physical and mental deterioration, Room 101 with its caged rats, the ticking metronomes and the luminous eyes into which Winston swam like a porpoise under the influence of drugs, the vast corridors of the Ministry of Love down which he rolled, confessing his crimes and implicating everyone he knew . . . It had all become so dark that his mind was overtaken by doubts.

Could he continue? He devised another way of seeing

his predicament, although somewhere beneath his conscious mind he knew it to be a form of rationalisation: the faster he finished the book, the sooner he could get himself to the sanatorium, where his best chance of survival lay. Or he could drop it all now, he supposed. He could ask Rees to drive him off the island to hospital the next morning, there being a ferry at eight a.m. But the temptation quickly faded. Once in hospital, he knew all writing would end – Dick would see to that. And what if he never recovered? Without the book, he would be just another minor author who died young, leaving a legacy easily overlooked, no matter the success of *Animal Farm*. Unfinished, his book – now a series of scrawls unintelligible to anyone but himself – would be reduced to ashes, and he to dust, a lonely ghost uttering a truth nobody would ever hear.

*

Early November. He screwed the lid back on the pen and dropped both it and the heavy manuscript onto the floor. The pen rolled across the sloping boards until it was arrested by the lip of the rug. The revisions were finished. His mind was now prepared for the sanatorium. There was just one thing left to do: type the third and final draft. No other person could understand it in its present form, and a typist working alone, even the most professional, would surely be too tempted to muck with the many neologisms. A skilled stenographer under his eye could type the final draft in a fortnight, he guessed; Warburg should be able to find him someone suitable.

He wrote to the publisher, but days drifted by without

anyone picking up the telephone. Frustrated, Orwell turned to his literary agent, Leonard Moore, who had persuaded Gollancz to publish *Down and Out in Paris and London* all those years before and had never let him down. Moore immediately found him someone with good references: Miss E. Keddie of 47 Barkston Gardens, Kensington, SW5. She was willing to travel to Jura for seven pounds a week plus expenses, typewriter supplied. Then Warburg's editor Roger Senhouse insisted Miss Keddie wouldn't be needed, as his niece, who had contacts in the secretarial world, assured him she knew typists who would jump at the chance to work with the famous author of *Animal Farm*. Orwell instructed Moore that his girl would not be needed.

He was unable to get out of bed for some days, so Ricky began delivering his mail to his room. Finally, a letter arrived from Senhouse.

> It is excellent news that you have found time to revise the novel. The tinge of disappointment is apparent in your letter when you state that the stress and uncertainty of the threat of your wretched disease comes through in the writing, and perhaps cannot be expunged to your liking. The astonishing feat of putting 'finis' to the work is surely a triumph. On the matter of the typist, give me three more days and you will know the result. Certainly we won't let you down, whatever happens.

A triumph? Not if you could see the state it's in, he thought. There was something about Senhouse's letter – a familiar inexactness and evasion – that told him he would have to type it himself, and do it quickly, or he would miss his chance to get off the island before the winter.

★

27 November. He was right – Senhouse had failed to follow through – and so he had taken on the grisly task. He had reached the end of his capacity for sitting at his desk – usually an hour, sometimes more, depending on his tolerance for the pain – but found he could string the working day out through the trick he had taught himself in the sanatorium years before: typing in bed. It sounded more difficult than it was. First the machine had to be balanced on a tray on the lap, which until you got used to it made the process rather like typing in a lifeboat on a choppy sea. Then the papers – four sheets and three carbons – had to be threaded through the platen for each page, so as to provide copies for himself, Warburg, Moore and the American publisher, Harcourt Brace. It was a job that had to be repeated some four hundred times.

He'd been at it now for a fortnight or so, every day the same grim mathematical task: four thousand words, twenty-four thousand type-strokes or spaces, two hundred carriage returns, ten changes of paper, all made more difficult by the decrepit nature of his typewriter, which was now close to the end of its life.

Working in bed had some advantages: pillows, for instance, could be arranged so as to position the manuscript for convenient reading; one easily kept warm; and it was a simple thing to doze off when one got tired. He tried to block from his mind Dick's warnings about the effects on his respiration of all the bending, stooping, sitting up, shifting of pillows and moving of arms. Each change of paper and each line of type must have required an additional cubic foot of oxygen – enough, all up, he suspected, to fill a blimp. It was deadly fuel for the bacteria multiplying in his lungs – but then again, hadn't Dick told him the drugs had wiped them out? Pleurisy, influenza, a bad cold – all were equally possible culprits.

He picked up the typing where he'd last left off: O'Brien's words entrapping Winston to join the Brotherhood. He looked at the draft and decided to alter it.

> 'You will have to get used to living without results and without hope. You will work for a while, you will be caught, you will confess, and then you will die. Those are the only results that you will ever see.'

He worked for another three hours, almost without pausing, surprising himself with his stamina and progress, both of which were now varying from day to day but were perceptibly declining. It was only when he was totally overwhelmed by fatigue, his body suddenly taking on the weakness and translucency of jelly, that he collapsed into the pillow to endure the broken, painful sleep of the permanently ill.

★

In the days that followed, he started working downstairs. As the icy winter storms began to howl and smash into the farmhouse, the temperature plunged; by now he had run out of paraffin for his portable heater, and his breath had started condensing inside his bedroom. The only necessities now not in short supply at Barnhill were brandy and gin, and he doubled his ration. He continued on the couch in the living room, swaddled in blankets next to the fireplace, whose damp, oozing peat gave off a feeble warmth. The house seemed bleak and empty, the only other occupants now being Ricky along with Avril and the new farm manager, Bill Dunn. Dunn, a veteran who had lost a leg in the war but had mastered his artificial one, had come to the island to learn agriculture, and though some years younger than her, had taken up romantically with Orwell's sister.

He was almost finished, which meant that confronting the novel's biggest conceptual problem could be put off no longer. The products of his fevered mind on the island and in the hospital – the painful injections, Winston's physical deterioration, the torture scenes, the rats – had, as he'd suspected, given the novel a bleakness that bordered on the Gothic. Had he avoided sounding like H.G. Wells only to end up sounding like Edgar Allan Poe?

A thought, which he knew was a false thought, now entered his mind. He could change the ending. Winston could confound them, live on while still harbouring his secret hatred of Big Brother, return to his old job, perhaps even be reunited with Julia, have his appearance altered through plastic surgery and live on as a happy prole – the things, he rationalised, the Hollywood movie moguls would insist upon in the unlikely event the novel became a bestseller. He dropped the crazy thought after just a few seconds. He'd tried it before, in *Keep the Aspidistra Flying*, and it hadn't paid off. Even Waugh had stopped writing like that. One could have nostalgia for the past, but not for the future.

He confronted the manuscript again and resumed typing. He was just a page or two from the end, having reached the scene where Winston was alone with his thoughts at the Chestnut Tree Café.

> Almost unconsciously he traced with his finger in the
> dust on the table:

The line that followed in his manuscript was '2+2=5'. He centred the next line and typed on. His Remington being one of the portable versions, it lacked the '+' and '=' keys, which meant the symbols would have to be added by hand. He typed '2' and hit the space bar three times, then another '2'. He paused, then picked up his pen and made the additions straight onto the page in the platen.

$$2+2=$$

It was the decisive moment. If two and two make five, there is no hope. Winston has been brainwashed completely, resistance has been proved futile, the party will always win, stamping on the human face forever. But make it equal four and Winston wins! As the bullet is entering his brain, he is still capable of logic – and therefore of thoughtcrime, of opposing Big Brother.

'To die hating them, that was freedom,' Winston had thought.

Now the power of deciding the future lay in his hands.

Until that moment it was as if the book had somehow been controlling him, and that his fate lay in its hands. His right index finger hovered over the keyboard. But hitting '4' would mean something else, too. It was a saccharine tablet whose chemical sweetness would rob the novel of its integrity. Hit '4' and you would descend into worthless sentimentality – the idea that purity of mind is all that counts; that freedom is possible even when jackboots walk the streets, when loudspeakers still screech out commands and posters of the leader hang on every wall. Hit '4', it occurred to him, and the lessons of Spain and the recent war would be forgotten.

You couldn't deliver a warning about the future by offering it up as a utopia; that was Wells' mistake. No, it was too late for backtracking. To get people to alter the future, he had to terrify them. With a resolve born as much of mental tiredness as of certainty, he pressed down decisively on the keyboard.

$$2+2=5$$

★

The next day, he typed the last line.

> He had won the victory over himself. He loved Big Brother.

Should I? he thought. Why not – he had always done it. He advanced the paper by three carriage returns and locked caps.

THE END

★

4 December 1948. Four copies of the completed typescript were lying face-down on his desk. He got out a roll of white ribbon and, with a knife, cut four equal lengths, which he used to bind them up. He placed three copies into envelopes and addressed two of them to Moore, who was dealing with the Americans (two in case one was lost in the post), and one to Warburg. The fourth was his copy. A shower enveloped the farmhouse, but passed quickly. Peering through the upper-storey window, he noticed there were not one but two rainbows, parallel to each other. One rainbow, with its pot of gold, was obviously a good omen. But what might two rainbows herald? His mind started working on his next book.

Two days later, he waved from the same window to Avril and Dunn as they drove up the track in the repaired lorry towards the island's only post office, at Craighouse, taking with them the packages. He was not well enough to see them off outside.

The next morning, trying to get up from his bed, he collapsed.

FOUR

- I -

Secker & Warburg, 13 December 1948. Fred Warburg summoned his secretary for dictation, lit a cigarette, which he attached to his customary long holder, leaned back in his chair and began. 'Heading: Report on *1984*. In numerals. Strictly confidential. Underline that, please. Strictly confidential. First par. This is among the most terrifying books I have ever read. The savagery of Swift has passed to a successor who looks upon life and finds it intolerable . . .'

The dictation took a full hour. When he was finished, Warburg requested that copies of the typed report be sent to the author and to everyone involved in the production of the forthcoming book. 'Give Farrer's copy to me.'

Warburg considered his executive David Farrer to be his shrewdest judge of a book's potential. Some hours later, with the typescript of his own report and Orwell's new novel in his hands, he went to Farrer's office and instructed him to drop whatever he was doing and read both immediately. Could he report within two days? The reason for the urgency was left unstated, but there could be only one explanation: Warburg had a winner.

Two afternoons later, Warburg, his cigarette holder

again in his mouth and a whisky glass in his hand, sat with his feet on his desk, reading Farrer's assessment.

> My reaction to a book which has been highly praised by someone else in this office is liable to be highly critical. It was in a fault-finding mood, in consequence, that I approached the new Orwell, which perhaps lends additional force to my statement that if we can't sell fifteen to twenty thousand copies of this book, we ought to be shot.
>
> . In emotive power and craftsmanship this novel towers above the average. Orwell has done what Wells never did, created a fantasy world which yet is horribly real so that you mind what happens to the characters which inhabit it. He has also written political passages which will set everyone talking and an extremely exciting story – the arrest is superbly done; the mounting suspense in Part II is perhaps more nerve-racking even than the horrors of Part III; as for those horrors, I believe they are so well written that, far from being put off, the public will gobble them up. In fact, the only people likely to dislike *1984* are a narrow clique of highbrows.
>
> *1984* might do for Orwell what *The Heart of the Matter* did for Graham Greene (it's a much better book) – establish him as a real bestseller.

Warburg pounded his fist on the desk.

★

Jura, January 1949. He was lying prone, finding that sitting up constricted his breathing too much. His arms felt weak, but he was able to hold Farrer's report above his head for long enough to read it. *1984* as a title looked strange; better to spell it out – he must tell Warburg. Splendid to eclipse Wells; Warburg's top man Farrer seemed to know his stuff, but what, he wondered, was Warburg himself thinking? He picked up and started reading Warburg's report:

The political system which prevails is Ingsoc = English Socialism. This I take to be a deliberate and sadistic attack on socialism and socialist parties generally. It seems to indicate a final breach between Orwell and socialism, not the socialism of equality and human brotherhood which clearly Orwell no longer expects from socialist parties, but the socialism of Marxism and the managerial revolution. *1984* is among other things an attack on Burnham's managerialism; and it is worth a cool million votes to the conservative party; it might well be a choice of the *Daily Mail* and the *Evening Standard*; it is imaginable that it might have a preface by Winston Churchill after whom its hero is named . . .

I cannot but think that this book could have been written only by a man who himself, however temporarily, has lost hope, and for physical reasons which are sufficiently apparent. These comments, lengthy as they are, give little idea of the giant movement of thought which Orwell has set in motion in *1984*. It is a great book, but I pray I may be spared from reading another like it for years to come.

He was stunned and horrified. So Warburg's Tory instincts had finally surfaced! How could someone like Warburg, who knew his political positions so intimately, get its message all wrong? Sadistic attack? Final breach with socialism? A preface from Churchill? Loss of all hope? Didn't Warburg get it? Winston wasn't Churchill; he was an everyman.

He looked at the typewriter on the desk. It was only a yard away but may as well have been a mile. If only he could reach it from the bed. He pushed away the blankets and made to move, but could barely lift his torso from the mattress.

★

Inevitably, leaving the island was a cock-up. The immediate objective was Ardlussa, where he was to lodge overnight before catching the mail van to the ferry at Tarbert. Given the state of the track – normally barely passable, but now treacherous after gales that had brought the sea up over the farming land in places – it would have been sensible to leave early, before the weather and the darkness closed in. But, as Bill Dunn knew all too well, that was not how they did things in the Blair family.

With the rain thrumming loudly on the roof and the windscreen wipers unable to cope, they sank into the track, where the heavy and underpowered Austin 12 became stuck fast. Bill and Avril couldn't ask Orwell to get out and help push – and so, soaked through, the couple made the trek two miles back in the gathering darkness with their boots full of water to collect the lorry, while he sat in the rear seat with Ricky, talking and eating boiled sweets. By the time they returned it was dark. They attached tow ropes to pull the Austin out of the mud, but it wouldn't budge.

Unless they could get the car unstuck, he would have to either walk two miles in the freezing rain or spend the night in the car, which had sunk to its axles in the mire. The first option was suicidal and the second extremely unwise. To make things even more impossible, the track ran through a peat bog which oozed with sticky black goo, so that it looked like the sands around a ruptured oil well.

Avril and Dunn appeared to have given up, and he watched as they sat in the front seat of the truck, contemplating what to do. Then Dunn appeared at the window of the Austin. The rain had become heavier, pounding on the cabin roof, making even shouted conversation difficult. 'There's nothing for it,' Dunn mouthed. 'We'll have to go around.'

'May as well go ahead and stake all on zero,' Orwell replied, as cheerfully and loudly as he could.

Through the fogged, watery windows, he watched as the giant ex-army truck inched its way past the car, almost scraping the paint in an attempt not to drift too far into the bog. Miraculously, it manoeuvred its way around and back onto the stony track. Avril draped an oilskin over her brother's head and guided him to the truck's cabin, then went back for Richard. After a bone-jarring ride they reached Ardlussa around ten p.m. He was utterly exhausted but bucked by the belief that civilisation and medical science were now less than a day's journey away.

★

Everything seemed to go wrong. Cranham, the sanatorium – twelve guineas a week, operations and medicines extra – was a swindle. Its rows of wooden huts were meant to convey the impression of Swiss vitality and fresh air, but in fact suggested an Arctic labour camp. Dick turned up and advised them to give him more streptomycin, but the terrible side effects returned and they were forced to stop. All that was left was the usual advice: do nothing, see no one, stay completely still.

He couldn't do it, because he wasn't finished with the book yet. There were the proofs to correct – two sets, actually, thanks to Harcourt Brace's decision to set their version without waiting for the corrected Secker & Warburg proofs. Then the Americans wanted to call it *1984* instead of spelling it out in words, and wanted the metric measurements replaced by imperial ones; they could do the first, but not the second. He was too tired to fight against the many minor stylistic changes they wanted for American readers. 'Protuberant' instead of 'Negroid' lips, for example, seemed reasonable. But there was only so far he was willing to go. There was no end to the damage the philistines who ran the book trade could do. Giving in to their every request would see the book ruined. He knew what publishers were like and what drove them: money. The way Gollancz had mucked with his early novels . . . Even Warburg had cut his preface from *Animal Farm*. Well, he wasn't having it again.

★

Cranham, February. Only the twice-daily mail punctuated the monotony of life, now that he couldn't do any serious work. Letters streamed in from those who had heard about his condition and wanted to buck him up: his old lunch companions Malcolm Muggeridge, Anthony Powell and Julian Symons, as well as Koestler's sister-in-law Celia Kirwan and the usuals like Astor, Rees and Moore.

This morning one had arrived from an unexpected source: Jacintha Buddicom – tender-hearted Jacintha, who had abandoned him to Burma with all hope denied so long ago. She had only just realised who her old childhood friend Eric Blair was: the famous George Orwell, author of *Animal Farm*.

Receiving her message was like an electric charge that set his memory to work. He steadied the borrowed typewriter on his lap – his own weary machine having finally succumbed – and began to write to her. 'Ever since I got your letter I've been remembering and can't stop myself thinking about our young days and things put out of our minds for twenty or thirty years . . .'

★

Shiplake, near Henley-on Thames, June 1920. It was the opening day of the coarse fishing season and the weather was perfect for angling. He arrived at the station in a woollen suit and puttees, a cap on his head and his fishing rod and tackle box in either hand. Jacintha was waiting for him at the agreed spot. She had given precise instructions in her neat handwriting: turn left outside the station; walk three-quarters of a mile down Mill Road to where there's a gate with a top bar missing; take the path across the field; go down a hedge-grown lane, then a track between bushes to the lock; walk along the riverbank . . . At last came the gently sloping meadows below Shiplake Court – the big country house that belonged to the local gentry. It was their spot; they called it the Golden Country.

He found her near a clump of elm trees that stretched down to the river. In the muddy water by the bank he could see carp lying under the surface, sunning themselves, and as he looked further out he saw a huge Thames trout sail by. He loved these muddy English fish with their ruddy Saxon names, which he had memorised from his angling book: roach, rudd, dace, bleak, barbel, bream, gudgeon, pike, chub, tench. It was approaching midday, and he cast in and rigged his rod on the edge of the water, using a forked branch driven deeply and solidly into the mud for a prop. Then he sat under the trees with Jacintha. Their excursions to the spot had started years before – during that last great summer before the war – when they had picnicked while Avril, Jacintha's sister Guinever and her brother Prosper played at fishing close by. Now, for the first time, they were alone.

Jacintha produced a slab of chocolate, broke it and handed him half. The sunlight filtering through the innumerable leaves was hot on their faces, and they could smell wild peppermint growing nearby. A bird alighted on a tree five yards from them and started singing. They both lay back, crushing a bed of bluebells, and listened.

'What bird is that?' she asked.

'Thrush, obviously.'

The bird trilled out its melody and flew away.

'Now, you promised me a new story,' she said, closing her eyes, but he could tell she knew he was looking at her. They had done this since they were children, usually gothic horror stories by Edgar Allan Poe or Beatrix Potter's animal tales.

'I've brought a long your favourite, *The Tale of Pigling Bland*—'

'We're far too old for that, Pigling Eric,' she said, giggling. He loved it when she called him this. She was right: they were now seventeen and nineteen, and would have been chaperoned, had their parents not been so disorganised and Shiplake's riverbank so far from the remit of the villa civilisation and its moral enforcers.

'I guess you're right, although you're never too old for a good animal story. Just think of *Gulliver's Travels* and those smart horses. It's easier to have sympathy for an animal than a human. I've read it—'

'Yes, I know, every year since you were eight.'

'It's *that* good; you should try it.'

'You promised me a story of your own. Practice: that's the only way you're going to become the famous author you've always said you'd be.'

He looked at her as the sunlight played on her subtly smiling face. Her eyes were still closed, and wisps of her long, brown hair had strayed over her left cheek. Although he had grown considerably in his four years at Eton, making him noticeably tall, the maturity of her body caused a sense of inferiority to lie heavily on him.

Her eyes opened – they were light brown, which he had never registered before – and she looked up at him sweetly. He had an urge to kiss her, but as always there was something about her that forbade his affections.

She clapped her hands. 'A story, as you promised me!'

He reached for his tackle box and pulled out something he had written on the train journey home from school. 'This is called *The Eton Masters' Strike*.' Lying next to her, conscious of her breathing and her scent, he read, holding the exercise book in front of his face to shield his eyes from the sun. '"Mr Baker received this morning a telegram from headquarters (unavoidably delayed owing to the fact that the telegraph girl's hair slipped under the receiver). The Ushers and Teachers Union had come out on strike in sympathy with the washerwomen, bootmakers and bottlewashers who are demanding nationalisation—"'

'Gosh, you *are* political these days, aren't you?' she said. As he continued, she snorted sceptically from time to time to tease him.

'"Two youths, who had gone out early for a walk and who were complacently sitting by arches discussing the respective merits of Lenin, Trotsky and Boguslavsky, were the only two in the school who did not realise what had come to pass."'

'*Red* Etonians? Oh, Pigling, that's just too much!'

He continued reading, with his usual collection of funny voices and intonations. The story, which he could now see was silly and very juvenile, had a happy ending: the masters went out on strike and the students were overjoyed at having gained an endless holiday from schoolwork.

She laughed. 'A utopia! But I can't figure it out – are you a Bolshevist or are you sending them up?'

It struck him that he didn't really know. Under the influence of the younger masters, who had returned radicalised by the war, the college had come to resemble an adolescent version of the Paris Jacobin Club, but he had remained largely aloof from what his friend Connolly had taken to calling 'Eton's doomed little experiment in human happiness'.

'Anyway, it's quite a coincidence, this,' she said.

'What do you mean?'

'Well,' she replied, reaching into her bag, 'I've brought you something.' She pulled out a parcel wrapped in brown paper, and passed it over to him. 'It's my father's old copy – the one you used to borrow from me all the time, remember?'

He unwrapped it. *A Modern Utopia*, by H.G. Wells.

'None of us wanted it anymore and it was listed for the village fete, but I couldn't let that happen, could I? Especially when you promised us all as children that you'd write a book just like it someday.'

He remembered. He'd stopped reading Wells a year or two before, and the stories had slipped from his mind. He felt disappointed. This was a gift you give a childhood friend, not a—

She cut off his thoughts. 'Are you alright, Pigling Eric?' Suddenly the nickname wasn't so appealing. 'I thought you'd be thrilled. Or at least mildly pleased.'

'I was rather hoping for something else.' He paused.

She thrust her cheek towards him, pulling it away after his lips had brushed it for what he counted as barely a fraction of a second, then she stood and made for the fishing line, which appeared to have a snag.

★

With his letter finished, he signed off: 'As we always ended so that there should be no ending. Farewell and Hail, Eric.' After reading it over, he picked up his pen, remembering there was something else they had always said to each other. 'Nothing ever dies.'

★

Cranham, March. The American Book of the Month Club wanted it, which was another way of saying he was about to become rich and famous. But there was a catch; there was always a catch when someone wanted to give you money for no additional effort. They would only publish if he agreed to remove the book within the book – Goldstein's testament – and most likely the Appendix on Newspeak as well.

He wrote to Moore: 'I can't possibly agree to the kind of alteration and abbreviation suggested. It would alter the whole colour of the book and leave out a good deal that is essential . . . I should be much obliged if you would make my point clear to them.'

The weeks passed in a state of helpless frustration. On 8 June, *Nineteen Eighty-Four* was published in Britain, and five days later in the United States. In the following days he was flooded with telegrams of congratulation. Greene, Muggeridge, Waugh and others including the Tawneys visited him. Lawrence Durrell and Huxley wrote.

His old friend Tosco Fyvel, a literary editor, also turned up in person. Although it was June it was still cold and wet, the sort of day in which all play in county cricket would be lost. Peering from his pillow, barely able to

– 261 –

crane his neck forward, Orwell watched him cross the field under his umbrella, unable to hide his contempt for the surroundings. When Fyvel stepped inside the room a look of fright crossed his face. By now Orwell was used to the effect his cadaverous appearance had on others. The false reports about his apparent good health weren't helping. He lay flat on his back, emaciated, his waxen skin clinging to his bones – like one of the inmates of the Nazi camps in Germany.

'Comrade.' Fyvel offered a feeble smile. 'How nice to see you.'

'Forgive me if I don't sit up, Tosco. Don't be alarmed; it's just my lung. Not a relapse, just pleurisy. The disease itself hasn't been progressing.'

'Well, that's good to hear,' he said, but sounded doubtful.

'Things aren't so bad, you know. To tell you the truth, after the effort of writing the book, I've been looking forward to some decent bed rest, like old Boxer. As you can see, it's quite cosy here in my pasture.'

A sudden draft came through a gap in the window, chilling the air.

'The book – I've read it, George. It's marvellous. I've got a feeling it's going to be the making of you.'

'You know how much I value your opinion, Tosco. I wish I could share your enthusiasm for it.'

'You're not serious, George? You can't be. It's being hailed as an absolute triumph.'

'It's just that I've had a read of it myself. There's not much else to do here than read, as you can appreciate. I'm afraid I rather ballsed it up.'

'Absurd.'

'No, I'm right. It's this damned illness. Made me rush it. I thought it might have turned out too gloomy and pessimistic, but I didn't have the energy for another draft. Now I've read it, it's obvious that not rewriting it one more time was a mistake. The Tories are going to say it's anti-socialist, of course.'

'They'd say that regardless.'

'Yes, but it's more pessimistic than I intended. Positively gloomy. Our side will get little solace.'

'Muggeridge and I thought it was funny. We said so on our radio talk.'

'Yes, I heard it, thanks for the plug.'

'Well, what would you change now, if you had the energy?'

'That's the problem, Tosco, I don't have the energy.' He paused.

'Any change would have to be subtle, you see, but enough for readers to get the point without some syrupy ending.'

'Hollywood's bound to supply that eventually. But I think you've got it just so.'

'There should have been a tiny ray of hope – at least a hint that the party is fallible.'

★

The next day, Warburg visited.

'Hello, Fred,' he said, doing his best to sound cheerful. Warburg had awoken him from a nap.

'Sorry for waking you, Sergeant.'

'At ease, old chap. Help me, will you,' he said quietly, motioning for his visitor to prop him up on his pillow.

Every surface close to the bed was stacked high with newspapers, books or heavy porcelain bowls. The typewriter box was on top of a wardrobe, next to a fishing rod and reel. Warburg plumped the pillows and helped Orwell up – all, Orwell noticed, while holding his breath.

Orwell sat back again with an audible gasp. 'What good news do you bring, Fred?'

'The book's a runaway train, George. It's going to eclipse *Animal Farm*'s sales in a matter of weeks, maybe even days.'

'Splendid,' was all he could manage.

Warburg flourished a file triumphantly. 'The reviews are stunning, George. It's a triumph. A real bolter. Everything tells me it's going to be a bestseller. Even Number 10 has asked for a copy.'

'Hope Attlee hasn't heard what I called him.'

'Oh?'

'A recently dead fish before it has stiffened, or something like that. My memory's not so good at present. Anyway, rather unfair. One gets carried away with similes.'

'Everyone loves it. Even the dead fish, it seems.'

Orwell nodded, and pointed to the pile of cables on the bed, sent over from New York. 'But they've got the book all wrong, Fred. All wrong.'

Warburg seemed to ignore this as he cleared a chair of books and notes and sat down. 'Ninety per cent positive, George. I've never seen such good reviews, at least since *Animal Farm*.'

'Have you read *Tribune*'s notice? The left can be so damned defensive.'

Warburg opened his file and began reading out a series of underlined passages from press clippings, theatrically flinging them onto the bed after reading each one. It was a well-worn routine which Orwell knew was meant to buck him up. He listened obediently.

'From V.S. Pritchett: "impossible to put down". From Lionel Trilling: "profound, terrifying and wholly fascinating". From Julian Symons at the *TLS*: "thanks for a writer who deals with the problems of the world rather than the ingrowing pains of individuals, and who is able to speak seriously and with originality of the nature of reality and the terrors of power". From Veronica Wedgwood: "It is no doubt with the intention of preventing his prediction coming true that Mr Orwell has set it down in the most valuable, the most absorbing, the most powerful book he has yet written."'

Orwell nodded his approval. 'Yes. Just so.'

'I must read you the communists' line.' Warburg fumbled with another sheet. 'They're calling you . . . here it is, "the maggot of the month"!'

Orwell smiled. 'They're fond of insects in the CP.'

'Yes, I thought that might cheer you up. They think it's anti-communist and anti-socialist.'

'The problem is, Fred, that's what the capitalists are saying too.' With an effort, he reached down to the pile of cables on the bed. He shuffled through them, then put on his reading glasses.

'Here it is, the *New York Times*. The novel is "an expression of Mr Orwell's irritation at many facets of British socialism, and most particularly, trivial as this may seem, at the drab grey pall that life in Britain today has drawn across the civilised amenities of life before the war".'

'An American driving around in a big motorcar in California might get that impression, George.'

'Well, he'd be wrong. The book is not anti-Labour or anti-socialist, as they well know. They're being dishonest, Fred. They're all at it. I've got extracts here from the *Wall Street Journal*, the *New York Daily News* and more. Here's the *Economist*.' He waved the magazine at Warburg. 'They should know better. I won't have my Spanish comrades thinking me a traitor. All those fine young chaps, dead! I want it corrected.'

'Let them read into it what they want, George, as long as they buy the book. If the capitalists like it, well, it'll sell twice as many copies.'

'Damn the sales, Fred. I'd like you to send a cable on my behalf, setting the book's message straight.'

'Criticising critics – let me tell you, it never pays, never. A book has to stand, and a reader will interpret it as he wants. That's how it works. If you haven't made your point clear, think of it as a bonus for the reader – they can all see something in it to approve of.'

'The same reason you left out the preface in *Animal Farm*!'

'Politics and literature have to meet halfway. You said something like that yourself once, George.'

Orwell sank deeper in the pillows and closed his eyes. He was now struggling to fill his diminished lungs. 'Fred, I have friends in the Labour government. Apparently even Attlee. What do I say to Bevan and Cripps?' He paused. 'Fred, I don't want to have to say it again. I will not have this book misunderstood. Look at what it has done to me!'

He took three long, shallow breaths, and opened his eyes. Warburg looked away. 'If you won't send out a statement clarifying my position and the intent of the book, I'll get my agent Moore to do it.' He slowly reached over to his bedside table and picked up his pen and some of the hospital's letterhead paper. 'I can't write at present, Fred,' he said. The paper shook in his weak grip.

He could see that Warburg now understood: there weren't going to be any more novels. The publisher accepted the writing materials and found himself in the unusual position of taking dictation.

'My novel *Nineteen Eighty-Four* is not intended as an attack on socialism, or on the British Labour party,' Orwell began, 'but as a show-up of the perversions to which a centralised economy is liable, and which have already been realised in communism and fascism. I do not believe that the kind of society I describe necessarily will arrive, but I believe (allowing of course for the fact the book is a satire) that something resembling it could arrive. I believe also that totalitarian ideas have taken root in the minds of intellectuals everywhere, and I have tried to draw these ideas out to their logical consequences. The scene of the book is laid in Britain in order to emphasise that the English-speaking races are not innately better than anyone else, and that totalitarianism, if not fought against, could triumph anywhere.'

He stopped, then began thinking as intensely as his tired mind could manage, knowing he likely wasn't going to get another chance. Warburg made to screw the lid back on the pen. 'I'm not quite done, Fred.'

'Yes.'

'The moral to be drawn from this dangerous nightmare situation is a simple one: don't let it happen. It depends on you.' He paused. 'That's it, Fred. I want it put out in England and the United States. Will you see to it for me?'

Orwell sank back into his pillows and closed his eyes, utterly exhausted. Finally, he had the feeling the job was done.

★

University College Hospital, London, late October. A woman had finally said yes to him: Sonia Brownell, who had begun visiting him while he was at Cranham. The idea had originally been his, but the event had been harried to its conclusion by her – at the encouragement, he suspected, of Warburg, who probably thought being married might keep him alive for longer. From Sonia's point of view, he could see, marriage to him had a lot going for it. Sex wouldn't be required – probably not even kissing, given his TB – which solved the problem of his current physical repulsiveness. Anyway, whatever duties being his wife entailed, she wouldn't be encumbered by them for long. Richard would be looked after by Avril; Sonia didn't have a natural affinity for children. He, or at least his estate, was going to be wealthy, meaning she would finally have the literary name and the independent income she craved.

At Warburg's suggestion, he had been moved to University College Hospital, which was the TB specialist Morland's beat. Sonia was allowed to see him for an hour a day; everyone else got only twenty minutes. This was his only contact with the world. He had become too weak to write anything but the shakiest scrawl; his energy was coming to an end, and, along with it, his words. Room 65 was little more than a cubicle, with a single armchair, a telephone, a basin and a commode, but it was private, and she fussed about, tidying his usual mess.

'What's the matter?' she said brightly. 'You look positively gloom-making.'

'I've finally got all this money, and you . . . And now . . .'

'Well, you're to stop that at once,' she said in her bustling manner. 'People get over TB all the time.'

She went to the shelf, selected two teacups, wiped them with a cloth, then poured them both a brandy. As he took his first sip, she closed the door, pulled across the curtain of the door's glass window – UCH was the sort of place where they made allowances – and took off her cardigan. She then unbuttoned her blouse almost totally, exposing her lack of a bra. She came close and allowed him to slip his hand onto her bosom. It was as far as anything could possibly go, and along with the sudden shot of alcohol it cheered him up. 'Any way,' she smiled, 'what an easy life you've had, darling. Think of me, giving up my best years as a coolie to that horrid little beast Cyril Connolly.'

For her sake, he momentarily accepted the fantasy that he might live. 'How do you think you'll spend your time now?' He moved his hand across to her other breast.

'As your slavey, of course, when they let you out of here.' She gulped down her brandy.

'I mean apart from that. You know I don't expect you to be any sort of stay-at-home. You must still have a career. A life. I'll insist upon it.'

'I can be your secretary and typist, to start with. I

imagine that will keep me busy enough.'

'How I could have used you a year ago.'

'And your manager. You don't want to be wrangling with publishers. You want to be writing.'

'Will you promise me one thing? In case . . .'

'Depends on what it is.' She stepped back and buttoned up.

'Don't let them say *Nineteen Eighty-Four* was too dark. I was unhappy with all my books, really, except *Animal Farm*. You see, I was running out of time. There were changes I contemplated but wasn't able to fully consider.'

'What changes?'

'To the ending.'

'You would have altered the ending?' The literary editor in her was awakened.

'I would have written it better. I don't mean have Winston and Julia freed to live happily ever after or anything of that sort. Something understated, to get my meaning across.'

'What meaning?' She refilled both their glasses, giving herself more than him; there was only so much he could stand. 'Tell me.'

'It's hard to say exactly. One feels so tired.'

She shifted the chair closer. 'You must try, darling.'

While he thought – even thinking now required an effort – the alcohol reached his mind and suddenly made the world look more cheerful. 'I wanted everyone to understand that I believe freedom will eventually win. That man can hold out against anything. That it doesn't all have to happen again.'

'How so?'

'I probably shouldn't have made Winston submit so completely at the very end.'

– II –

University College Hospital, 20 January 1950. It took a while for the nurse to find a vein, or at least enough meat in which to pump the syringe. He reckoned he had reached the lowest weight a man of his stature could be without being dead. They were giving him something. He thought it might be a sedative, but then again, maybe it was a new treatment. Such great advances were being made in America . . .

He pushed the idea from his mind and thought of his approaching trip to Switzerland. It was Morland's idea, although he hadn't been giving him much in the way of treatment recently. No doctor had seen to him for some weeks now, which he took as a judgement. He couldn't stand mountains, even spectacular ones, but had finally relented and agreed to go. There was no point in dying without exhausting every possibility, especially when you had another book in you – and today he was sure he had at least another five. Anyway, he'd heard there were fantastic trout in the mountain streams near the Swiss sanatorium, and a new fishing rod lay at the foot of his bed. The chartered flight was to leave in five days.

Sonia wasn't there, reporting a bad cold – the last thing

a man in his condition needed. She hadn't been to see him for a couple of days, since the solicitor had visited them to finalise the will.

It wasn't the prospect of being dead that disturbed him; it was the act of dying, which he expected was going to be painful. But they were letting him make the journey to Switzerland, so he must be alright for the moment. He even felt better. Perhaps, at last, his lungs were healing; maybe that clean, high-altitude air would work its magic. The prospect of the trout made him look down to the fishing rod with special longing, and then up at his typewriter, ready in its carry case. There was that essay about Conrad, and that smoking-room story that he'd made notes for, and a big novel about the end of the war that he'd plotted out in his mind.

His eyes closed. It must have been a sedative.

Yes, his lungs were getting stronger. He was no longer in the hospital but on the bank of the stream, near Shiplake, with the warmth of the sun on his back and the springy turf beneath his feet. It was the Golden Country. He looked around to see the dace cruising beneath the surface, and, further along, a great carthorse of advanced years meditating peacefully in the pasture. He knew that in a clearing close by, surrounded by elms, which were swaying in the gentle summer breeze, Jacintha – or was it Eileen? – lay naked on the bed of bluebells, waiting for him. The world, life itself, had been awakened from the dark slumber of winter to be as it should be once again: eternal summer. There were no dictators screeching lies in front of the spotlights, no truncheon-wielding guards in their jackboots, no loudspeakers babbling out lies, no cork-lined prison cells where the lights burned all night, no endless war with its destruction and poverty, no mass graves to be argued about, and no hidden microphones recording his every movement. People like him could write again, freely, not having to hide themselves away in attics, waiting for the secret police to kick in the door in the middle of the night and deliver a bullet to the back of the neck. They could love whom they liked and not have to live alone. The truth of their lives would not be altered or erased from memory. His torment was at an end. Everything felt smoothed out, his story was laid bare, all was forgiven.

Then he was looking at himself, from a distance, and he could see himself smiling. A thought gripped him: this man he could see, living free and happy – was it really him? Or was it . . .?

Then he realised with a shock: it wasn't him with the sun of freedom on his back; it was his son. It wasn't the present or the past he was gazing upon; it was the future. He cried out in his feeble voice: 'Richard! Richard! Richard! Richard!' Once more:

'Richard!' He woke with his lungs unable to fill, and the feeling of sliding down, down, fifty fathoms deep.

★

London, 21 January. It was a bright cold day in January, and a million radios were striking thirteen. The BBC news let the bells of Big Ben ring thirteen times, before the reader began the bulletin: 'The death occurred in London today of Mr George Orwell, the author, at the age of forty-six.'

EPILOGUE

The Alcuin Press, Welwyn Garden City, December 1949. With a sigh, the compositor, wearing his ink-stained blue overalls, looked at the order that had come from upstairs. If there was one thing he hated, it was publishers who requested changes to the text after the formes had been stereotyped. That's what the galleys were for, wasn't it, picking up final corrections? Well, he was damned if he was going to reset any of this. And anyway, with the cost, it was out of the question – the boss would never allow it.

What he was about to do was crude, but doing it well required a degree of skill and brought a certain satisfaction. The essence of the task was to alter the existing metal type without letting the reader see that any change had been made. It had to look as if what was there before had never existed, and what was there afterwards had been intended all along.

He checked the carefully written order slip again, noting its instruction:

29 0/39 2 + 2 = 5 SHOULD READ 2 + 2 = [bla n k]

It was simple enough. When the type had been set, the compositor must have mistakenly added the character '5' to line 39 on page 290. He could see why it was a mistake – it was an absurdity. The author must have meant '4', but orders were orders; perhaps there was a good reason to leave it blank.

He scanned the large metal plates spread out before him. By a stroke of luck, it turned out to be an easy job: '5' was the last character on the last line of the page, which meant that, when it had been removed, there would be no tell-tale blank space. He reached into the bag at his feet and pulled out a mallet and a small round iron bar. Carefully lining up the '5', he gave the tool a tap, flattening the character into the soft metal. Next he inked the plate and pressed a sheet of paper to it, using a hand roller.

Peeling it back, he looked at the altered line. His aim had been slightly off and he'd also removed part of the equals symbol, which now looked rather deformed. It was a bugger but couldn't be helped. The rectified passage now read:

Almost unconsciously he traced with his finger in the dust on the table:

$$2 + 2 =$$

AUTHOR'S NOTE

The Last Man in Europe is a work of fiction, but one that attempts to keep as close to the historical facts as is possible without sacrificing the dramatic requirements of the novel form. My main sources are the twenty-volume *Complete Works of George Orwell,* edited by Peter Davison (Secker & Warburg, 1998), an extraordinary piece of scholarship unlikely to be surpassed for any modern writer any time soon, and the materials in the Orwell Archive at University College London.

There are many fine biographies of Orwell from which I have learned much, particularly Bernard Crick's *George Orwell: A Life* (Penguin, 1980), Gordon Bowker's *George Orwell* (Abacus, 2003), which overtakes Crick 's biography as the most comprehensive account of the subject, Michel Meyer's *Orwell: Wintry Conscience of Generation* (W.W. Norton & Company, 2001), which rescues Orwell from sainthood, and D.J. Taylor's *Orwell: The Life* (Chatto & Windus, 2003), which sheds the most light on Orwell's human side. Taylor's occasional new discoveries of letters, photographs and film are illuminating. *The Unknown Orwell* by Peter Stansky and William Abrahams (Constable, 1972), although pre-dating the others, remains a valuable insight into Orwell's early years. Two collections of reminiscences about Orwell provided valuable first hand accounts of the man: Steven Wadhams' *Remembering Orwell* (Penguin, 1984), and Audrey Coppard and Bernard Crick 's *Orwell*

Remembered (BBC, 1984). I have supplemented these with considerable research of my own, including by putting on my boots and walking through Orwell's world, about which I have written elsewhere ('Big Brother is still watching you across here', *Sydney Morning Herald*, 5 April 2014).

Some events and quoted passages have been compressed for the sake of simplicity. Orwell's letter to his adolescent sweetheart Jacintha Buddicom, for example, is an amalgam of two letters sent to her in February and May 1949 (*Complete Works*, vol. XX, pp. 42–44 and 119–120). Eileen Blair's final letters to her husband are shortened and include an element of pathos taken from her final letter to her friend Lettice Cooper (*Complete Works*, vol. XVII, p. 104). The correspondence between Orwell and Fredric Warburg has been shortened throughout.

Some of the events of Part I draw on *The Road to Wigan Pier* and *Homage to Catalonia* and the semi-autobiographical novels *Keep the Aspidistra Flying* and *Coming Up for Air*. Flashbacks to Orwell's schooldays rely on his 1946 essay 'Such, Such Were the Joys' and Part II of *The Road to Wigan Pier*, as well as on Cyril Connolly's *Enemies of Promise* (Penguin, 1979) and Jacintha Buddicom's *Eric and Us* (Leslie Frewin, 1974).

Occasionally, scenes have been liberally reimagined or wholly created, but these are based on a reasonable degree of probability and evidence: the ILP rally at the Kingsway Hall, for example, closely follows reports in the party's newspaper, *The New Leader*, and while there is no evidence Orwell attended it, he did attend other similar ILP events. There is no conclusive indication that Orwell read the account of the rigged trial and execution of Yagoda, Rykoff and Bukharin in *The Times* of 16 March 1938, with its manufactured evidence and uncanny resemblance to the Party's case against Jones, Aaronson and Rutherford, but we do know that he followed the 1938 show trials closely while in the Preston Hall sanatorium in Kent. While my novel's numerous dream sequences are obviously invented, Orwell's last literary notebook contains a little-known entry describing his 'death dreams', in which he has 'a peculiar feeling of happiness and of walking in sunlight', as well as his 'ever-recurrent fishing dream' – dreams which became more frequent whenever his health deteriorated and he despaired of recovering (*Complete Works*, vol. XX, p. 203).

While the conversations in my novel have been imagined, many contemporaries commented on Orwell's habit of rehearsing the contents of his forthcoming writings in discussions with friends and colleagues.

Every reader will have his or her own interpretation of the meaning of *Nineteen Eighty-Four*. My story attempts to demonstrate my view that Orwell's nightmare future was not an imaginative work of science fiction (a genre he often criticised) but an amplification of dangerous political and intellectual trends he witnessed in his own time. The fact that something similar had happened already – in the forms of fascism and communism – gives even more force to Orwell's warning that they can happen again, if we let them.

Two other points need mentioning. First, in his introduction to the 2003 Penguin edition of *Nineteen Eighty-Four*, Thomas Pynchon suggests the coincidence of the birth years of Winston Smith and Orwell's adopted son, Richard Blair – 1944 – may have been deliberate, raising the possibility that Winston is at least partly identified with Richard, and that the novel's message was aimed at Richard's generation. While this can't be proved, I have fitted it into my story in a way that allows Orwell to clarify the date of his story – 1984 – and the novel's purpose: to send a warning to the future.

And second, in preparing *Nineteen Eighty-Four* for publication in Orwell's *Complete Works* in the 1980s, Peter Davison argued that the last scene of the novel was altered by a printers' accident during the creation of the second edition of late 1950: that the '5' in the formula $2 + 2 = 5$ had 'dropped out of the printer's forme'. This mistake, he believed, was reproduced in all subsequent UK editions until 1987, though not in the US editions. In my research for *The Last Man in Europe*, I discovered that the change occurred far earlier – in the second impression of the first edition, published in March 1950 – and was likely deliberate. Importantly, this printing was almost certainly being prepared while Orwell was still alive. If this alteration to the text was made at Orwell's request, the meaning of *Nineteen Eighty-Four* is altered in a significant way: Winston is still capable of thoughtcrime when the longed-for bullet enters his brain. The addition of this subtle strain of optimism is consistent with Orwell's belief (stated most succinctly in his 1946 essay 'Second Thoughts on James Burnham') that totalitarian governments would eventually be destroyed in the name of freedom (*Complete Works*, vol. XVII, p. 283). For a full discussion of this point, see my 'Note on the Text' in Black Inc.'s new edition of *Nineteen Eighty-Four*, published to coincide with the release of this book.

ACKNOWLEDGEMENTS

My thanks to Richard Blair and Orwell's literary agent, Bill Hamilton of A.M. Heath, for taking the time to read my book in uncorrected proof form. My gratitude also to Chris Feik and Julian Welch at Black Inc. for recognising the potential of my idea, guiding its development and ensuring it emerged into the world in the best possible shape. Your astonishing dedication to the editing task is warmly appreciated.

I have a number of other people to thank for their assistance and encouragement: Carolyn Fraser, for her expert advice on the printing of *Nineteen Eighty-Four*; the artist Cameron Hehir, for helping me visualise Orwell's world; Robert Seatter, Head of History at the BBC, for allowing me to visit the site of Room 101; the staff of the Heritage Collection Reading Room at the State Library of Victoria, and the staff of Islington Libraries, for trusting me with their precious books and artefacts; Kim Williams, for pulling some strings on my behalf and for his generous and inspirational gift; Zoe McKenzie, for the wonderful use of her writer's retreat at Sorrento; Matthew Pennycook MP and Vicar Chris Moody, for organising a tour of the crypt of St Alphege in Greenwich, Orwell's air-raid shelter during the Blitz; Stephen Hepburn of Coventry Books and the team at the Avenue Bookstore, for their superb support of local authors; Chris Barrett and Angela Buckingham, for hosting me during my exploration of Orwell's Paris; Tim

Soutphommasane, for his interest in this project and his kind gift of an important text; and the principal, teachers and children of Albert Park College, for inviting me to speak on my research into Orwell at their 2016 literary festival.

Two close friends deserve special mention: Emily Millane, for her constant encouragement over half a dozen years, and Anthony Kitchener, who never once wavered in his enthusiasm for *The Last Man in Europe*, and never relented in his demands that I drop everything to finish it. Only the best friends continue to believe when all rational reasons for doing so have disappeared.

Finally, Toby, Teddy and Fiona, who for years have endured stoically my disappearances into my own Room 101 to write this book. Boys, I dedicated the last one to you, so this one is for your mother! So, Fiona – for you with love and appreciation.